Ella's
Ice
Cream
Summer

Ella's Ice Cream Summer

SUE WATSON

Bookouture

Published by Bookouture
An imprint of StoryFire Ltd.
23 Sussex Road, Ickenham, UB10 8PN
United Kingdom
www.bookouture.com

ISBN: 978-1-78681-169-1
eBook ISBN: 978-1-78681-168-4

For Delilah

Chapter One

Facebook and Funerals at Forty-Four

'Kim Kardashian came into the shop today,' I said, helping myself to vegetables and smiling like a woman in a stock-cube commercial.

No one looked up.

My plan that evening had been to enjoy a 'proper family dinner', but my two teenagers and my mother (yes my mother!) were on their bloody phones. All three of them had been glued from the moment they sat down and I'd produced my delicious, laboured-over chicken fricassee.

'I said, Kim came in to buy a frock. Kanye was with her...' I added, 'wanted something she could wear down the British Legion next Friday night... in blue.'

'Oh blue, that's nice,' Mum muttered, her face screwed up into her phone (held only a millimetre away from her eyes).

'Put your glasses on, Mum, you'll ruin your eyesight,' I said, hearing the mother in my own voice, and wondering at what point our roles had reversed. I hated being a nagging parent, let alone a nagging daughter, but it seemed I was everyone's mother these days. I just felt like I was giving to everyone all the time and getting nothing back.

Mum looked up, then directly at me. At last, a reaction!

'Am I going to someone's funeral tomorrow?' she asked, feigning ignorance.

'No, the funeral's Tuesday, Mum,' I said, thinking here we go again!

'Oh maybe I'm going on Tuesday then…'

'Yes that's right, it's Sophia's funeral on Tuesday.'

'She never said – has she invited you as well?'

'Yes, she's your sister – and therefore my aunt.'

'I know that, silly,' she said, her face clouding over. 'So, she invited you?'

'No, sadly she died before she could send out the invites,' I replied sarcastically.

Mum's sister Sophia had passed away very suddenly the previous week and despite having been estranged for many years Mum had, quite understandably, been affected by this, though at the moment you couldn't tell, because she was engrossed in her phone. I wondered if she felt guilty that she hadn't seen her sister for so long. Apparently Sophia had been ill for some time, but Mum had no idea and had continued to harbour ancient resentments and the sisterly slights of decades. When we had the phone call to tell us of her death, Mum went into shock and cried, which surprised me, I hadn't realised how much she'd cared for Sophia – yet still she didn't want to talk about it. I'd known Sophia quite well as a child, and was also upset about her death and hoped it might help Mum to talk through what had happened all those years ago. I'd never understood what it was that had caused the sisters to fall out, but they hadn't been in contact since I was a teen and if ever Sophia's name was mentioned, Mum became suddenly forgetful. Her 'memory loss' wasn't real, it was definitely Sophia-related – and involved pretty much every conversation around her sister. One minute Mum was fine, perfectly lucid and able to recall anything from five minutes to fifty years ago, but then at the very mention of Sophia, she would slip into her version of forgetfulness. This wasn't serious, I knew she hadn't really forgotten, but it was annoying, especially as the logistics of getting to the funeral had to be discussed – apparently on a daily basis, because she appeared to have forgotten.

Mum continued to swipe her phone and take me further into her foggy world; 'Ella, there was a funeral last week too, I think...'

I looked up at the kids to see if they were with me – they weren't. No surprises there!

'Yes, Mum,' I said, 'that was Gladys's funeral.' I was suddenly stung by her sadness; she'd lost three friends and her sister in the same number of months. Is this what I had to look forward to in old age?

'Dropping like flies,' she sighed, 'the bloody WI will be wiped out by August at this rate... mind you those mini quiches were nice at Gladys's wake.'

'Nothing says rest in peace like mini quiche,' I smiled.

She giggled; we still shared the same sense of humour, even if hers was at times of her choosing.

The past few months had been a social whirl for my mother on the funereal finger-buffet front. She'd even started giving marks out of ten for hospitality and making notes about her own guest list and table arrangements for when the time came.

'That reminds me,' she said, looking up from her chicken fricassee. 'I don't want her from number 42 at my wake, she'll eat us out of house and home. Have you seen the size of her? Never warmed to that one, always thought she was better than she was.'

'Don't worry, Mother, your guest list will be vetted,' I said, tongue in cheek, but she wasn't listening.

'That's where I met that Eric again after forty-five years you know… at Gladys's funeral. Shame about those egg sandwiches…'

'Yes, I was there – it was a good day for Eric but not the egg and cress.'

The numerous funerals of Mum's friends and family were the only type of social event I'd attended this year – and it was June already. I think it was safe to say I wasn't setting the North West social scene on fire.

'Well I hope the buffet's better at Sophia's,' she muttered. 'I doubt there'll be any mini quiches. Sophia liked to keep everything traditionally Italian, so there might be some nice pasta.'

I nodded. 'Something to look forward to,' I monotoned. Was this it? I was only forty-four but was this all that was left for me, being my mother's plus one at funerals? Was the odd fancy canapé at a party for the dead followed by my mother's post-mortem (no pun intended!) of the buffet all I had to look forward to? I wanted to cry… and drink gin.

Despite pretending she was fine, Sophia's death had definitely shaken Mum's foundations. Their estrangement was rather puzzling, having once been very close they apparently fell out over a box of teabags when I was a baby, which caused a rift leading to a ceasing of all communication when I was twelve. It made no sense, I'd never understood what happened and how a box of teabags sometime in the 1970s could have such far-reaching effects on a family. But Mum's reaction to her sister's death made me realise that the tear in their relationship had cut far deeper than she'd ever revealed.

When I was younger I'd accepted the 'teabag' explanation but now doubted such a chasm had been caused by something so trivial. Sophia's death had brought the whole thing back to the surface and I hoped to finally discover what had really happened between them. This wasn't proving successful so far as Mum refused to discuss it and when I'd pushed her, she said she'd forgotten, which I didn't believe for one minute.

The only safe conversations around Sophia were about our summers spent at Sophia's ice cream café in the little Devon village of Appledore. She and Mum had moved there from Italy with their parents when they were young, and Mum loved to talk about the walks on the beach, the village characters and, most importantly, the different flavours of ice cream they used to make by hand. She remembered all this in detail, but apparently couldn't recall why she'd fallen out with her only sister, just a vague reference to teabags which didn't seem to stand any scrutiny when I pushed for details.

I had my own memories of wonderful holidays as a child, 'helping' my aunt make ice cream while listening to her stories of Sorrento, where 'the lemons are as big as your head'. I wasn't sure about these mutant lemons but Mum confirmed this to be the case, and her eyes would go misty as she recalled the place she was born. Sophia was four years older than Mum and had been almost eleven when they'd left Sorrento. Mum always seemed rather peeved that Sophia considered herself 'more Italian'.

'Waving your arms about and shouting "Mamma mia" every five minutes doesn't make a person Italian,' she'd say. But Sophia's accent, the hand gestures and the constant switching between English and Italian fooled me as a kid into thinking I was in Italy when I visited her in Devon. And later, I loved listening to her memories of 'home'. 'We used to sit outside in the year-round sunshine after school drinking lemon granitas and strawberry gelato,' Sophia would tell me, whereas Mum couldn't remember quite as much about 'the old country', as she called it. Consequently, Mum's interpretation of her 'Italian culture' was bordering on Mafioso, having been honed from *The Godfather*, *The Sopranos*, and, more recently, *Mob Wives*. Her Mafioso repertoire was varied, and I doubt she understood what most of it meant, but liked how it sounded. It was mostly harmless but hadn't gone down too well at the ladies luncheon club when, in a vaguely threatening tone, she informed Dorothy Ramsbottom: 'You can get more with a nice word and a gun than you can with a nice word.'

Though Sophia's Italian accent was more genuine (and less New Jersey) than my mother's, the two women were very much alike – slipping into the lilting accent whenever they spoke of home. In their voices I heard the rustle of lemon trees, a warm Mediterranean breeze rolling over the sea, and constant summers of simmering heat, soothed only by fruity gelato.

They'd been dragged from their Italian birthplace by my grandparents, who'd moved to Devon after the war. My grandfather was a

Devonian and having met my Italian grandmother while stationed in Italy had eventually brought the family 'home' to Appledore, a sleepy little village in North Devon. My grandmother made the most amazing gelato and they took advantage of the burgeoning youth culture of the sixties and started a small ice cream and shake bar, which eventually became Caprioni's Ice Cream Café.

When my grandparents died, they left the café to their daughters, where both sisters worked happily together until Mum had me and Dad's company transferred him to Manchester. We moved up North and Sophia bought Mum out of the business, going on to build the café into a huge local attraction with her husband Reginald. People would travel for miles to try Sophia's home-made ice cream and exotic sundaes.

I was remembering the piquant taste of the apricot and amaretti ice cream when Mum broke into my reverie, 'Ella, do you think they'd play Barbra Streisand?' she was saying as I helped myself to more fricassee, which seemed to have disappeared even though the kids hadn't taken their eyes from their screens.

'When?'

'Tuesday, at Sophia's funeral. Me and your dad loved "The Way We Were"; they could play it as I walk out of the crem.'

Fortunately I didn't need to answer and point out it was Sophia's moment, not hers, because her phone pinged. Mum's eyes were now drawn back to the screen like an alien returning to the mother ship.

'Nan, are you sexting Eric again?' Josh asked, without looking up from his screen.

'That's enough, Josh, your nan is not…'

'Oh yes, I am. Josh showed me how to take photos on my phone and I've been sending Eric a few pictures.'

I glared at Josh, now smiling to himself.

'What sort of pictures, Mum?' I asked, almost not wanting to know. Honestly, she was more of a liability than my two teenagers.

'Oh just ones of me naked.'

'Oh, Mum, no…' I started, almost choking on my dinner. I reached out my hand to touch her arm and talk her through the potential problems of the internet. I'd imagined having this conversation with Lucie, my nineteen-year-old daughter or even my eighteen-year-old son but not my seventy-eight-year-old mother. Then I saw the three of them laughing at the shock on my face. She was joking. Thank God!

'Honestly, you lot,' I said, rolling my eyes. 'And Josh, after the incident at the WI I'd hoped you *wouldn't* be assisting Nan in her quest to conquer the internet.'

Since Mum inherited her iPhone from Josh there had been several misunderstandings and embarrassing incidents. However, the worst had to be when Josh had told her that texting and sexting were the same, and in fact it was technically correct to refer to texting as sexting. One can only imagine the looks passed down at the OAP computer class, the library and the ladies luncheon club. Who knows what regional outrage was caused by my son's hilarious wheeze? But it seems things really kicked off when a speaker came to the WI to do a talk on 'technology and texting for beginners'. Right on cue, Mum informed the room that she spent 'many a happy evening sexting the vicar'.

This resulted in me receiving a call from a very concerned Reverend James, worried people might be under the impression he was 'grooming' my mother.

I'd placated the vicar, and apologised profusely to the ladies of the WI, but as long as Mum had that phone in her hand I knew it wouldn't be the last apology I'd have to make. Oblivious to the drama she was causing, Mum had continued to cut a swathe through social media, but with little idea of what she was doing. And judging by the abuse she'd recently tweeted to Dame Judi Dench (damning and disgusting words apparently meant for Donald Trump – it was easy to see how the two could be mixed up!) it was a matter of time before she was barred from Twitter. God knows what poor Dame Judi, a national treasure, made of being called 'a big orange fascist' by my trolling mother.

'Mum, all I'm saying is please check who you're tweeting before you tweet, and don't put comments or pictures online that you don't want the world to see,' I said, for the hundredth time.

'I'm not on the bloody line, I told you I'm doing the sexting,' she snapped.

'Mum, after all that stuff with Reverend James, please tell me you know the difference between sexting and texting?'

'Like you do?' Josh giggled.

'Of course I know the difference,' I said, not that I'd ever sexted in my life.

'And so do I,' Mum spat. 'Sexting is sending a picture of someone's big penis in the post, isn't it?'

Oh God, 'big' and 'penis' are not two words you want to hear your mother say, let alone at dinner in front of your kids. I looked over at Lucie and Josh for help, I don't know why.

'Don't ya just hate it when mums and nans try and talk technology?' Lucie muttered while apparently trying to dump her boyfriend by Instagram – is that a thing? I'm not even sure I'd know if I'd been dumped by Instagram. I pondered momentarily on this. Did an aggressive emoji suddenly appear on your phone, or perhaps there was a particular ring tone that signified the end of a relationship? 'Hit the Road Jack', or Chopin's 'Funeral March', perhaps? If not I was going on *Dragons' Den* to claim the idea the following week.

I sat at the head of the table presiding over my oven-to-table-ware while my mother and children all just continued in their own little worlds, oblivious. I'd assumed that as the kids grew up things would calm down and I might have 'me time' again. But my mother had moved in with us the previous year after a nasty fall while attempting the Argentine tango during *Strictly*. I pointed out that just because Louise Redknapp had scored three tens for hers it didn't mean Mum had to copy step for step – instead I just told her to come and stay with us. I'd expected this to last a matter of weeks, but four months later it seemed Mum was happy with us and had no plans to leave any time soon.

I confess I found it quite claustrophobic to have my mum living in my home. Nothing I did was quite up to her standards, from the way I cleaned the kitchen to the way I added tinned tomatoes to pasta sauce. Mum was an excellent cook, and when my dad was alive they'd have dinner parties every week where she presided over a beautiful table. Her specialities were Italian dishes, sizzling chicken cacciatore, creamy carbonara, and her buttery, aromatic home-made garlic bread was to die for. I would never compare myself to Mum in the cooking arena, but I'd tried, with my packet mixes of Italian classics. These were abhorrent to my mother, who made her feelings quite clear about my chicken parmigiana when she emptied the contents of her mouth into a napkin shouting 'Che palle!' which apparently in Italian means 'What balls!' After that I gave up trying to please her and it was usually rushed eggs and oven chips thrown together after a day at work. However, I used my culinary muscle to make desserts and ice cream; this was my area of expertise thanks to my childhood holidays in Devon helping Aunt Sophia in the family café. Mum never complained about my lemon meringue pie ice cream, or hot fudge sauce made from scratch and poured over home-made vanilla ice cream. But she rarely complimented me either – I simply had to assume the empty dish was sign of her approval.

'Mum, can you lend me thirty quid?' Josh was now saying.

'No, because I'm paying for pretty much everything else in your life – so unless it's a necessity I won't be adding thirty quid to the financial haemorrhage I'm currently suffering.'

'Okay, take a chill pill, Ma,' he laughed.

'I will "take a chill pill" when you come up with a phrase that isn't straight out of the nineties,' I said in a quick and fabulous comeback. Pleased with this, I leaned over my dinner to give Mum a high five, but not only did she leave me hanging, she cowered.

'Mum, don't leave me hanging, give me five,' I was saying, trying to sound like my kids and refusing to be ignored.

'Oh, Ella, we don't do high fives any more, we do fists,' she wafted her hand dismissively at me and returned her gaze to her phone.

'I suppose Josh told you that?' I asked, clearing the plates.

'Yeah, Nan's been fisting the vicar haven't you, Nan?' Josh piped up.

I gave him a warning look before going into the kitchen, a round the table discussion on fisting was just a step too far, but he was too busy showing Mum something on his phone to notice.

Being around Josh and Lucie had introduced Mum to a whole new online world, and her interest had suprised me. She had never really been very technically minded, she could barely text before she moved in with us, so her new-found silver surfer status had taken me aback somewhat.

'Online I'm not old,' she'd told me when I asked her why she was so keen to join Facebook and Snapchat. 'On here I'm not invisible – I can be anything or anyone I want to be.'

I understood how she felt, and as being online had given her a new lease of life, I was prepared to put up with any teething problems, of which there were a few. Like when I'd decided to go to the gym and asked Lucie to take a before and after picture of myself in my pants and greying old bra. This was an impromptu idea to give me motivation and obviously for my own use, hence the less than glamorous underwear. But Lucie didn't bother to delete it and when Mum 'inherited' her phone she'd managed to unwittingly post me all over Facebook in cellulite and old underwear. It was days before I noticed – but my ex-husband Richard and his floozy had seen it straight away and 'liked' it – the bloody cheek.

And it wasn't just the internet she approached with little caution – I don't even want to think about the time she phoned a live radio show thinking it was her friend Molly. She managed to inform the listeners of *Manchester Live* that 'Ella hasn't had sex since her husband left – and that was seven years ago!'

What she didn't explain was that celibacy was my choice (well, mostly). The kids had been disrupted enough by the divorce, so my aim for the past twelve years had been to stay put, keep calm and earn enough to keep us all going. I didn't want to bring another man into their life and wanted to make sure they were settled and happy before I even considered chasing my own rainbow.

And despite Mum now adding to my stress, I did owe her big time. Not only had she been a good mother, she'd always been there for the kids, and had been very supportive when Richard had walked out on me twelve years earlier. My husband's departure had hurt like hell and that hurt soon turned into a bitter, unrelenting rage. But Mum had talked me through those long nights of tears and blame and soothed me as she always had.

I'd hoped this evening we could have a nice family meal together, share what had happened that day, dip into each other's lives a little. Life was short, the kids would be gone soon and this would all disappear with them, this life I'd been making for the last twenty years was suddenly slightly defunct. But any hopes I'd had of having one of those perfect family meals I'd witnessed so often on my friends' Facebook feeds had disappeared somewhere around the moment we'd all sat down.

Over the years I'd had the privilege of seeing my friends' amazing meals out, amazing meals in, awesome husbands, spectacular long-haul holidays and stratospheric kids. I'd lived through their new kitchens, holiday sunsets and celebratory cocktails – and I'd had enough.

'I'm fed up with my so-called friends on Facebook rubbing my nose in it,' I'd complained to my friend Sue. 'I don't mind being bombarded by photos of people who've achieved something – a degree, an abseil for charity… even a cute new puppy, but who has the arrogance to think anyone is interested in their new Aga? It's an oven, get over it,' I'd said.

'Oh the Aga queens,' my friend Sue had laughed. 'They might have a shiny new oven but while they're making toad in the hole, their husband's doing the same with his shiny new girlfriend.'

'You're talking about Dick…'

'I'm not.'

'No I mean The Dick, my ex. He was doing that toad in the hole thing with Miss Perky while I was slaving over a bloody oven. He's now smeared all over Facebook lying next to her and her fake breasts outside their bloody villa in Spain.'

'Forget Dick and fake breasts. You should start to follow my friends,' she'd said, 'at least they're honest – most of them spend Saturday nights crying into their ready meals about the fertility of life.'

'Futility?' Sue often got words mixed up.

'Yeah. And trust me, if you saw Lily Johnson's page filled with loopy cats and lonely dinners it'd really cheer you up – raw baked beans on toast with real moggies. Your life's a bloody carnival compared to hers.'

I knew I wasn't the first person to look at the manufactured lives and touched-up photos of my friends online and feel resentful. No one could have so many holidays, so many meals out and so many 'awesome' times with friends in their new sodding kitchen, could they? All I ever did in my kitchen was wash, cook and clean, what an interesting Facebook feed that would make. It wasn't like I was jealous. I didn't want 'shiny things' – but I'll admit, those online sunsets gave me glimpses of a world beyond my back door and the little dress shop where I worked. And I felt like I was missing something.

It all started in the nineties when I was young and carefree, with my life and career before me. I had so many plans: a pastry chef in Paris, a gelato queen in Rome, a sweet shop in London. I wasn't sure, but I knew whatever I did it would be something sweet. Then I'd met this handsome, charming guy who asked me to marry him. As soon as he gave me the ring, I gave up my dreams.

It wasn't Richard's fault, he was the fork in my road – and I was the one who made the choice. But years later, my fork in the road felt like a fork in my chest when he dumped me and the kids for a life of fake breasts and luxury with his glamorous boss. And as two became one to the sound of champagne corks popping under a hot Mediterranean sun, I just went through the motions of feeding, loving and nurturing our kids – alone. But now the kids didn't really need me any more, except at meal or money times. And I'd begun to realise that the more you do, the more your kids take you for granted. I'd become invisible, the ghost mother in the house. No, my life wasn't the kind to brag about on Facebook, unless a photo of a pile of clean laundry and a packet of fish fingers does it for you?

Then, just when I thought my destiny was decided for me and I was hurtling towards middle age with nothing to show for it, something happened.

Chapter Two

Mad Mothers and Mini Quiches

After my failed family dinner the previous evening, I woke to scrape fricassee crust from my oven before work when a letter landed on the mat. Mum and the kids were still in bed and when I opened it I squealed loudly, causing Mum to rush down the stairs thinking I'd hurt myself.

'What on earth…' she was saying, tying her dressing gown cord around her waist.

'It's Aunt Sophia…' I said.

'It can't be, she's dead…'

'No, I mean, it's from her solicitors, Mum.'

'Oh, is she in trouble?'

'No she's left me "a portion of her business" in her will.'

Mum and I looked at each other and her hand flew to her mouth. 'Oh no…'

'Oh yes. It's Caprioni's Ice Cream Café, Mum… I think she must have left it to me and Gina.'

Mum pulled her lips tight in deep disapproval. 'Well that's not going to work, is it?'

Mum had never liked my cousin Gina, Sophia's only child – she'd always said Gina was 'fickle '.

'I don't understand,' I said. 'Why would she leave anything to me?'

'Nothing to understand,' Mum snapped. 'Don't get involved is my advice. Mark my words, Gina will ruin that business. Leave well alone, Ella.'

'Oh Mum don't spoil this… it's quite exciting. I'm not going to turn down an inheritance just because you fell out with Sophia and you don't like her daughter. I loved them, and I loved the café, I had some happy times there.'

As a child I'd visited Appledore once a year for two weeks – and it was quite, quite wonderful. The only downside had been that my parents had never joined me; Mum and Dad would drive me there, leave me for the fortnight and collect me at the end of my stay. I never questioned this when I was young because it was the way it had always been done; it was only later I realised it was because of the feud between my mum and Sophia. As for Gina she was my beautiful, older cousin who I looked up to from being tiny. One of my earliest memories was of Gina swirling clouds of strawberry ice cream into cones behind the counter. She would have been in her late teens, dressed in a bright pink uniform, lipstick to match – and to me, she had been a goddess.

Mum was looking increasingly more worried now. 'Don't get involved in the café, Ella, you can't live in the past. And Gina will probably want to sell up anyway – hates hard work that one.'

'It would be a shame to sell it, Mum – this is a family business. I'm sure Gina must have some thoughts…'

'I bet she will, that one. She'll turn up, cause trouble, take the money and run.' Her lips tightened. 'Ella, you wouldn't go and work there, with her, would you?' she asked, suddenly seeming very old and vulnerable. 'We're happy here, love – it's not like you could commute is it? And we can't all move down there, we don't want to uproot again and...'

'No, of course not, Mum, I've got a good job here at the shop, and we've got a nice home. Perhaps Gina and I could rent the café out? I was thinking... if we make any money from this we might be able to redecorate, new wallpaper?' I heard myself say, but I wasn't really feeling it. 'I have to go down to Devon next week for the reading of the will. I imagine Gina will be there so we can talk then.'

I didn't want Mum to worry. I had no idea what this might mean but finally I felt I had something exciting to tell the kids. And that evening after work, I suggested they all went with me to Devon to find out just what the inheritance involved.

'Wow was she rich, has she left you shedloads of dosh, Ma?' Josh asked, for once taking more interest in me than his phone.

'No... just a portion of the business – the café.'

'So, you don't reckon it's worth a million pounds then?' Lucie looked at me.

'No, it's only a little café on the front, we'll probably just get someone to run it for us... or we could sell it?' Just saying this made me feel a little guilty – Aunt Sophia and Uncle Reg had worked very hard to build that business and in its heyday it was the meeting place for everyone locally. Selling it to someone else would feel like a betrayal.

'So why don't we all go together to Devon? We can stay in Appledore,' I said. 'I could take next week off work, we're really quiet at the moment, Sue won't mind – I can go and see the solicitor about the will and then we could spend a few days there. What do you say… sounds like a plan?' I was quite excited at this prospect, I might even have some 'awesome', family time of my own to put on Facebook. But then I looked at the kids, now both staring at me with identical faces – I wish I could say the look was joy, but it was bordering on repulsion. Mum was adding the sound effects at the side, tutting loudly and making negative sounds under her breath, clearly as unimpressed as the kids regarding a trip to Devon.

'You could get to see Aunt Sophia's ice cream café,' I added desperately.

I'd always wanted to return to the café but told myself as a single, working mum I didn't have the time or money, which was true. But the main reason was that I knew that Mum wouldn't have liked me going down there and fraternising with 'the enemy'. I'd never been back since the last summer I stayed when I was twelve.

'Remember those wonderful ice creams, Mum,' I sighed, 'a whole summer of strawberries in every cone.'

Mum rolled her eyes; she didn't see the place through the same strawberry-coloured lenses as me. She clearly wasn't as keen to relive the past and put ghosts to rest either.

'I'm looking forward to seeing Gina.' I turned to Lucie and Josh, trying to get them on board. 'My cousin Gina was a Hollywood starlet,' I said proudly, to which my mother hissed like a snake.

'Starlet? Hardly. She ran away from home, couldn't cope, I'm surprised she stayed in America, she never stuck at anything that one.'

The fact that Gina had fled the country to become a film star in LA had always been the stuff of dreams to me. She was like something out of a Jackie Collins novel to my teenage self and I copied everything she did or said on my return home – which really annoyed Mum. 'Does Gina chew gum like that?' she'd ask, or 'Why is your skirt so short, God forbid you don't want to end up like Gina?'

After I stopped going to Appledore I wrote to Gina a few times once she'd moved to LA. She sent the odd postcard back, but it always felt a bit awkward when Mum got to the letterbox first and stood in the hallway with it clutched to her bosom and a betrayed look on her face. She never said anything, her lips were so tight she probably couldn't – but she glowed disapproval and, quite honestly, it was almost a relief when Gina stopped writing to me. I missed the postcards from Hollywood – but I understood, Gina probably had a life filled with screen premieres and dress fittings with no time to write postcards to her boring teenage cousin. Though I continued to check the post box throughout my teens, just in case.

We heard snippets about Gina over the years. We knew she'd married a millionaire and lived in a fabulous Bel Air mansion, which I hoped might endear her to Mum, but it seemed to have the opposite effect. Mum didn't want to talk about her and soon changed the subject if I brought her up. But I kept an eye on my glamorous cousin. I'd googled her name and found the odd picture, but after lots of searches I had to conclude that she liked her privacy, and who could blame her? She was living a life of Hollywood royalty in a Bel Air mansion. As a child I'd always thought Gina looked just like Marilyn Monroe – her pale skin and bleached blonde hair was quite different from the rest of the family with our dark hair and Mediterranean olive skin. The only thing that betrayed Gina's heritage were dark, fiery eyes and, if family folklore (well Mum) was anything to go by, she'd had a fiery love life too.

When I'd stayed at the café, she'd always been so kind, like a big sister, and as an only child I appreciated that. She would paint my nails and show me how to use a lip pencil and that last summer she'd bought me a bra, which had gone down like a lead balloon with my mother. It was pale pink, frothy lace and perfectly acceptable for a twelve-year-old girl, but seeing the delicate 30AA cups as the gateway to an orgiastic future, Mum confiscated it and I was soon back in my thick, white vest.

I remember Gina taking me swimming at the beach once towards the end of my holiday, I was sad I wouldn't see her for a while, as we were both leaving later that day – me back to grey Manchester and Gina back to her glamorous life in the US. It was a warm, sparkly day and Gina was wearing a scarlet bikini, looking every inch the movie star, her hair was full and blonde and everyone was looking at her. I remember feeling so proud that this captivating creature who lived thousands of miles away in a magical place was my cousin, and my friend. We were having a wonderful time splashing each other in the sunshine when Mum suddenly appeared on the horizon. She was supposed to be collecting me later – these pick ups were always arranged with military precision to avoid the feuding sisters crossing each other's path. But today Mum had arrived early and was storming across the beach, waving and shouting. I couldn't understand what she was saying, so I waved and smiled back – surely everyone was as happy as me that day? It was only as she came closer that I realised she was angry and I was embarrassed and unsure what to do as she hauled me from the sea, wrapping a huge towel around me.

'Gina, she could have drowned,' she was yelling. 'Are you stupid? You know how dangerous it is when the tide's in, you could both have been swept away.'

Gina protested, but Mum always had the last word. As I looked on, shivering in the towel, I was unable to comprehend my feelings, but now I know I was burning with humiliation for Gina.

I tried to talk to Mum about it on our return, but the very mention of my cousin made my mother's chest puff out, so I gave up. I rarely spoke to my mother about my holidays in Appledore, and after that I didn't say a word – I didn't want to upset her or get Gina into trouble again. As an adult, I find my mother's behaviour even more difficult to comprehend. I don't recall the sea being particularly rough that day, and there were other children younger than me alone in the sea. So why did Mum embarrass us both and admonish Gina like that? As a mother now myself, I've often thought how lovely it would be for my kids to have a 'Gina' figure in their lives – she was always exciting, so much fun.

And I wasn't about to let my mum's ancient feud ruin my chance of happiness now. Gina had been one of the main reasons I'd loved spending time in Appledore. And it was wonderful to think that we might spend some time there together now, as older women. I wasn't the little twelve-year-old wrapped up in a towel, shivering by the sea while my mother told me what to do. I was perfectly capable of making my own choices about whom I spent time with. I just wished the kids, and Mum, would join me on this new journey.

'Go on, come with me to the Ice Cream Café?' I asked the kids, while trying to ignore the steam of resentment coming from my mother. 'I used to love it there, little rickety tables, a great big plastic ice cream cone outside. I used to call it "The Giant's Ice Cream," that made my aunt laugh,' I sighed.

Mum didn't respond and the kids barely lifted their heads, until, in the silence, Lucie looked up. She had a pained look on her face.

'Mum, don't take this the wrong way, I mean a few years ago we'd have loved a big plastic giant ice cream cone somewhere in Devon, but we're a bit old for all that now. You just go... and read the will and have a nice time.'

With Sophia's will I had a sudden yearning to return to the holidays of my childhood, and I longed to share some of the past with my own kids. Everyone tells you that you don't have your children for long, but when it happens, when they grow up and leave it's a shock. I wanted to preserve what was left of my precious time with them, put it in a jar and close the lid for a while. They'd been my reason for living and as much as they'd needed me over the years, I realised now, I needed them too.

'I just thought... it would be good. A trip down memory lane, a last holiday as a family... by the seaside?'

'Yeah, but we're heading off ourselves soon…' Lucie said, a gentle smile on her face, desperately trying not to hurt me.

I smiled back, I understood, but how I longed for those bygone days when the children would be so excited about going on holiday they couldn't sleep the night before. When did my children grow up and leave me behind?

I wanted to preserve what was left of my precious time with them, put it in a jar and close the lid for a while. They'd been my reason for living and as much as they'd needed me over the years, I realised now, I needed them too.

They'd been my anchor, but it was time for them to move on – because there was a big old world out there just waiting for them. I'd passed them the baton, I hadn't conquered the world so they had to do it for me, and they had far bigger summer plans than a few days in Devon.

Lucie had finished college the previous year and been working to save up to go away and Josh was doing his A levels. In a few weeks Lucie was going with friends on a gap year starting in Thailand and Josh had just found out he'd been accepted for a summer volunteering programme in Nepal with his girlfriend. Their plans were made, their bags packed and I was proud of them, if a little disappointed that they weren't prepared to indulge me for a few days first.

'Don't be sad, it's all good, Mum,' Josh smiled, as he passed me carrying his plate into the kitchen. He touched my shoulder and enunciated this clearly, like I was about a hundred years old.

'Oh sweetie, I'm not sad,' I lied. 'I'm delighted you two have an exciting summer ahead… real grown-up adventures without your mum,' then I added weakly, 'Yay!'

I suddenly felt very alone. I'd been buoyed by the news of the inheritance, going back to Devon, spending time with my family and now I just felt hollow. My future stretched out before me and there was no one else in it. The emptiness must have shown on my face.

'Soz Mum,' Lucie smiled and I put on a brave face; I didn't want her to feel bad.

'Oh no, don't apologise, darling, I want you to go, what you're doing is wonderful… brilliant. I just thought perhaps we could fit in a little family trip first,' I said, my voice fading.

I felt Lucie's wave of pity wash over me and realised if I wasn't careful, the healthy dynamic between me and the kids would alter and I'd become 'poor mum, waiting at home'. I never wanted to be that.

'Well, if you guys are both off around the world, I guess me and Nan will have to do Devon on our own?' I sighed, making a brave face at the kids' holiday rejection.

'We can do the funeral and then the will,' I said, attempting to sell it like a two-centre holiday. 'Mother and daughter time, eh Mum?'

My mother looked up from her meal and touched my hand gently. 'Sorry love, I can't come to Devon…'

'What about Sophia's funeral?'

'I can't.'

'She's your sister.'

'I know, but she won't be coming to mine, so I'm not going to hers.'

'Mum, what are you talking about? Of course she won't, she's dead,' I said, irritated by this churlishness; 'Why are you being so mean, I can't believe you're still holding a grudge.'

'I just don't want to go back there, I don't want to. You can't make me,' she said, sounding like Lucie whan she was about five years old.

'There may be mini quiches?' I tried.

'Not for all the mini quiches in M&S,' she said sadly.

She clearly didn't want to return to Appledore. So turning the funeral/will trip into a nostalgic family holiday, eating ice cream, sand between our toes and sunshine on our faces wasn't happening.

'Well, I still need to go,' I sighed, realising I was daunted at the prospect of going back to Appledore alone. What had happened to the Ella I knew, the one who planned to chase my dreams and make life my adventure as my glamorous and successful cousin Gina had?

'You can be anything you want to be,' Gina used to say, 'don't let them tell you any different.' And she was living proof that you could pack your bags and find that rainbow, but then she had never had any children. She hadn't spent the last twenty years cooking and cleaning and nurturing – in between shifts at work. Kids have a habit of holding onto your heart, stopping you from running away.

But now I was left behind on the shore waving everyone else off. I'd been so busy encouraging my kids to live for today and have an adventure, that I'd forgotten to book one for me.

Chapter Three

Toyboys, Tinder and Tropical Moments

The following morning I arrived at 'Fashion Passion', where I worked, feeling quite bereft. I parked up and climbed out of the car, eager to discuss my 'inheritance' possibilities with Sue my boss, who was also my friend. A former hairdresser, Sue had once been the proprietor of 'Curl up and Dye' in the Midlands, but after meeting a toyboy on Tinder, she'd sold up, lost her head and moved to Marbella. Six months later, she was back in the UK, most of her life savings gone, along with the toyboy, all she had to show for it was a tan.

After what she called 'my Tinder trouble', she moved up north where property was cheaper and opened 'Fashion Passion', with what little money she had left. Sue's aim had been to transform a rather stale dress shop into what she said would be a 'classy and extinguished venue', she'd meant 'distinguished', as I said, she often mixed up her words. Unfortunately, Sue's taste was not to everyone's liking and one woman's 'classy' is another's 'Big Fat Gypsy Wedding'. Sadly, much of Sue's stock involved a million sequins, lots of shine, and required a good cleavage and an ample reserve of courage.

That morning I walked into the carpeted interior with its glitzy brocade walls with rows upon rows of blingy dresses and felt instantly comforted. I took off my coat, heading straight into the little kitchen at the back of the shop to put the kettle on.

Sue was standing in front of the fridge with the door open; being a lady of a certain age with what she referred to as 'ravishing hormones', she often did this to calm the hot flashes, her 'tropical moments'.

I turned to her about to embark on my inheritance hopes, empty nest and Devon trip, when I saw she'd been crying.

'Oh Sue...' I started. I was as protective of her as she was of me; being in a confined space filled with flashing sequins eight hours a day had brought us very close. 'I thought we'd agreed Tinder will only break our hearts,' I said using the royal 'we' and sounding like a TV life coach. 'I thought we'd agreed the places to meet decent men are mixed gender book clubs and hanging around the foyer of the Ship Inn on "widowers" Wednesday?'

'Oh it's not Tinder, I wish it were, love... but that's a thought, I'd forgotten about "widowers" Wednesdays at the Ship, I could do with a nice rich man without a wife.' Then she reached for the custard creams, and I knew we were in trouble; Sue watched her figure and rarely ate sugar, but always turned to custard creams in a crisis.

'What is it, love?' I said, turning on the tap and filling the kettle. This was clearly going to require tea – lots of it, along with several more packs of biscuits.

She closed the fridge door and began fiddling with her rings.

'It's... the shop, Ella.'

I stopped what I was doing and looked at her, my mouth suddenly dry.

'We haven't been bringing in enough to cover the overheads, and now the bank wants money and the landlord wants his rent and I... just don't have it. I just kept hoping every week I could turn things around, but I'm so sorry, Ella...'

I couldn't believe what I was hearing; 'You mean, "Fashion Passion" might have to close?'

She nodded.

'But can't you just get a loan...'

She shook her head; 'We're past that stage, my love.'

'Oh Sue, why didn't you tell me, you must have been so worried.'

'I was, but you've had a lot on these last months with your mother moving in and I didn't want to add to your worry, I thought everything would sort itself out.'

'So... what's going to happen?'

'It's all over, oh my lovely shop.'

With that she burst into tears and I hugged her tight as she sobbed on my shoulder and the kettle began screaming, an echo of my own feelings inside.

Sue had taken me under her wing a few years before, promising to show me the ropes of high fashion, love and life. But if the toyboy trouble and the sea of sequins was anything to go by I should have known that Sue had little knowledge of fashion or passion. We sold very little, and despite her previous financial woes, I'd assumed she had capital and could afford for us to make minimum profits, allow customers to drink tea, chat for hours and buy nothing. But that obviously wasn't the case, and as customers used the place like a social club, and Sue entertained them all, pronouncing on everything from Lady Gaga's costumes to the new pasties at Greggs – no one was spending. In fact, the only person that spent anything in the shop was Sue – and that was on the mountain of tea and biscuits she doled out.

I really felt for Sue, but selfishly this also translated into panic for me. I needed this job, we couldn't survive on the pittance The Dick sent for the kids and I wanted to cry too, but had to stay strong for Sue.

'It's all my fault, I've always been erotic with money,' she said through her tears.

'Don't blame yourself, you're not *erratic*,' I said, 'the high street's in decline, blame the government.'

'This was my nest egg,' she sighed over a calming cuppa a few minutes later. 'When my ex-husband walked out with that tart I made a go of the hair salon, but then there was my Tinder trouble and…' she took a sip of tea. 'But listen to me going on you're a single mother – what about you, love? How are you going to manage?'

I told her I'd be fine, I even joked that as my kids were going away my food bill would be less and I'd be better off financially. This wasn't the case, in order to keep a roof over our heads I'd agreed to pay the monthly mortgage payments. When he left, my ex had said he wanted half the house when it was eventually sold, but until that time I could live in it with the kids. It had always been a struggle to make ends meet, and to make things worse I'd just paid for both the kids' flights on my credit card. My stomach swirled with worry as I tore open another packet of custard creams, desperately trying to recalibrate and work out what I needed to earn to cover my monthly outgoings.

Sadly there were very few local businesses left in our town, so it wasn't like I could just finish work here and find another job down the road. I suddenly had no income, and was responsible for two kids, a mortgage and a mother. The only slight glimmer of hope on the horizon was the possibility that my inheritance might offer me half a business to sell or earn from. Yes I might be in dire straits now, but I did have the prospect of the Ice Cream Café twinkling on the horizon.

I'd been worried about going back alone to Appledore, I didn't know what I might find there, and Mum's reluctance had made me even more unsure. But now I had no choice but to go there as soon as possible and find out about the café and what it would mean financially. I'd been through worse than this: I'd been left alone with two young kids and no money and I fought through that, so I could do it again. This wasn't about me, this was about my family and I was going to face all my fears to keep them going and be the mother, daughter, provider I'd always been. And in my heart I felt that one way or another it would all work out and this inheritance might just help me through a sticky patch. Little did I know.

Chapter Four

Fake Teak and Melted Memories

'Mum, tell me truthfully, do you miss Sophia?' I asked, as we had a last cup of tea before I set off for Devon. It was very early in the morning, but Mum had got up with me, and made me some sandwiches to take. I felt like I was going on a school trip.

'Sophia?' she answered, pouring boiling water onto teabags. 'No, I don't miss her now; I haven't seen her for so long. I miss when we were kids, when we played together, then later when we moved to Devon we had some fun. We were very popular with our schoolmates – something to do with our family owning a café that made ice cream,' she laughed, bringing two steaming mugs to the kitchen table while I finished off my toast. It was rare to hear Mum talking fondly of the past, and especially of Sophia, but at the end of the day they were still sisters.

'Do you ever wish you'd stayed in Devon?' I asked.

'Ooh no. Your dad and I wanted to get away, we needed a fresh start, and when he was promoted and transferred to Manchester our prayers were answered.'

'But the café? How did you feel about leaving it?'

'Sophia had made her mark on it by then, I'd not worked there for a long time – three miscarriages can put you off your stroke,' she added sadly. 'Then you came along and I wanted to be with you, my precious daughter,' she squeezed my cheek.

As a mother myself I couldn't imagine what it must have been like to lose three babies, and even now I saw the pain etched on her face. But the experience had made her the mother, and grandmother, she was – caring, loving and ferociously protective when it came to me and the kids.

'I've been a good mum haven't I, Ella?'

'The best, Mum, the best,' I smiled. It was a mantra often heard from Mum; she seemed to need reassurance that she'd done the right thing, that she'd been good to me and I always answered the same, 'The best, Mum, the best.'

She seemed sad this morning, I wondered if she might change her mind about coming to the funeral.

'Are you sure, about today?' I asked.

She nodded, quite adamantly.

'Mum, do you think on her death bed Sophia might have forgiven you for whatever…?'

'No. We vowed never to speak to each other again, and it worked. No point raking up the past, Ella.'

This made me feel sad, and despite Mum's dismissal I knew it must have affected her. The sisters were once so close, and until recently they were all that was left of what Mum called, 'the Devon branch of the Caprioni Dynasty'.

I asked Mum again why they hadn't stayed in touch, but her forgetfulness, like her Italian accent came and went.

'You can't expect me to remember details about something that happened over forty years ago,' she said, dismissing the feud like it was nothing.

It seemed that whenever I mentioned the café and Sophia, or even Gina, my mother's memory completely deserted her. And I wondered, not for the first time, what it was that made her want to forget? I tried to respect her need for privacy, but it bothered me. However, I didn't have time to get into this now, I had a train to catch, so I stood up and began to gather my stuff together for my day in Devon.

'What are you doing?' Mum asked, suddenly.

'I'm just putting some stuff in a bag, I'm going to Devon. Sophia's funeral? The will?'

'I'm not going.'

'No, I know, but I am.' We had discussed this many times.

'Don't... please don't go.'

'Mum, she's my aunt. I loved her and she was always good to me – she's thought of me in her will. I have to pay my respects.'

'But you might not come back?' she said, a haunted look on her face.

'Mum, I'm back this evening, I have my train booked.' I knew this was just another way for Mum to ask me not to go, but she seemed genuinely scared and it upset me. But even if I'd wanted to stay I couldn't, I had to say goodbye to Sophia. Apart from Gina I was the only other family member who'd be there. I'd also arranged to hear the will on the same day, it made sense, the solicitor was happy to do it and it saved me an extra journey, not to mention another train fare. I didn't want to worry Mum about our dire financial situation, but this inheritance might be the only way out of it.

And so, on that sunny June morning at 5 a.m., I went against my mother's wishes and set off for Devon.

I sat on the train wondering again what it was that kept my mother from attending her own sister's funeral. Mum had once told me they'd been very different growing up. Sophia had apparently been 'the bad sister' who'd left school early and fallen pregnant at nineteen. As a child, I'd once overheard my mum talking about how 'Sophia had a shotgun wedding', and I'd assumed this meant a Western theme with cowboys and saloon girls. It had all happened in the late fifties, the family were staunch Catholics, and Mum said they never forgave Sophia for 'the shame' of being unwed and pregnant. My grandmother eventually accepted Uncle Reginald, but in the early days had refused to go to the wedding. Clearly Mum was as stubborn as her own mother when it came to Sophia.

But as far as I was concerned my aunt had been a wonderful woman and she seemed as excited as me when I went to stay, giving me special treats, allowing me to mix the ice cream and serve behind the counter. I loved the freedom of life in Appledore. Mum had always been so protective of me, never wanting me to stray far without her, always supervising everything I did. 'You might burn yourself,' she'd say if I tried to make her a cup of tea or offered to help in the kitchen.

In Appledore, Sophia allowed me some space and there was a delicious independence in being able to walk to the shop along the front alone. I could play on the beach with new-found friends, and even make tea and coffee – in fact it was asked of me when Sophia was really busy. 'Put the kettle on, love,' she'd say, from behind a sweet, swirling vat of ice cold vanilla. And I didn't scald myself once.

I was a late and only child for Mum and after the problems she'd had carrying babies to term, I know I was precious to her. But the result of her overprotectiveness was that she always kept me on a tight rein and I still trod those safe lines as an adult – never taking risks, always playing it safe. Now I could see how limiting this had been for me. Perhaps if my mum had allowed me to make some mistakes and let go a little I'd be a different person? I might have taken more chances, more opportunities and not been scared to do something different, to have an adventure.

I kept reading on Facebook that I had to do one thing that scared me every day (and I don't think going to see *Blair Witch 2* counted). But from being young I'd always associated taking risks as hurting my mother – I'm sure many people felt this way, but it made me scared to do anything. I wanted to wake up in the morning and wonder where the day would take me, and have something other than cooking, cleaning and working to think about. But all I wondered was where my life was going.

I arrived in the sleepy little village of Appledore mid-morning, and as I stepped from the taxi I felt all my worries slipping away. Wandering through the cobbled lanes of pastel shops and houses, strung with pretty bunting, I felt a tingle. The place hadn't really changed much, a few new shops had popped up, the pub had had a makeover, but it wasn't hard to remember things as they were.

I headed for the church where Sophia's funeral was to be held, memories of my aunt filling my head and heart. I looked forward very much to seeing my cousin, imagining her dressed all in black, looking impossibly glamorous but probably distressed, it was her mother after all. I wondered how often she'd been able to visit from LA, and if she felt guilty about Sophia dying without any family around her. Despite Mum's harsh words, I knew she felt bad about not being around for Sophia, and again wondered why she and Mum had fallen out so terribly. I wondered too if there was more to Gina's leaving for LA all those years ago – was it purely to seek her fame and fortune or had something driven her to leave Devon?

These were questions I'd asked myself (and my mother) many times, but to no avail. And on arrival at the church it didn't look like I'd have the opportunity to ask Gina any of those burning questions. I studied every face in the congregation but couldn't see her anywhere. The only sign of Sophia's daughter were a dozen red roses: 'To Mum, RIP.' I was incredibly disappointed not to see my cousin;I was also upset to think she hadn't turned up to her mother's funeral. Mum and I had our ups and downs, but missing her funeral would be unthinkable.

I spotted a friend of Sophia's who used to come into the café – she was much older now, but I recognised her. I asked her if Gina would be coming along later and she looked at me like I was mad; 'Gina? No, she says she's too busy with work to get here... well, you know Gina.'

But it seemed that perhaps I didn't know Gina after all?

And later, as I stood at Sophia's grave, I cried quietly for the sister who wasn't there and for the daughter whose life was clearly more important than her mother's death.

I left the church service with little time to spare – and a desire to avoid another funeral buffet – and headed for the village and the reading of Sophia's will. I had to assume if Gina wasn't at the funeral she wouldn't be at the reading of the will either, which was frustrating. I'd hoped we could discuss what to do with the café, especially as this was important to me in terms of a possible income. But walking along the front, I gently pushed away my worries for now, I was back and it felt surprisingly good. The air was fresh and salty and the tide was in, glittering in the sunshine under a big blue sky, and I stood on the edge of the promenade allowing myself a few minutes to take it all in.

This was a special place, and I felt like I'd come home to this lovely little village where the sea ended and the sky began. I'd often come back here in my mind, and I missed it, but hadn't realised just quite how much until now. I'd been tempted to come on family holidays with the kids and Richard but felt I would be betraying Mum so it had been easier to stay away. I looked out at the vast expanse of sky, big and blue, the seafront shops and houses in complementary pastel shades behind me. And after a breath, I began to walk along the front. In the distance, the sign was blowing in the gentle wind coming from the sea: 'Caprioni's – The Ice Cream Café'. I was transported straight back to being six years old and my first memory of being here alone, without my parents.

The café closed about 9 p.m. each night and Gina would put the jukebox on and the two of us would dance in the middle of the café. I remember the heady mix of Bowie, Blondie, The Police, Gary Numan, The Village People as my six-year-old feet tried to copy my older cousin's graceful, sexy moves. Then the sweet scent of warm chocolate drenching cold ice cream as we made our own sundaes. Illicit ice cream, made to measure in our own creations – lemon, peach and strawberry with raspberry sauce; chocolate and tiramisu with fudge; peanut butter and maple syrup. Gina and I would make all kinds of weird and wonderful concoctions – we didn't follow the menu and broke every rule, layering fruit with chocolate and peppermint before hurling on a million sugar sprinkles. Sometimes we'd go along the freezer putting a blob of every ice cream and every kind of syrup into sundae glasses and creating a spectacle of colour and crunch and creaminess. Two kids in a candy shop, literally. We'd then take a spoon each and share the towering confection, until we couldn't eat any more. Afterwards, Gina would reapply her lipstick and I'd watch, entranced, my lips moving with hers as she slicked on strawberry gloss. Gina was everything I ever wanted to be.

During those summers, Aunt Sophia showed me how to make the finest ice creams, sharing old family recipes her parents had brought over from Italy, inspired by the seaside town of Sorrento. I loved her gentle accent, the way she rolled her Rs and the dramatic hand gestures. She stirred and poured and tasted, delighting in the ice-cold crunch of hazelnut, the rich coffee liqueur and creamy mascarpone of tiramisu ice cream, the sweet-sourness of lemon granita. I hoped Sophia had written the old Italian ice cream recipes down or they would be lost for ever, and back here now, I couldn't bear to think that I'd never taste Sophia's gelato again.

My eyes sought the pink and green striped café awning I remembered so well, and I looked beyond my immediate eyeline to find it, eager to get back there. I felt the years peel away as I recalled black and white Athena posters of good-looking boys on Vespas, girls drinking milkshakes, chrome coffee machines, a jukebox and peppermint green and pink tables. As a child I was convinced this was the ice cream equivalent of Willy Wonka's factory, and those tables would taste as sweet as candy canes.

And I could taste the cold bliss of the ice cream now as I approached the café; every shade and flavour of swirling creamy ice whipped and piled into oblong tubs behind glass, just waiting to be chosen. My child's eyes would dance across the creamy rainbow, my memory and taste buds aching for the previous summer's joy. And they never let me down, sharp Sorrento lemon, ice green pistachio, pastel pink raspberry drenched in a fruity sting of scarlet strawberry purée, all as lovely as I'd remembered. My mouth was watering now, my tongue tingling at the thought of the special shelf above the ice creams where jars upon jars of jewel-like sugary treats glittered. From spiky citrus sherbet to clunky chocolate buttons – they made ice cream sing when layered in a tall glass and drenched in syrup.

Arriving outside Caprioni's, I stopped abruptly, my ice cream memories melting as I saw immediately how much the place had changed. The strawberry ice cream pink paintwork was now puce, dirty and peeling, and the once beautiful windows were steamy and filled with fluorescent star shapes advertising cones of chips and burgers. But where were the ice cream posters, the huge pictures advertising the summery sundaes, the delicious waffle cones stacked with a rainbow of flavours and sprinkles? What had happened to the beautiful café of my childhood, the one I'd kept in my head all these years, the one I'd dreamed of returning to one day? I held my breath as I walked towards the door, just hoping inside would be just as it had been thirty years before.

Chapter Five

Magnums, Cornettos and Day-Glo Disillusion

I was shocked, this place had been so well preserved in my memory I'd stupidly assumed it had remained exactly the same. But the fifties seafront glamour of my memories had been replaced with Day-Glo disillusion.

I opened the door and stepped inside, hoping that the interior wouldn't be so bad... it was worse. I was horrified to see the peppermint-coloured tables had been replaced by fake teak. I looked further, praying for a miracle, but the counter was grubby glass containing wrapped biscuits and muffins that had seen better days. What had happened to the ice cream café? I hadn't even seen a tub of vanilla let alone the exotic flavours my aunt used to make.How bad things must have been for Sophia, here all alone, no family, just an ailing business. I suddenly felt a surge of overwhelming grief for my aunt, and a sense of hopelessness that it was all too late.

The guy behind the counter was reading a book and looking distinctly uninterested in his surroundings. I didn't blame him, this was like a death to me – Caprioni's had been my past and a place I'd often escaped to in my head and now it was gone.

'Yes?' he said, clearly annoyed by the interruption.

'I'm Sophia's niece,' I said.

'Whoopie do,' was his response. He didn't even look up from his book.

'I have an appointment... I've come to meet with the solicitor, Mr Shaw.' I waited for his response, I thought he might be surprised we were meeting here rather than the solicitor's office, but he didn't flinch.

'Through the back, the second door on the left,' he said, enunciating this loudly and clearly like I didn't speak English.

'Thank you,' I sniffed and walked through the café, averting my eyes, unable to look any more at the neglect, the awful transformation, while trying not to breathe in the grease and mashed potato that hung in the steamy air. Just before I opened the door to go through into the back of the café, I turned and called over to ask if they still sold ice cream.

'Yeah,' he said, without looking up. 'Magnum or Cornetto?'

'Nothing thank you,' I said, realising we'd not only lost Sophia, but every last remnant of Caprioni's Ice Cream Café.

An overwhelming feeling of sadness enveloped me once more as I opened the door and walked into what I knew would not be the Narnia-like vision of the past I'd hoped for. The kitchen where Sophia had once made that wonderful ice cream was quiet and empty, the surfaces covered in dust, no ice cream maker, no huge bowls of whipping cream and crates of eggs, just boxes filled with paper cups and cheap serviettes.

I couldn't see any sign of the solicitor, so just waited, leaning on the cleanest part of the countertop near dusty boxes and stacks of ledgers just imagining the past. So much had happened here. Sophia had lived and worked a lifetime in this kitchen, and her own father before her, from the minute they arrived one chilly spring day from their home in Sorrento where the lemons were as big as your head.

I was bereft, I felt like I'd lost a piece of my childhood. Could I have done something to save this place before now? I'd never visited, never stayed in touch with Aunt Sophia, I just put my memories of Appledore in a jar and preserved them there, in order to protect Mum, but perhaps in recent years I should have been stronger.

My own family history was here in these walls, stuff I didn't know and would probably never know now, and along with the loss I felt this huge weight of guilt descend on me. My aunt was dead and the family café lost and I'd allowed it to be washed away with the tide, refusing to engage with it because it might hurt my mother's feelings. But with Gina away, I had been the nearest thing to a daughter Sophia had – and I'd neglected her, along with the café.

I hadn't written to Sophia except once, in my twenties, to ask if she had an address for Gina in LA. I'd explained that I hadn't told Mum I was writing, but that I wanted to keep in touch with Gina. Sophia had eventually written back and said 'it probably isn't wise for you to contact Gina – it will just bring everything to the surface. It's best for everyone that we make a clean break.' I was confused and heart-broken and never tried to contact her again, but now, seeing the decline in this once beautiful place, I regretted that. I should have visited Sophia to see how she was, listened to her as she talked of 'the old country', lost forever now.

Sophia's stories had died with her, along with the secrets of her ice cream made. Sophia kept those recipes in her head, a secret only she knew. And sitting in the café kitchens now waiting for the solicitor to arrive I felt myself deflate. Despite saying I wouldn't want to actually run the ice cream café, I suppose I'd harboured a dream to come back here and take on a thriving ice cream empire, if only as landlord. But having seen what the café had become, I doubted Gina would be interested in trying to resurrect the past, I wasn't sure it was even possible, given the state of the place. My cousin had her new life in LA, away from sleepy old Appledore, and she clearly wasn't interested in the past – she hadn't even made it back for her mother's funeral.

Perhaps we could sell after all? God knows, I needed the money now I didn't have a job, and it would give me some breathing space before I found work. Yes, that would be the safest, most sensible thing to do.

But hadn't I always done the safest, most sensible thing – and look where it had got me? Instead of being an out of work single mother with no career I could be queen of my own ice cream café with plenty to post on my Facebook page? I could come to Appledore and save Caprioni's from its fake teak and stale muffin death? I daren't even hope for something like this… it wouldn't be my decision anyway, even if we had equal shares, it would ultimately have to be Gina's choice.

Just as I was wondering if the solicitor was a no-show, I heard a door opening and closing. Someone was shuffling through into the kitchens – an old, greying man in a suit with a dickie bow probably, the kind my mother met through her various dating apps. But when Mr Shaw, from 'Shaw Associates', wandered in I was amazed. He was late thirties, with a five o'clock shadow and hair that looked like he'd just been caught in a tidal wave – which it turned out he had... well almost.

'Sorry I'm late, I was on a dive,' he said as he plonked a very battered rucksack onto the counter.

'Ben,' he reached out his hand to shake mine; 'I'm Ben Shaw from Shaw Associates.'

'Well that's a new one,' I laughed.

He looked bemused and scratched his head as he looked at me.

'I mean – "sorry I'm late I was on a dive" isn't an excuse I've ever heard for a business meeting,' I smiled and he smiled back, a dimple on each cheek.

'I thought you'd be older,' I said. 'Are you the actual Shaw Associate?'

He laughed. 'One of them. Though my father's the real deal – it's a family business. We used to be Shaw and Son, but then I left and he decided to kill me off,' he laughed, 'then I came back, so he decided I was an associate.'

It looked to me like he'd been forced kicking and screaming into the life of a lawyer and would really rather spend his days in the sea.

'So, was the dive good?' I said, like I knew about these things.

'Challenging, cold tide, lack of visibility, but then it's Devon, not Hawaii,' he shot me a longing look as he opened up his ruck-sack.

'No, I don't suppose it is. So you're a diving lawyer?'

'More of a lawyering diver,' he said, then looked puzzled; 'if that's a thing.' He smiled again and those dimples appeared and I thought, Oh yes… that's a thing.

'You're lucky I didn't turn up in my wetsuit,' he smiled.

I reckoned I'd be luckier if he had, and tried to pretend I hadn't just swept my eyes from head to toe imagining him in tight rubber. I didn't know what had got into me, it must have been the emotions of the day coupled with the sea air, I hadn't entertained thoughts like this about any man for a long time.

I looked away as he took off his jacket, I hadn't been in the proximity of a good-looking man for a while and there was only so much I could take. He rolled up his shirt sleeves and lifted himself onto the kitchen counter – with rather muscular forearms. I gasped, I really hadn't expected the family solicitor to be in tight faded jeans, and a T-shirt emblazoned with – 'The Deeper You Go the Better it Feels'. I had to look away.

'So, have you explored Appledore?' he said, settling onto the countertop.

'Not this time, I used to know it well, but today – I came straight from the funeral.'

'Oh yes, of course, sorry about your aunt. My father was there.'

'Oh that's nice,' I said stupidly, not really quite sure what the protocal was regarding funeral attendance. 'Thanks for fitting in the reading on the same day; it saved me making several journeys.'

'Yes, well your aunt was organised, she knew what she wanted and was quite specific, which makes my job easier.'

'I imagine when she wrote the will she didn't expect the business to be quite so... run-down,' I said.

He nodded and shrugged.

'I don't know why but I just expected it to be exactly the same as it was when I was younger.' I sighed. 'Rows of ice creams, music playing, people coming and going. Silly really, to think things stay the same...'

'No, it hasn't had the best time since Sophia became ill... a couple of years ago, she kind of gave up.'

This saddened me, the very idea of a woman as strong and fiery and passionate as Sophia giving up. But she was old and unwell and had no one to help her, and I felt another wave of guilt engulf me.

'I don't understand why she changed everything... the lovely colour scheme, the tables...'

'She didn't have the energy to continue making ice cream on a daily basis and the café needed a lot of maintenance work, so she turned it into a place for coffee and snacks, had it all whitewashed and moved in some new tables, the old ones were falling apart.'

'That's sad,' I said, imagining those beautiful, ice cream coloured tables lying in the bottom of a skip. Then I looked at him. 'But teak?'

'Okay, it seems she would have rather violated it than closed it,' he looked at me and half-smiled, waiting for my reaction. I laughed; I liked his sense of humour.

'And the customer service leaves a lot to be desired,' I added.

'Ah, so you met the staff? Marco's okay once you get to know him, he was close to Sophia and I think he's pretty cut up about the way things have gone.'

'Well he's not helping matters – he's positively rude.'

'Yeah, but he stuck by Sophia and the café. From what I understand, she just wanted the place to tick over so when she died she'd be leaving a going concern to sell. Her daughter's miles away and…'

'Oh… so Gina will want to sell?'

'I believe so.'

'Aunt Sophia took such pride in this place, worked long hours and she ate, slept and drank ice cream… and now? It all feels like it was for nothing.'

'Yeah I know,' he said, then he smiled again and those dimples made an appearance. 'When I was a kid I lived for Saturday afternoons in the summer, walking along the front with my dad to Caprioni's for a cone.'

'Yes – those home-made waffle cones, crisp and thick with an undercurrent of treacle,' I said, licking my lips.

'You hadn't tasted raspberry sauce on your 99 or hot chocolate fudge on your sundae until you'd tasted Caprioni's,' he smiled, gazing ahead like he was back there. It was nice reminiscing with someone who remembered the same things as me. I could almost taste the vanilla, a soft pillow of creamy white, the perfect canvas for oozing raspberry sauce or a blanket of hot chocolate fudge. 'Ice cream has never tasted as good since. I wonder if that's because it really was the best, or it's just the way we remember it?'

'I reckon it's a bit of both – it was the best, but even better through the mists of memory,' I said.

He suddenly seemed to remember why we were there and reached over for his bag, which was open, with sheets of paper sticking out: 'So, let's get down to business,' he said, pulling out a pile of notes.

'Gina wasn't at the funeral,' I said, 'so I don't suppose she's going to come for the reading?' I asked, gesturing at the dusty kitchen surface like it was a boardroom. Despite the state of the café, I was sitting on a cloud of wonderful memories and suddenly my mind was racing ahead. Just being here was awakening something inside me, a sense of hope, like magic. I suddenly felt invigorated, inspired – could I convince Gina not to sell? Could the two of us bring this café back to life? My mind was suddenly downloading all kinds of craziness – we could get a loan from the bank to do it up and Gina could stay in her mansion in LA while I ran the café?

Ben Shaw was studying the documents on his knee and shook his head absently; 'No, Gina couldn't make it, a very busy lady apparently.'

I could tell by the way he said this he didn't really approve – and, if I'm honest, neither did I. Gina was the only daughter and Sophia's next of kin and I was surprised and a little disappointed in her. I don't care how busy she was, she'd missed her mother's funeral. I'd come all the way from Manchester and would be going back the same day – the train fare had cost a fortune I didn't have, whereas Gina could just get on a plane without worrying what it would cost. I imagined her millionaire husband had his own plane.

I couldn't allow myself to resent Gina because she wasn't there for her mother, she had her reasons, and besides there was enough judgement and hurt in this family to last a lifetime. I wanted to move forward and work in some capacity with Gina; we hadn't fallen out with each other, we were just victims of our mothers' small-mindedness and inability to forgive.

Ben carried on shuffling through a pile of papers, as my fingers tapped on the table impatiently.

'So, put me out of my misery,' I said, trying to sound light-hearted and jovial, but probably sounding like some scheming relative grasping at my dead aunt's inheritance. I was just keen to know the score – exactly.

He was scratching his head again, and as he lifted his arm I noticed the old T-shirt he was wearing had a hole under the arm. He really didn't look like a solicitor. Eventually he looke d up and I swear he seemed surprised to see me. 'Oh sorry, yes you'll be wanting to know what...' He went back into his rucksack and produced more paper and sat for another eternity before clearing his throat and beginning to read from Sophia's will.

There was lots of legal jargon which I didn't understand – and I have to say I wondered if he did. But finally he came to the bit about who were the recipients of the estate. He said 'thereof' rather a lot while reading this but I heard only the line; 'I leave The Ice Cream Café business to my daughter Gina to do with as she thinks best.'

I was waiting for my name to be 'appended', or whatever the legal term was, but my name wasn't mentioned, and I couldn't help it – I was shocked. Of course it made perfect sense that Gina would be given the café or a large part of it, but having been told I'd been left a 'portion' of the business I'd assumed I'd be part-owner with my cousin, but that clearly wasn't the case. So why was I here?

'Ben, this is all quite as it should be and I'm sure Gina will do as she thinks fit,' I started, wanting to cry and shout 'where's mine!' but restraining myself. 'I'm just wondering what you meant in your letter about me receiving a portion of the business,' I said, trying not to burst into tears, my dreams of an Ice Cream Café empire or at least some extra money sliding down into oblivion like melted mint choc chip.

He lifted up a finger in a 'wait', gesture. He then began rustling around in his jean pockets, pulling out various odds and ends including part of a snorkel until he finally produced a set of keys. 'Follow me,' he said, and set off back into the café. 'Sophia was keen for you to have this,' he was saying over his shoulder as we walked. 'She said you always liked it when you stayed for the holidays.'

Great, I thought – it's the ice cream cone; I always loved the giant plastic ice cream cone that stood outside the café. This will be useful when we're homeless. I shall be returning to Manchester with a 7-foot ice cream cone strapped to the roof of a taxi. Who says bad things don't happen to good people?

Ben was now disappearing outside through the front door, so I pulled my coat around me and followed him. I just needed to know what Sophia had left me and if it was the giant 99 cone how I would get it onto the 16.42 from Barnstaple without taking someone's eye out. I could find myself in the cells overnight for assault with a deadly weapon.

Walking along the front, the blast of cool, salty air caressed my face and began to calm me. I was reminded of being little and walking along here in jelly sandals, Gina's hand in mine, the sun on my face and on my bare knees, the salty tang in my nostrils.

'Let's blow away those cobwebs,' Gina used to say and we'd walk along the estuary, looking out to the sea, sometimes so far away. Gina would point to America (well that's where she said it was, over the sea) and tell me that's where she lived, with all the film stars in Hollywood. I could feel the memories crowding in as the cobwebs cleared in my head, following Ben down the street, still puzzled as to where we were going as we walked further and further away from the café. Did Aunt Sophia own more businesses? Was I about to become a Devon property magnate? Dare I hope I might finally be able to put photographs on Facebook of me lounging by a pool in a five-star hotel paid for by my property portfolio? I doubted it, but a girl can dream.

Ben suddenly stopped and waited a moment while I caught up like he'd just remembered I was behind him. Maybe he had actually forgotten me and was heading off on another dive?

'Where are we going?' I asked, but he just looked slightly puzzled and started walking again. Eventually we reached a small group of outbuildings round the back of the Seagate pub. He sorted through the bunch of keys he was still holding, an act as chaotic and frustrating as his paper sorting – and eventually he found the one he was looking for. I stood behind him holding my breath as he approached a smallish garage and started to unlock the door; it clearly hadn't been opened for a while because it was very stiff and took two of us to pull hard on the door handle, but we finally lifted the door and slowly but surely what was inside revealed itself.

'It's Reginaldo,' I sighed, trying not to cry with disappointment.

Chapter Six

Wild Times in Sapphic Seas

I was unable to hide my disappointment that this was Reginaldo, the Caprioni ice cream van and not my portal to another, financially secure life. Reginaldo was very old, and clapped out having trundled around the Devon streets in the summers of my childhood. I looked through the windows, remembering days helping in the van. I could almost hear the sound of its tinkling tune bringing hordes of salivating children, like Pavlov's dogs, running blindly along the pavement.

'I used to sit here in the passenger seat with Gina while my Uncle Reg drove us along the sands,' I smiled, feeling tears prick my eyes. 'It was so... exciting...'

'Reginaldo?' Ben laughed at the name, standing back with a bemused look as he weighed up the rickety old vehicle in front of us.

I explained that Uncle Reginald wasn't Italian, but when my grandmother died and Sophia and Reggie stepped in to help my granddad he bought the van for Reggie. My granddad wanted his son in law to feel a sense of ownership, along with a little Italian authenticity.

'Well, I'm glad you like Reginaldo, because he's all yours,' Ben said.

'Oh. Really?' I was touched, but I couldn't imagine why she thought I'd know what to do with it and quite frankly I felt like I'd been handed the booby prize. I felt like I was starring in one of those old TV game shows where the presenter would say, 'look what you could have won,' before revealing what I'd actually won. Coming to Appledore had taken me back to the past, what had been and what might have been, and despite a reluctance to even try to renovate that awful, dilapidated café, I'd fleetingly contemplated a different life. With Gina as a sleeping partner who knows, we might have been able to restore the café to its former glory? But even that glimmer on the horizon had now been taken from me. I had nothing to do with the café – all I had was this – a rusty old van. This wasn't going to make my fortune, or even help with a few mortgage payments, it probably wouldn't even start. I couldn't help but feel deflated.

'So are you going to be driving her along the beach this summer?' Ben was saying, a permanent smile on his face as he walked round the vehicle, kicking her tyres and playing with the wing mirrors. I winced every time he did this, expecting poor old Reginaldo to crumble. 'It would be great to see Reginaldo back in action,' he said, longingly.

'No, I couldn't control a beast like him. I can only just manage my Fiat – this would be like driving a juggernaut, and it's practically Jurassic – it must be a hundred years old!'

Ben laughed; 'Yeah, he's seen better days, but according to the documents he's roadworthy. Your aunt kept on top of the MOTs each year and apparently gave him a spin every now and then.'

I felt a softening inside. This had clearly been a labour of love for Sophia, who'd kept the van going for her husband even though he'd died years before. Theirs was a true love story, with all the passion and wanting that often comes when a couple have to fight to be together. And here was Reginaldo, a symbol of Uncle Reginald's success at becoming part of the business – and the reason Sophia's family finally accepted him. Uncle Reggie had loved the café like his own, and together he and Sophia had built it into something even better, and despite my disappointment, I knew my aunt had left me something very close to her heart.

But how could I take up the challenge, what the hell was I supposed to do with it? Apart from having no clue how to run an ice cream van, I couldn't drive it round the mean streets of Manchester, it was meant for a sunny beach. Besides, taking Reginaldo away would be a terrible thing to do, he was part of the fabric of this town, so many people here must have had similar childhood memories to me; I could see by Ben's reaction, this van was like an old friend. But even if Reggie stayed here, I couldn't – I'd need rent to live in Appledore, and I still had the mortgage repayments at home to cover. Then there was Mum and the kids to think of – it was just too complicated to consider.

All this was going through my head as Ben opened the door of the ice-cream van and we both climbed inside. Again it wasn't living up to my memories, everything was covered in at least a year of dust and the windows were so filthy you couldn't see in or out. It seemed that Reggie had seen the last of his days in the sunshine on Appledore beach.

'You could spruce him up, give him a lick of paint...' Ben was saying.

'I can't really afford to invest any money in him, I recently lost my job.'

'Even better, you need a job and here he is – look what the universe gave you,' he said, gesturing towards Reginaldo as if he were the answer to my prayers.

'Mmm it's not quite as simple as all that, I've got kids... commitments at home in Manchester.'

'Oh that's a shame, I liked the idea of renovating an old ice cream van.'

'Yes it would be lovely, but I need to be sensible,' I said.

'What do you want to do with him then?' Ben asked, deep disappointment now etched on his face. 'The guy who owns the garage let Sophia keep him here, but now she's gone he'll probably want his garage back.'

This was an added problem, not only had I just inherited something I didn't really want, I had to find somewhere for it to 'live'.

'I can't afford to pay for storage...' I started.

'It breaks my heart to say it, but you could scrap him I suppose, wouldn't be worth much but...'

'Oh God, no! It would be like murdering Uncle Reggie – I couldn't do that.' The van may have been no use to me, but I couldn't send him to the scrapheap.

Ben laughed. 'My mate's a mechanic, I could ask him to look it over for you and he'd probably have an idea about what it's worth. He might even know someone who'd take it off your hands,' he suggested.

I thanked him, I wasn't going to be able to come down here again for a while and if Ben could sort things out for me it would save a journey. I felt slightly bereft at the thought of giving Reggie up but what else could I do? At least Ben could find him a nice home and save him from the scrap heap. I was grateful, and just kept gazing at the van, running my hands along the sills, allowing myself one last, lingering glance at the lovely old thing. I couldn't help but think how like a proud old man he was – past his prime but waiting patiently to be useful again. Then my head took over, told me to stop being such an idiot, and I swallowed hard and waved goodbye to Reginaldo for the last time while trying to hold back the tears that had suddenly and inexplicably welled up.

'So... you have kids?' Ben asked as we closed the garage doors.

'Yes Josh and Lucie, eighteen and nineteen – what about you?'

'No, my life doesn't have any kid sized spaces - but I have Jimmy... my snorkel,' he said. 'I travel light, I'm here for the summer and then I'm off to Hawaii to dive for the winter.'

'That sounds lovely,' I sighed, 'to be able to just pack your snorkel and set off for another ocean.' I could just imagine this guy's Facebook pictures, he'd put all those Aga shots to shame.

'Yeah... I can't complain. I couldn't live without the sea, it gets to you, you know? I work with my dad for a few months, save a bit of money, live at home – then go off again. It works for me.'

'You sound like my kids, they're going off for the summer, my daughter's planning on spending a whole year away, and my son's volunteering in Nepal for the summer, but who knows when I'll see him again once he's gone. They don't really need me around any more, but Mum will... I think. Mind you she's recently joined a dating website to have some "fun", but as she's seventy-eight it's a little daunting – for me more than her,' I laughed.

Ben was now leaning against the garage door listening. He was smiling, interested in what I had to say, he wasn't looking at his phone or downloading music and he wasn't wearing earphones and tuning me out, as far as I could tell. This made a nice change for me.

'Selfishly, I'd rather hoped Mum was done with men and was prepared to accept the life of singledom, but she's made of sterner stuff,' I added. '"I'm determined to have an adventure," she said, and Josh, my son, helped her to upload her profile and photo onto "Grey and Gorgeous". Anyway, typical Josh, he'd had one eye on his Xbox, so instead of offering herself to the members of "Grey and Gorgeous", mother became an active member of the "Gay and Gorgeous" website. Needless to say, after mother's third "date" with a lovely lady called Den with love handles and a penchant for welding, I felt the need to step in and investigate. It didn't take Miss Marple to work out that she was offering herself for "wild times" and "uncomplicated fun" to every ageing lesbian within a twenty-mile radius. I suggested she stop agreeing to go on dates, and take her profile down immediately, but then my kids said I was making "hetero assumptions" and I mustn't assume my mother was straight because "gender can be fluid".'

Ben was laughing now; 'Caught between two generations.'

'Exactly! And it's a minefield honestly, my kids are a constant reminder that the world is changing and everything I thought was fact might not actually be true.'

'That sounds scary,' he said, supressing a smile.

It was nice to have someone listen to me for a change and he seemed to find my story amusing. So I continued to tell him about my mother's inadvertent dip into Sapphic seas, which ended when she discovered Frederick on Facebook and decided her gender was pretty stable after all.'

'You've certainly got your hands full, Ella,' he said, when I'd finished. 'I see now why moving down here would be impossible.'

'Yes, then there's the social whirl, I have a carousel of funerals to attend with my mother, usually followed by several washes and an evening meal to serve,' I said, checking my watch, 'it's all glamour – oh and my train's leaving soon, I'd better get off.'

I'd been chatting so long I'd not realised the time and was re-lieved when Ben offered to drive me to the station rather than have to wait for a taxi. 'I want to hear more about your mad mother and your crazy life in the north,' he laughed as we climbed in his car. It was an old mini and once seated I felt like my bottom was on the ground. It reminded me of driving through Salford as a teenager with an old boyfriend. Or was it just being with someone like Ben that was making me feel young again?

His eyes were firmly on the road as we set off and I took the oppor-tunity to survey him close up. It was a long time since I'd been alone in a car with a man – and it might be a while before it happened again, so I savoured every moment. Nice firm legs in jeans, sexy stubble and raggy cuffs on his jacket, the car smelling of sea salt and sun cream. I could have travelled for miles like this, but too soon we'd arrived at Barnstaple station. We agreed that Ben would look at options for buyers and then I would make a decision as to the fate of poor old Reginaldo before we exchanged numbers and I ran for my train.

By the time the train pulled away from Barnstaple, I was telling myself to forget the last few hours, go home and face reality. I would send out my CV to all the local shops and ask around to see if anyone had any work – anywhere. I tried hard to summon up enthusiasm, but all the way home I watched the trees flash past as Devon disappeared into dusk and all I could think about was Appledore and Aunt Sophia's delicious gelato.

The memories were bittersweet – the relationship rift between Mum and Aunt Sophia had torn everything apart and ultimately left Sophia alone. Her husband died, Gina went off to live her own life, and Sophia stayed behind only for her hard work to disappear like sand between her fingers.

I thought about how my own life was currently doing the same. My kids were leaving, I'd lost my job and I was set to be a divorced unemployed single parent living with her mum who at seventy-eight had a better social and romantic life than I did. My dreams had been dealt a blow in Appledore too; I hadn't got to see Gina, I'd hoped for a share in the café but instead I was now returning home the not-so-proud owner of an octegenarian van.

Was there still time to do something more with my life and get that Facebook fantasy? Should I just play it safe and not risk losing what little I had, or should I throw caution to the wind and embrace what apparently the universe had given me? Perhaps this was my adventure after all?

Chapter Seven

Lovely George Clooney and Cheryl Cole-Thingy

The trip to Devon had opened my eyes to the possibility of something else and no matter how hard I tried I couldn't let it go.

I tried to forget the salty air, the long, golden beaches and the hot, ice cream summers of my childhood, because I had real life to deal with and a monthly mortgage to pay. I had to get a grip; there was no huge windfall, no ice cream business and no Gina. Yet the other part of me, the one who had run into the sea with Gina, and made crazy, towering sundaes, dared to wonder... what if?

The following weekend both my kids were leaving for their summers away, and I had to be in the present and just make sure they went with everything they needed, and one of those things was a happy mum.

Once everything was sorted with the kids then I would call Gina – I didn't have a number for her but I was certain I could make contact – surely Ben would have a number she could be reached on? Yet I didn't feel that my life was in the right place to speak to my successful, beautiful cousin just yet. I wished I could call her and say 'Yes I'm doing well, I am CEO of a company, my husband and I just celebrated our silver wedding and we're all off on a family holiday to Cannes.' I'd follow this call up by emailing photos of the company, the family and the holiday, just like the ones I saw on Facebook. But with a failed marriage, no job and a soon to be empty nest, I didn't have the confidence to call – and there were no photos to show off with. One thing was for sure though – whatever happened to me, I wasn't going to make the same mistakes our mothers had made and leave it too long to make contact.

Meanwhile, I had a lot of other stuff to think about, from the kids' passports, to toiletries, to malaria tablets to condoms (I'm a realist). I had an awful lot of other people's requirements filling my head – and my shopping basket – and having these things to worry about was keeping my mind off the real trauma that my babies were leaving.

Eventually the time came for Lucie to leave and I drove her to the airport while Josh slept in the back of the car (I'd asked him to come along, worried I might need physical and emotional support). Mum had been upset about Lucie leaving; she was as protective of them as she had been of me. So I'd suggested she say her goodbyes to Lucie at home rather than waiting around at the airport, and seeing her leave which might be more painful.

'Now keep in touch won't you... it's easy and free on Facebook,' I said as I drove her to the airport.

'Yes but I'll only communicate with you on there if you stop putting on lame posts about that old man,' she groaned.

'Who, lovely George Clooney?' I teased. 'I only wrote that he was my dream guy. It's not like I posted my naked breasts all over the page.'

'Oh gross,' Josh muttered from the back seat, waking up groggily at the horrific prospect.

'Which reminds me,' I said, 'talking of old people posting naked body parts, I'm not very good online and Josh leads her astray, but can you still keep an eye on Nan's online activities while you're away?'

Lucie smiled; 'Yeah, don't worry, I'm always across that shit.'

'Good.'

'But I reckon we're one photo away from her getting her Instagram shut down,' she warned. 'And someone should take her Twitter off her.'

'Not Donald Trump again?'

Lucie pulled a face; 'Putin.'

'Oh Christ, really? And to think until recently all I had to worry about was her having a tattoo on her bum like Cheryl Cole-thingy and plastering it all over the net.' I could only dream of those halcyon days, when all I worried about was my mother appearing on a niche tattoo-porn website. Now I was concerned about the KGB living in our loft and what to pack for my thirty-year stay in Siberia.

'Oh the Cheryl tat was funny.' Lucie smiled, gazing ahead like it was a lovely moment of nostalgia.

'No it wasn't, I had to convince her that just because "the lovely girl off *X Factor*" had a rose on her arse it didn't mean she should.'

'But she wasn't going to have it on her arse...'

'That's not the point, Lucie. She's seventy-eight, she shouldn't be thinking about tattoos... or arses for that matter. Talking of which have you heard from your father?'

'Not since 2007,' she said.

Great, that meant The Dick hadn't made any financial contributions to Lucie's trip.

'Anyway, who says Nan can't have a tattoo?' she said, picking at her nails. 'It doesn't matter how old you are, it's Nan's body even if she did want it on her arse...'

'Stop talking about your nan's arse, it's disrespectful,' I said, and we both giggled. And I giggled so much I started to cry because I was going to miss Lucie so damn much and I had to pull over and Josh had to drive while I sobbed on the back seat.

And later, when we waved her off at the airport I could think of little else but my little girl three years old in pigtails with a lisp – and it felt like yesterday.

Two hours, several frappuccinos and a box of tissues later, I was still a nasty mess but managed to drive home with Josh as navigator. It was less scary than letting him drive.

We were just pulling up outside the house and I'd gathered myself together, when he started talking about Aarya, his girlfriend, and how much he liked her. This was unusual for Josh, he'd rarely shared his feelings with me since he was little, and suddenly he was telling me all about his relationship. This revolved around how kind, beautiful and clever Aarya was and how he saw their future together, which was lovely. He told me Aarya meant Princess and she was 'just like an Indian Princess with her long dark hair and beautiful brown eyes'. I was amazed, this was the first time we'd spent longer than ten minutes talking – the last time didn't count because he was asking for money with his earphones in.

'She's going to miss her little dog, Delilah, while we're away,' he said.

'Aah, well I suppose they could Skype?' I joked.

'She won't be able to – her parents are refusing to look after Delilah while we're gone,' he sighed theatrically. It was then it dawned on me that this wasn't perhaps about my son opening up to his mother after all.

'Oh that's a shame,' I said, 'but I'm sure someone will take care of her for Aarya while you're on your travels.'

'Actually Mum… we wondered if you'd like to look after her? She's so cute… she's a tiny Pomeranian…'

'I've seen Aarya's photos and Delilah is very cute, but I've got enough on my plate, Josh. I don't need another mouth to feed.'

'She just needs TLC, she's very old, Mum – she's only got one eye.'

'Josh I've got enough with a human OAP who needs TLC – I don't need a canine one.'

I glanced across and he was looking at me with big eyes.

'And you can't use emotional blackmail, or anything else in your armoury – Aarya's dog is not my responsibility, therefore the guilt trip won't work.' I pulled hard on the handbrake for emphasis and climbed out of the car.

For once Josh didn't answer me back, but meekly followed me into the house where my mother was sitting on the sofa. She had the volume on high and was engrossed in some *Jeremy Kyle* drama.

'But Mum…' Josh started again.

'No,' I said, stopping him before he could tell me some shaggy tale about how this amazing dog had rescued Aarya from a burning building.

Mum was watching the TV, engrossed as a heavily tattooed bloke threatened to punch another heavily tattooed bloke, and by the way she was bouncing I reckoned she was joining in.

'Ooh it's like the wrestling,' she gasped, one hand to her mouth, the other on the sofa arm to steady herself in the excitement. 'Did Lucie get off okay? I was trying to take my mind off her leaving by watching a bit of Jeremy.' I had to smile; I didn't think a bear pit filled with angry people being verbally tasered by the presenter was quite the sanctuary mother implied.

'Yeah Lucie was fine, not sure about me though,' I smiled, wandering over to the sofa and sitting next to her.

Mum put her arm around me, a mother comforting another mother; 'I've shed some tears too, love... our little girl going all that way,' she sighed, dragging herself away from the on screen action to give me some attention in my hour of need.

'I know. Hard to believe, isn't it?' I sighed, resting my head on her shoulder.

'Well she's living her life – she's going off to find herself a nice young man... and it's about time you did.'

Mum seemed to see my single status as some kind of deformity that had to be fixed – or hidden. Only recently she'd introduced me to her new friend Doris, who she'd met at a tea dance, explaining, 'No, she doesn't have a husband any more, she let him go.' This was said like I'd sacked him, or been careless and lost him at sea, when it was him who walked out on me. I hadn't chosen this status, it had been forced upon me, and Mum held the old-fashioned view that a person wasn't complete without a partner.

I pulled away, 'Not everyone's looking for a date, Mother.' I hated myself for snapping at Mum but sometimes I wished she'd stop the constant reminders that I was single, like I didn't know.

'Shall I put the kettle on, ladies – two teas?' Josh was saying in an unusually ingratiating voice, walking into the kitchen.

Mum and I both looked at each other. I was surprised he knew where the kettle was, let alone making the tea.

'What the bloody hell's wrong with him?' Mum said, one eye back on the TV. 'Is he on those drugs, do you think?'

'I hope not,' I said, horrified.

Then she turned away from the TV and looked at me soberly. 'His girlfriend's pregnant by another man.'

'Christ no... but I thought everything was perfect, that he loved her,' I felt sick. This was so unlike the Aarya I knew. 'Where did you hear that, Mum? Was there something on Facebook?'

'No.'

'So how do you know?'

'Jeremy Kyle told me,' she said, pointing at the screen like I was mad.

'Oh you mean *him*. The tattooed man's girlfriend's pregnant?' I sat back, breathing a sigh of relief and tucking my feet under me.

'Yes.' Mum looked at me and rolled her eyes like I was the one who'd caused the confusion.

Before she could fill me in on any more TV scandal, Josh entered the room with a tray and cups of tea and biscuits, something I'd never known him do before. I was beginning to wonder if my mother was right. Was my son under the influence of some illegal substance?

'You okay, Josh?' I asked, trying to look discreetly into his eyes for dilated pupils as he put the tray down on the coffee table.

'No... I'm not, Mum.'

'Those drugs,' Mum muttered under her breath, 'he's on that "canarbiss", Ella, they're all on it now.'

'Thank you, Mother, I can handle this...' I started, hoping she'd go back to tattooed Tommy and his mate still giving Jeremy Kyle a hard time.

'It's everywhere isn't it, Joshy?' God, the woman never stopped. 'Frederick and I were wondering if we should try it, might calm my arthritis and his dodgy hip.'

'Not ganga, Nan,' Josh said, 'you'd be all over the place.'

'Ha, I am anyway,' she sighed and returned to the TV.

'Mum, I'm... worried,' he looked at me under his lashes.

'Oh love, what about?' I asked, as he settled down on the arm of the sofa. I touched his arm. 'You can tell me... are you worried about going away?'

He nodded slowly and my heart swelled.

'Oh love,' I said, putting both arms around his waist. He may be taller than me, and think he's all worldly, but he was still a little boy at heart, a little boy who was going to miss home, miss his mum. And I was going to miss him too.

'Thing is – if Aarya doesn't find anyone to look after Delilah she says she can't come away with me.'

'Josh,' I said in gentle chastisement. I pulled away and took a sip of lukewarm tea – he hadn't even boiled the kettle properly.

'But, Mum, Delilah's so cute... and she can take the place of me and Lucie – keep you company while we're away.'

'I've got Nan for company – when she isn't romancing her latest fling Frederick. Besides, no one could take the place of you and Lucie, even a cute dog.' I had to assert myself over this dog business.

'But Mum, we leave on Wednesday – and it's not like you're going anywhere is it?'

'Oh no, it's not like I'm going anywhere. In fact, I'm going nowhere,' I said, but Josh was now on his phone, lost to me, and I looked around the room, the phrase echoing in my head. 'I'm going nowhere.' I'd felt this dip the minute I'd hit the grey Manchester streets; they didn't compare to the sunshine pastels of Devon and the sea.

'So what do you say, Ma?' I heard him say, waking me from my reverie.

'She's the cutest little dog,' Mum muttered, now on her phone too.

'Josh, have you just texted Nan to say that?' I asked.

'No Mum, I wouldn't do that... I tweeted obviously. Nan knows how important it is to save a life, don't you Nan?'

'Yes, my love,' she said. 'I retweeted it,' she was smiling at her grandson like he were a god. I don't know how I was expected to keep my kids under control when my mother ruined them both.

Josh could get anything out of me, he was sweet and charming and had a way of playing the vulnerable card beautifully, but not this time.

'I've got some stuff to do,' I said before either of them could say any more and headed upstairs, leaving them to their Twitter campaign. I was more concerned about a job right now than a dog. I headed upstairs to dig out my old CV and search job websites, something I hadn't actually done yet. Until now I'd thought I might have some money, one way or another, via Sophia's inheritance, but even if Ben's friend managed to sell Reginaldo for me he wouldn't be worth much. This was now officially a financial crisis and I had to act quickly.

I was just settling down on my bed with all my paperwork when the phone rang; the voice on the end of the line said he was Dick's solicitor and he would be sending me some documents in the post.

'Clients often find the legal jargon a little difficult, so I sometimes call first to make it very clear,' he was saying.

'But we're already divorced,' I said, wondering why Dick's solicitor would possibly be sending anything to me. For a moment I wondered if something terrible had happened at his villa and he'd finally fallen in that pool and left everything to me and the kids. But then I remembered, this was The Dick and he would never do anything so thoughtful.

The solicitor started going on about deeds and agreements now and how I'd signed something several years ago to say I would buy Dick out of the house.

'Yes, I know,' I sighed, 'but he said we can stay as long as we need to. I can't afford to buy him out yet…' My heart was beginning to thump slightly and my head felt rather light.

I can't remember exactly what he said next, but the gist of it was that I'd signed an agreement promising to give Dick half the money for the house. And as the kids were now over eighteen I either had to move out or pay half of the money for the house to Dick.

So now I was jobless and homeless – with an ageing mother to support, could things get any worse?

I put down the phone and wept. This was the house we'd moved into when Josh was born, we'd been here almost twenty years; it was full of memories, some good and some Dick.

I wish I could say I couldn't believe he would do this, but it was classic Dick. He'd always been a selfish money-grabbing pig and even though this would affect his kids that didn't matter to him. His timing, as always, was spot on; I had nothing to live on, let alone pay him hundreds of thousands of pounds. I was upset, but more than this I was angry; all I could see in my mind's eye was his smug face and *her* perky brown breasts taunting me from Facebook. I couldn't allow them to beat me, I had to do something; I would not let them see me fail. I would stall for longer, and in the meantime I would show him. I'd make something of my life, in spite of him, and he could have his bloody money. I just wasn't quite sure – as yet – how I was going to climb this particular mountain.

Chapter Eight

Frogs and Snails and Puppy Dogs' Tails

I lay upstairs for a while thinking things through – I was furious with Dick, but I've always been a great believer that things happen for a reason. There were things I couldn't control and things I could and it was time to start working to find a way we could survive.

I made some notes, googled a few things and came to the conclusion that Dick might have done me a favour for the first time ever. Perhaps this final act from a man I once loved was the kick up the bum I needed for a fresh start?

Later, when I'd finally cleared the red mist, I told Mum about the solicitor's phone call, and after using some colourful adjectives to describe The Dick, she eventually calmed down.

'You could sell the house, give the greedy bugger his money and buy something smaller?' she said.

'Yes, I could, but we'd still need somewhere to live and I wouldn't get a mortgage for a new house as I don't have a job.'

She nodded. 'Perhaps I could get a job? I can sing you know.'

'Yes I know, Mum, but the Spice Girls have already split and I don't think Little Mix are looking for any more members.'

She giggled. 'Well, you never know, I still look good in shorts and I could show those young ones a thing or two.' Then she patted my knee. 'Try not to worry, you'll think of something, love, you always do.'

I loved her faith in me and tried to give her a reassuring smile as Josh wandered in from the kitchen, a sandwich in one hand, his iPhone in the other.

He looked at me and before he could say anything I snapped. 'NO. I can't look after someone else's dog, Josh.'

'How did you know I was going to ask…?'

'Because I'm bloody psychic – it comes with being a mother, your nan knows what I'm going to say next don't you, Mum?'

She was watching Jeremy again – series after series on catch up TV, tits, tats and trauma on a bloody permanent loop. Mum had watched *Mob Wives* in the same relentless way, a live streaming session of pseudo Italian abuse and vile death threats gushing into the living room. I spent one Saturday listening to botoxed New York women with collagened lips shouting things like: 'Check my bloodlines, I'm coming for you bitch.' That was a long weekend.

'The pierced people have been having three in a bed, Ella,' she was shaking her head. 'Disgusting… and now she's run off with his sister.'

'Mum, don't watch if it offends you.'

'It does… absolutely disgusting, but I have to know what happens,' she said, turning her back to me and resting her head on her hand to fully absorb the 'disgusting' sexual antics of Jeremy's guests.

Mum was happy in her own little world; she had a string of interchangeable boyfriends, lots of friends and Jeremy Kyle on the

TV. Lucie had gone and Josh was about to. This was a home filled with memories, I thought as I gazed around the room, but perhaps it was time to let go, stop using the house and the kids as an excuse to stay here? I remembered what Ben the solicitor had said about the universe providing the answer to my problem. I had no money and would soon have no home, so what was there to lose?

'Mum, just tell me what you've got against looking after a little scrap of cute fur while we're away?' Josh began again.

And before I knew it, I heard myself say, 'Because I'm going away too.'

Both Mum and Josh looked at me, yes, really looked at me – eye contact, phones down, everything.

'Away?' they both said in unison, as if it were the craziest thing they'd ever heard.

'Yes,' I said. 'Aunt Sophia's van is calling. I think I'm going to give it a go, a summer in Appledore selling ice cream on the beach? I could do a lot worse.'

They were still staring at me.

'Don't be daft, you can't do that, Ella,' Mum was shocked. 'You can't go all the way to Devon, what would happen to me?'

'You'd come with me, wouldn't you?' I hadn't given the practicalities too much thought, but Mum was a consideration, and welcome to join me on my adventure.

'Oh no, I'm not going back there – and I don't think you should either,' she looked momentarily scared.

'Why not, Mum?' I thought she'd come round to the idea, but she seemed so adamant.

'Because, you mustn't go.'

She said this without offering any explanation. I didn't understand, but she wouldn't be pushed and if she wasn't going to tell me why I shouldn't, then why shouldn't I?

'Mum, you said I'd think of something, and I have. The house is being sold, I have no job and I need to do something. Now.'

Throughout this exchange my son stared at me apparently genuinely concerned, which was nice. Unusual, but nice.

'Mum, you can't just go off on your own…'

'But, sweetie, *you* are.'

'I know but that's different, I'm young.'

I had to smile at this. 'Josh, I will be fine, just think of this as my own "gap summer", I'll be back by September.'

'You can't just go off and do stuff, where will me and Lucie go if we need to come back?' Josh said.

'Josh – I'm not stopping *you* from going away, so don't stop *me*.'

'I'm not,' he said, 'it's just… mums don't do things like that.'

'Well this one's about to,' I said. 'This is the first time in my life I'm doing something I want to do. And I'll still be there for everyone – I just might be on the end of a phone rather than in the flesh.'

In the few minutes I'd given in to my heart and decided to do this, the idea was growing on me. I loved the sound of summer by the sea, waking up to the sound of seagulls, sand between my toes, wind in my hair, and being me, just me.

'But what about Delilah… you'll be abandoning her as well as your family?' He was a trier my son.

'Honestly! Didn't you hear what I said? I'm not going to sit here and mind dogs and make tea and wait around just in case someone, somewhere might need to pop back from their own big adventures.' My family were everything to me and I didn't want Josh or Mum to think I didn't care, but I did need them to know how I was feeling.

Mum turned to look at me, alarmed, sounding really scared now. 'You can't go there Ella... you can't go there... Sophia will...'

'Sophia's dead, Mum,' I said gently.

'Don't go there,' she repeated, slowly.

For a moment I was concerned, I didn't want to upset her. 'Why, Mum?'

'Because... I don't want you to,' she was deadly serious.

'Mum, nothing's going to happen to me...'

She suddenly seemed to regain her composure. Her tone and expression changed, but it didn't feel real. 'Who would cook my tea?' she asked, with fake brightness.

I smiled and patted her arm reassuringly. 'Come with me and cook mine when I get in from the beach?' I said, liking the sound of days spent working by the sea.

'Over my dead body,' she spat, shaking her head vigorously, and I wondered for the millionth time what had happened to make her so hostile towards the idea of Appledore. Even now, with Sophia dead, she didn't want to return to that lovely place by the sea with its whitewashed houses and a tingle in the air.

'Mum, I wish you'd talk to me about this. Why do you feel such hostility towards Sophia... and Appledore? You were once very happy there, you and Sophia were close... I don't understand...'

'The past is the past. I'm not coming with you,' Mum said, folding her arms.

'Okay, well if that's how you feel and you don't want to talk about it I suppose I have to accept it.'

'Yes you do,' she muttered, her face red with anger or frustration, or upset… she was hard to read.

I wasn't going to weaken my resolve, and I also wasn't going to use my mum as an excuse not to do this. It was scary, a huge challenge, but I was going to go for it; 'I'm still going to go, Mum.' I saw her open her mouth to challenge me, but I carried on.

'So are you okay to stay here and show prospective buyers around the house,' I said. 'Perhaps you could even try and put them off to get us more time here,' I winked.

Her face softened, she liked a bit of mischief and I wondered in that moment if perhaps this might be good for all of us, a gentle push to move us forward. Who knew what my adventure would bring, but at least I'd be earning something, not worrying about money while waiting around for responses to job applications that might never come.

'I know it's not ideal, but I believe things are meant to be. There's a reason that Aunt Sophia left me that van, don't you agree, Mum?' I was hoping she might react to this, provide a clue as to why she'd been so against coming with me, so tried to bring her back into the conversation, but she just looked at me.

'I think it's an insult quite honestly… it was my family's business and she should have left some of the café to you. But no – we are left out in the cold – again!'

'But Aunt Sophia loved me, she wouldn't try to hurt or insult me. Why do you think she would do that?'

'Because she wants you to go back there, but she's not prepared to give you anything more than the van. She thinks you'll come running, like you used to when you were a child.'

I always had a feeling Mum might be jealous of my close relationship with Sophia and Gina. As a mum myself now I could see how it was easier for Sophia and Gina to give me more freedom, more treats, more late nights – they were like the weekend parent and never had full responsibility. For Mum this must have been frustrating watching me go off each year and have a wonderful time without her.

'Are you jealous? Is that what this is, Mum?'

'No, what rubbish. I'm not jealous of her, I just don't want you to go there, she always said you'd go back and now you are. And Gina'll turn up and cause bother and… oh love, just stay here?'

'Mum, I think you're imagining all this. Gina and Sophia were always kind to me, but it's like you don't trust Sophia, like she's luring me back and it will somehow hurt me. Why can't you tell me what's bothering you?'

'If you don't want to take my advice then just leave it be, Ella,' she shook her head and began scrolling through her phone.

'Mum, you're as bad as the kids, looking at your phone every time we try to have a conversation…' She wasn't going to tell me, but I kept on, knowing at times I probably should have backed off, I just wanted to understand where all this was coming from. 'Mum, why don't you try to move on, whatever it was, Sophia is dead now – can't you let all the bitterness and resentment go with her?'

What could possibly be so bad that she still felt like this to-wards her dead sister?

'No,' she said, turning off the TV as she left the room.

I didn't know what to say to her, I couldn't make up my mind if she had a legitimate reason to be worried or was just feeling un-loved. I tried not to let Mum spoil this – after all she'd always been protective, reluctant to let me fly.

'I just want to give it a go,' I said to Josh. 'I need a job and now there's the van – so why not do something I want to in a lovely setting?'

Josh shrugged, finally in semi-agreement... I hoped.

'I'll make sure I have internet connection,' I continued to try and reassure him. 'So we can Skype and call or text wherever you are. Just pretend I'm here if it makes you feel better.'

He nodded; 'If it's what you want, Mum?'

'I do,' I said, 'I really do.'

'Hey, Mum, you know what might help?'

I looked at him.

'Take Delilah with you, so you don't feel so alone.'

I laughed at his persistence. 'Hey, I'm travelling light, no dogs on board – the very idea of having a small animal around is out of the question, so please tell Aarya that Delilah the Pomeranian will have to stay where she is.' I reached for a biscuit from the tray; 'And I am adamant about that, Josh, no amount of emotional blackmail, charm or persuasion will change my mind.'

Later that week, as I took possession of Delilah, her toys, her four-poster bed, various bikinis (oh yes) and an Imelda Marcos-style number of dog shoes, I wondered just what part of 'adamant' my son hadn't heard.

The only good thing about Josh's departure was that he and Aarya were being driven to the airport by her parents, which made the goodbyes easier for me. I stood in the window waving Delilah's paw at the departing car and for the first time in a long time wondered what life had in store for me. For better or worse, things were going to be different – I was scared and excited and I could feel my heart beating at the prospect of the voyage ahead of me.

I put Delilah down and wandered the house, looking into the kids' empty bedrooms. Lucie's smelled of pear drops, and Josh's smelled of feet and sweat; frogs and snails and puppy dogs' tails, I thought as I closed the door. I was missing them already but happy they were doing what they wanted to do, discovering the world, living their lives.

I didn't feel lonely with the kids gone; I was used to them being out and about, or just in their rooms. But I always knew where they were (within a ten-mile radius) and it felt strange to think they wouldn't be coming home tonight. I'd often longed for some peace and quiet, but this was a little sudden and slightly unnerving. I was pondering this when I suddenly became aware of another presence, and looked down to see a little blonde fluffy face looking up at me. Delilah was a rescue dog who'd been mistreated, and she did indeed only have one eye, but it was the softest, brownest eye, and her little doggie smile touched my heart. Her expression seemed almost human, quizzical as she turned her head to one side then the other.

'Are you trying to work me out, Delilah?' I said, bending down to fuss her. 'Don't waste your time, sweetie, because after forty-four years I'm still trying to work me out.' I picked her up, holding her against my chest; she was so light and seemed so vulnerable. We'd both been plonked into a new world, a new life – and I think we were a little nervous about what might happen next.

'So what are you like at selling ice cream, Delilah?' I said to my-self as much as to the little bundle of fluff in my arms. She licked my cheek and her tail wagged like mad and I knew in my heart that it was time for both of us to have our own adventure.

Chapter Nine

Ice Cream and Flip-Flops down Avenues of Pleasure

The next day I called Ben Shaw and told him my plans.

He seemed very enthusiastic. 'Sounds like a great idea,' he said, 'and I'm sure as the ice cream van belongs to the café you could use the kitchens there for any storage or preparation you need.'

I hadn't even thought that far ahead, but it sounded like a great idea and it would be a pleasure to work there again. He also said I could have the keys to Sophia's apartment which meant I wouldn't have to worry about finding somewhere to stay. 'It's Gina's now,' he said, 'obviously she's not around and I'm sure she wouldn't have a problem with you staying there until you get settled in.'

It was wonderful, everything was falling into place; this was my adventure – my ice cream summer. It may be a disaster, but I was doing something that excited me, and I hadn't done that for a very long time.

And so a couple of weeks later, at the end of June, I packed the car and prepared for the six hour drive ahead.

I had intended to travel light, inspired by the sea and the way some people just move around the earth with no chattels. But despite my longing for spiritual freedom and a barefoot summer there was the not so small matter of Delilah's 'luggage' – a matching eight-piece set in pink and black polka dot that filled much of the back seat. Obviously she needed her throws and jewellery boxes too, and these were taking up half the boot. I'd hoped we could both turn up with a sarong and a smile, but Josh let Aarya loose on Skype and she'd insisted Delilah take all her outfits, 'just in case'.

'Ella, I'm missing her so much already... will you post all her pictures on Instagram so I can see my baby every day?' she'd asked. I understood, I was missing my babies too. But photos, every day? Really? I could only hope Aarya would become so involved in her work in Nepal that I may be able to have the odd day off from doggie selfies.

Mum was now standing on the step one leg in the hallway ready to sprint back in as soon as I'd gone; she'd downloaded *The Real Housewives of Cheshire* and was keen to 'get stuck in'.

'While you're away I'll show buyers round the house and tell them we've got rats and damp,' she laughed. I knew she was still unhappy about me going, but realising I wasn't going to change my mind she was putting a brave face on things. 'No, I know, I'll say there was a murder here and it's haunted,' she continued. 'No one will want to buy this house, I'll make sure of it – and then we can stay here and Dick can sing for his money!'

But when it came to me actually leaving she became tearful, and for a moment I almost caved in, until I remembered that though this was an adventure – I also had no choice. I'd had no luck so far in terms of getting a job and this was the only option right now to make some money.

'Call me any time,' I said, refusing to feel guilty as she stood on the step clutching her hankie.

'Now all the bills are direct debited, Mum, so there shouldn't be any problems,' I said, hugging her. 'And I've arranged an online shop to arrive each week, so no worries there.'

'I might never see you again… I might die before you realise you did the wrong thing going there.'

I ignored this, reminding her that she could change her mind any time and come with me if she wanted to.

She pursed her lips. 'Not while there's snow on the Himalayas.'

'Well, I'd love it if you did come and stay at some point,' I said. If she wasn't going to discuss this with me properly I had no choice, I had made the decision and I was going.

'Go on, you go and enjoy yourself… you'll soon find out what you're missing,' she shooed me away as I climbed into the car, but gestured for me to wind the window down for her parting shot.

I braced myself.

'Don't get too involved with people down there…' she said, her face was close to mine and she had that concerned look again.

'What people?'

'They talk… there's lots of talk, small town… don't believe anyone's lies.'

This bothered me slightly but I wouldn't let Mum see me weaken, this was my time, my adventure and I wasn't going to be put off. 'I don't understand… I want to make friends, I think it'll be good for me. You're always telling me to get out more, meet new people.'

'You can do that here.'

I couldn't hang around any longer listening to Mum trying to put me off. I waved and pulled away, wondering once more what she'd got against Appledore, its people and her sister. Perhaps my journey back there would reveal what had happened once and for all?

It was a long journey down the M5 and Delilah and I needed a couple of toilet breaks. I'd brought her travel bag with us which contained everything a doggie on the go might need, from a toothbrush to perfume (Jean Paw Gaultier and DCanineY of course), to spare pyjamas and the all-important diamanté-encrusted water bowl. I bought us both a bottle of water and poured hers into her bowl, much to the delight of a young family in the next car whose kids asked if they could take her picture. I took one too, she looked rather cute in her pink party dress, though later I was admonished by Aarya when she saw the picture on Instagram. 'Ella, she shouldn't wear her designer stuff for travel,' she messaged me.

I apologised and explained I'd never dressed a dog before, this was the first time – it looked like this was going to be a summer of firsts.

On arrival in Appledore I parked up and walked along the beach to Ben Shaw's offices to collect the van and apartment keys. This was the first time I'd been to the offices, and from the outside they looked like a typical, mundane solicitor's, grey windows, dark paintwork. I couldn't imagine Ben working here and tried to reconcile this place with the man I'd met on my last visit here. Having slipped Delilah into something stylish but casual after our long journey, I tied her up outside with her bowl of water and walked inside where Ben was sitting at his desk. He had both feet up, flip-flops on, reading a book and eating an ice cream cone, oblivious to anything around him. I stood for a few seconds wondering how to get his attention, and coughed slightly which did the trick. As soon as he saw me he leapt up.

'Whoa you scared me; thank God you're not a client.'

'I think I might be classed as a client?' I suggested.

'Oh… yeah of course you are. At least you're not my dad; I'm paranoid he's going to walk in and find me eating ice cream with no socks on.'

'There are worse things a man could do…' I said, looking at his bare feet, imagining them pounding on sand into the foamy sea.

'I suppose. God I hate this 9 to 5 crap, wish I was on a beach somewhere hot.'

'Don't we all?' I sighed, glancing down at his flip-flops. 'So ice cream and flip-flops are frowned upon here?'

'Yes, in fact any avenue of pleasure is frowned upon if you're my father – which I think we've established you're not?'

I laughed. 'No, I can't be, because I love ice cream and flip-flops and often stroll down avenues of pleasure,' I said, wondering what the hell I was going on about.

'You sound like my kinda girl,' he laughed.

I blushed and laughed along. Too much. In fact, my excessive laughter may have given him the impression I was slightly un-hinged. It was weird, but I couldn't stop – it's just that no man had said anything remotely flirty to me for many years and it threw me slightly. Eventually I had to style it out into a cough and he brought me a glass of water.

'Flip-flops and ice cream is an interesting choice for a solicitor at work… but hey it could catch on,' I said, once I'd composed myself.

'Yeah, that's what I say, I told my dad we should have dress-down days and a slide in the office like they do at Google, but there are only two of us, and he hates helter-skelters.'

'They aren't for everyone,' I smiled, realising that Ben was joking much of the time. In fact, he rarely took anything seriously, which was refreshing.

'Do you get your sense of humour from your dad?' I asked.

'God no, he doesn't *laugh*, but that's because he's been stuck in this office all his life, which is why I don't want to be.'

'I get that, I'm so looking forward to spending the summer outside. Which reminds me, I've come for the keys.'

'Oh of course, hang on.'

He was now shuffling around in drawers and his pockets, and after recovering several sets of keys and putting them back, he finally found the ones he was looking for. He handed me three sets: one for the van, one for the café kitchens and the other for the apartment I'd be staying in. Ben had contacted Gina and she'd agreed I could stay there rent free over the summer, which was wonderful. He also gave me some forms to fill in, which he'd organised regarding my trading on and around the beach.

I thanked him for all his help and he pointed out it was his job.

'In the meantime you just need to get set up and running as soon as possible,' he said. 'I'll rush through these papers and chase the process through. Summer isn't long, you have to make the most of it… that's my motto anyway.'

'Yeah and it's true – so why are you stuck in here?'

'My ticket to Hawaii won't pay for itself unfortunately. I'm off at the end of August and won't be back here until next year. And before you say anything, I know, I know, I'm thirty-nine, and I need to grow up. But there's nothing quite like being in the ocean, surrounded by turquoise… nothing.'

'Oh I understand totally. Look at me I'm forty-four and I've already done the growing-up thing and it got boring. Now I'm starting on my own adventure, thanks to you.'

'Me?'

'Yes, you were the one who said why not work in the van over the summer. I'd already lost my job, then my ex-husband decided to sell our home from under us, and I remembered something you said… about the universe providing the answer. For me that answer was in the shape of Reginaldo – so here I am.'

'Hey nice to know someone actually listened to me for once,' he smiled.

'So while I'm dreaming of Devon, you're dreaming of Hawaii,' I said, suddenly wanting to know more about this man.

'Yeah. I've dived pretty much everywhere, Australia, India, the Caribbean, but Hawaii, she's my dream. It's somewhere I've always wanted to go and it feels like my last chance, my final exam you know?'

'Yes, I do. I'm not doing anything as amazing as scuba diving in Hawaii – but selling ice cream from a van on a Devon beach feels as exciting as that to me!'

'Everyone's dreams are equally valid, Ella,' he said, and he looked at me with those eyes, like he could see into my soul. He had this lovely way of making me feel comfortable, happy – and that word, 'valid', made me feel like I existed again. I was enjoying his company again, but suddenly remembered I'd left Delilah outside and could only imagine the drama that would ensue if anything happened to her so as much as I wanted to stay I decided to drag myself away.

I thanked Ben and said goodbye, wondering if he had a girl-friend and hoping I might see him again.

As he walked me to the door, he opened it and Delilah leapt up as soon as I emerged into the sunshine, and in her delight to see me was twirling like a spinning top.

'Who's this?' Ben said, smiling and immediately bending down to stroke her. She licked his face and we both laughed at her rather overwhelming hello, and I couldn't help but notice the way his long legs folded underneath him as he sat on his haunches.

'This is Delilah,' I said, 'she's an older lady and she may only have one eye but she knows how to bat her lashes.'

'I reckon you're going to love it here, Delilah,' he smiled, ruffling her fur.

'We've already walked along the beach – it was great, there was much excited barking and digging – and that was just me!'

'Be careful, people round here are funny about barking women,' he laughed, and I was warmed by this. Ben Shaw seemed to laugh a lot, reminding me of how little I'd laughed recently.

I watched him playing with Delilah, the tall man and this tiny dog looked so funny, but he didn't care. I wanted to be like him, free and happy, my life in a rucksack ready to go at any time. I'd always felt restless, like I was looking for something – a final piece of my jigsaw. Perhaps Appledore would bring me that feeling of freedom I craved?

Eventually, I prised Delilah off Ben; for a moment I envied the way he was touching her nose with his and telling her how gorgeous she was. In that instant I'd have given anything to be a Pomeranian in a pink jumpsuit.

With much tail-wagging and waving, we said goodbye and Delilah and I headed off for the car, both a little flat from leaving Ben behind.

After driving round for quite some time and taking in a little more of the area than planned, we arrived at what was to be our summer home. It was a first-floor apartment, and when I opened that door the calmness hit me like a blowing sea breeze, filling my head with tranquillity. Sophia had bought this place a few years back, but I'd always stayed with her in her apartment over the café when I'd visited, so this was all new to me.

As I took in my surroundings I noticed the walls were painted white, the floor was warm oak and the living room lined with bookshelves. Vintage Italian posters were dotted about the light and airy room with starfish and mermaid sculptures displayed on one of the shelves.

The bedroom was a cool blue with a tiny window looking out onto the estuary, and the view was amazing, I could see what Sophia loved about this place. The beach was flat, squiggly lines, rivulets of water on sand, turning to glitter when caught by the sun.

Delilah and I loped back downstairs to discover the tiny little galley kitchen stuffed with Mediterranean pottery and pasta pans hanging from the ceiling. How like Sophia to bring a little bit of Italy to this lovely apartment. I could almost smell the warm garlic, and taste the red wine, thinking of Sophia stirring her special pasta sauce on the hob.

The walls were covered in familiar mosaic plates, the ones Sophia used to have on her kitchen walls in her place over the café. Sea blue and green ceramic jostled with jagged sunset oranges, the colours reminiscent of an Italian villa perched on the cliffs above Sorrento. For once I felt like I might just have made the right decision to spend the summer here in Little Italy, North Devon.

I was so grateful to Gina for allowing me to stay here and wondered what she planned to do with the place. But most of all I wondered what she was going to do with the café; I had to make contact with her as soon as I was settled.

It was late afternoon and the sun was still high in the sky when Delilah and I went into Appledore for supplies. A nostalgic tang of salt and sunshine hung in the air, holding the promise of a fresh new summer to come. We visited the lovely deli first, where we bought the ingredients for a light Italian-style supper. And with ice cream on my mind, I also bought eggs, cream and salted pistachios. I may have been in Devon, but if I was going to be staying in Sophia's Italian villa by the sea I would embrace the dolce vita.

The first thing I did once back in the kitchen was to make the ice cream for my Italian dessert. I whisked egg whites, mixed in the yolks, fresh cream and sugar, all the time trying to remember what Aunt Sophia had taught me. I could hear her now as I stirred the mixture, 'brava ragazza,' she used to say, which in Italian means 'good girl'.

I smiled to myself as I thought of her now, and before putting the plastic container into the freezing compartment of the fridge, I said, 'here goes Sophia!', and swirled in some pistachios. I wasn't sure it would work, I knew Sophia always used unsalted, but I could only find salted – this could be my first mistake. But we learn by our mistakes and this was going to be a rocky road, especially as everything was quite new to me. I'd made ice cream many times with Sophia, but without her recipes and her hand to guide me, I knew this summer would be a big learning curve for me.

Later that evening, I felt like Sophia Loren, sitting on my elegant balcony, eating succulent olives, creamy mozzarella and sweet cherry tomatoes. With Delilah at my feet, I sipped a crisp Italian white and took in the view, while letting my mind race across the beach and dive into the ocean.

This kind of peace was something I'd never experienced before. It was precious and I truly felt like I might find me again in all this. I used to be young, with ambitions and dreams, but life had become a conveyor belt dealing with everyone's needs. This was my time. And what a luxury it was just to sit there and allow myself time and space, uninterrupted by people or noise – just me, Delilah and the universe.

As I watched the sun sink into the silvery sea, turning it to honey beneath a pink sky, I sampled the ice cream I had made earlier in an elegant glass dish. The rich, sweet creamy base was cold and perfect with the spike of salty pistachios – not a mistake, a resounding success to my taste buds, and I was reminded of Sophia's conviction that everyone brought something new to a recipe, and I'd brought a little sass to this one. Perhaps I could fly without the safety net of Sophia's recipes after all? I could take a few risks, add my own twists and come up with my own take on flavours. I was in heaven, even the glass dish was perfect; it was as if Sophia knew exactly what I would need in that little kitchen – Mediterranean and old-fashioned in an elegant, Italian way.

As the sun set on my first day, it felt like a beginning of sorts. I had a place to stay, food to eat, Delilah was settled, and the sea was sparkling on the horizon. Eventually, when the stars came out to say hello and the air turned a little cooler, I wandered inside, went to bed, and slept through the night without waking for the first time in years.

Chapter Ten

Hot Cappuccinos and New Beginnings

Opening my eyes to a shaft of morning light beaming through the bedroom, I immediately wondered where I was. Then remembered with a flush of fear and pleasure that I was in my new life and I climbed out of bed to face the day and everything it held.

I wandered over to the window and marvelled at the early morning view. The sun was already up, and the tide was out, leaving a swathe of smooth beach on the estuary dotted with people. From my vantage point on the patio, I could hear the seagulls, make out the dog walkers, runners, a mother and toddler and an old man carrying a newspaper. I thought how wonderful it must be to live in a place where you could walk along a beach to the shops – then I reminded myself, this summer, I did.

I wrapped my dressing gown around me and contemplated calling Mum, then decided to have a cup of coffee first. It was a small thing, a cup of coffee and a moment for me before attending to everyone else – and the threat of a guilt cloud hung vaguely over me, but I didn't let it rain down. I was finally putting me first – and as selfish and outrageous and terrible as that was, it also felt pretty damn good.

Delilah and I sat on the balcony welcoming the same sky we'd parted with the evening before. Now it was bright and blue, never-ending and dotted with wisps of white cotton. I was enjoying this lovely calm when the doorbell rang.

Answering it, I was surprised to see Ben standing in the doorway with a smile on his face and a thick wad of paper in his hands.

'Good morning! I thought I'd hand-deliver your street trader's licence along with other deeply boring documents that I can barely look at because I might have to kill myself – or at least fall asleep,' he smiled.

I assured him I might also die of boredom if he dared to make me read them, but as a new business owner I would go through them and sign as necessary. I ushered him in and offered him coffee – he asked for cappuccino.

'Sorry, but I tried to work the cappuccino machine last night,' I sighed, 'but I can't get it started, you wouldn't happen to know how it works, would you?'

'I've had many cappuccinos in this apartment,' he smiled, 'but never actually made one, Sophia always made a fuss of me...'

I smiled, I liked that Ben was friends with Sophia, he was a genuinely nice guy and it made me feel a little better to know that despite having no family, she had friends here in her later years.

'That sounds like my aunt. She loved making a fuss of people, always the hostess, wherever she was, I swear she was born to own a café,' I smiled, fond memories slowly opening in my head like a flower. 'Did she sit on the patio to eat in the summer?' I asked. It was a small thing, but I wanted to know everything I'd missed.

'Yes, she did that often, and sometimes if I was walking along the beach I'd wave to her. She was a friend of my mother's, Dad too, and she was just such a big part of the community here, people were so fond of her.'

I wondered again why this popular woman who everyone seemed to love was disliked by her own sister. While I was here I might just discover what had torn them apart, but that was for another day, this morning was about cappuccinos and new beginnings.

'So you reckon you can get this cappuccino maker working?' I said, walking to the kitchen door.

'I can give it a go… oh and Sophia always had home-made little amaretti biscuits to eat with the coffee.'

'I don't have any of those,' I said.

He looked at me mock accusingly. 'Do you mean you haven't made a fresh batch for my arrival?'

'No, because I'm now officially a selfish, self-centred woman who is going to look after herself for a change – and that includes not making bloody biscuits at dawn for a passing solicitor.'

'Ouch,' he laughed, joining me in the kitchen, making it feel even smaller with the two of us in there. I rather liked that it was cramped as we had to huddle together over the machine, our bodies touching – which wasn't unpleasant.

'My girlfriend had one of these… I'll try and remember how turn it on…' he started.

Oh God he did have a girlfriend! Of course he did. I couldn't help but feel disappointed.

'So does your girlfriend bake biscuits for you every morning to go with that coffee?' I was already slightly jealous of the beautiful woman that might have Ben's heart.

'No, she doesn't.'

'Good for her,' I said, glad she wasn't a domestic goddess and completely perfect. 'She's not slaving over a stove for a man…'

'I haven't seen her for a couple of years.'

She was probably some amazing diving princess who jet-set around the world, checking in with Ben every now and then for passionate weekends.

'Playing hard to get is she?'

He laughed; 'Yes, very much so. She ran off with someone else.'

'Oh, I'm sorry, Ben.'

I felt awful for being so flippant.

'It's okay; it wasn't her, it was me… or something like that. I never stay in the same place long enough to get too attached. Women tell me I have commitment issues… but I do miss her cappuccino machine.'

I was glad he was single, I needed a friend here, and I didn't want some girlfriend getting the wrong idea.

'It's a bit rusty,' he was saying as he opened up the back of Sophia's coffee contraption. 'Probably not been used for a while,' he sighed. 'It must be a few years since I had one of Sophia's cappuccinos, I wouldn't be surprised if that was the last time it was used. But I think I can fix it – might just need a good clean. It'll take me a little while, but it's a good excuse to turn up late for work.'

'So your dad will accept the excuse that you're late because you were fixing a cappuccino machine?'

'Mmm probably not, but you're a client – so I can be doing all kinds of things for you.'

I could feel the heat rise up my body, and move to my face. Was he flirting with me or was this just innocent banter, as the kids referred to it? Aware my neck and chest were probably now flushed red with embarrassment I leaned forward on the countertop, trying to hide my mottled decolletage. 'You really are in the wrong job aren't you?' He was obviously practical and could fix machines, but give him a sheaf of legal documents and he was all over the place.

He shrugged and wiped his hands on a tea towel. 'Lots of people are in the wrong jobs – it's just about finding the courage to get out. At least, I've got something to escape to.'

'Wow, I'm running *away* to come here and you're running *away* from here – funny really.'

'Yeah – well that's life I suppose, we always want what we can't have,' he said, a wistful look coming over him.

'I know,' I said. 'I longed for peace and quiet and although I've only been here a day, I love it here, but I'm already missing the kids and my mum terribly! Silly isn't it.'

'They could always come to stay?'

'No, the kids are doing their own things, and my mother simply refuses to come.'

I'd called Mum on arrival the day before but she had been very monosyllabic and quite disinterested in my stories of how Appledore was still pretty, the sky blue and the sea bracing. But I kept talking, telling her about the new deli and the chocolate shop and how I'd made ice cream from a long-remembered recipe of Aunt Sophia's.

'And have you seen anything of Gina?' she'd asked softly.

I told her that Gina hadn't come over from LA yet.

'Typical, like a butterfly that one, she's probably found something more interesting to do.'

'Mum, Sophia's gone and Gina's thousands of miles away – whatever happened a long time ago just isn't relevant any more…'

'Yes and the past needs to stay long ago, there'll be all kinds of gossip in town, but only those involved know the truth.'

'If I knew what it was, I could put a stop to any idle gossip,' I said, seeing an opportunity to lure my mother into spilling the beans.

'No. You just keep out of it, water under the bridge,' was all she'd said, and I'd had to leave it at that.

I'd felt guilty leaving her, even though it was what she wanted, and talking about her and the kids brought a lump to my throat; I knew, like everyone else, I sometimes took my family for granted.

Ben was now taking the cappuccino machine into the living room and laying it on a tea towel on the floor. Delilah had rushed over to help and he was rather distracted giving her the required attention (she was quite the princess). So guessing this might take some time, I offered him a cup of instant coffee until it was fixed. He seemed eager to stick around and I wondered if it was because he enjoyed my company as I did his – or if he just didn't want to go to work.

I went into the kitchen and boiled the kettle, thinking about that last conversation with Mum.

'Ben, have you ever heard any gossip?' I called through into the living room.

'All the time,' he called back. 'But we deal in divorces, deaths and house sales – it's a hotbed down at Shaw Associates. Sadly I'm sworn to secrecy.'

I laughed while pouring the steaming water into our mugs. 'I can imagine, but I meant gossip about the Caprioni family, about Sophia... Gina... my mother?'

'No, nothing interesting or scandalous, if that's what you mean, but like I say, I couldn't tell you if I did. I would have to kill you.'

'It would be worth it for a snippet about the scandalous Caprionis.' I said, walking in with two steaming mugs of coffee and placing his on the floor. It felt natural to sit down next to him, but at the same time vaguely inappropriate, too intimate perhaps? But I did it anyway, and he didn't flinch, he seemed comfortable, so I stayed.

'Nothing scandalous, just the Mafia connection, oh and there was that brothel, the gun running and the drugs.'

'Oh we all know about that,' I laughed. 'I want to know the real serious stuff – like why my mother and her sister stopped speaking to each other and why my mum's so paranoid about my cousin Gina. Even on Sophia's death bed there was no reconciliation.'

'They're Italians, have you never watched *The Sopranos*?'

'No, but my mother has, again and again, she is pure gangster. I'm not quite so hardcore, but I've watched *The Real Housewives of New Jersey* and those brawling Italian mamas don't hold a light to my family's lifelong vendettas.'

He sat back on his haunches surveying the machine from a distance and then looked at me. 'I suppose, like all families, there were fallouts, but being Latin-tempered they took it beyond the grave.'

I watched him take a sip of coffee, which was too hot and caused him to spill some on the floor, splashing the sofa and my pale pink dressing gown along the way.

'I'm sorry, Ella, so clumsy of me,' he said, standing up, his own sweatshirt now coffee-stained.

'It's fine – it seems to be something you excel in,' I laughed as he sat back down.

'Yeah, my mum used to say I wasn't meant for a house, my legs are too long and I should be running on a beach or splashing in the sea. She was right. Funny, every time I accidentally hurl a glass to the floor or spill a drink spectacularly, I think of Mum and wonder if she's watching and shaking her head.'

I was smiling and he looked up from the machine, biting his lip, his forehead slightly furrowed over the technical problem he was encountering. And suddenly our eyes met and the sun came out, his smile spreading across his face as I felt mine do the same and for a moment we just bathed in mutual happiness. The sun was streaming through the window, the sea was glittering on the horizon and a really nice guy was sitting in front of me. It didn't get much better than this.

As is often the case, this lovely moment was followed by a rather awkward silence while we both recalibrated our thoughts. I was aware Ben was watching me and I wondered if he'd really turned up just to give me my street trader's licence? He hadn't alluded to it since he'd arrived and had just left it on the sofa, which was making me wonder what was happening here.

'I made ice cream,' I suddenly said, because the silence was too much and I wasn't sure if this was awkward or not. Perhaps Ben was just having one of his confused moments and he wasn't staring at me at all?

'Oh wow! Are you going to do home-made ice cream for the van?' he asked.

'Yes of course, Sophia would turn in her grave if I sullied that van with profanities like Magnums and Cornettos.'

I went into the kitchen, returning with a swirl of salted pistachio ice cream in a bowl, and handed it to him. He took it from me, his fingers brushing mine and sending hot waves of electricity through every nerve. Any longer and it would have melted the ice cream.

'Oh wow, this is like nothing I ever tasted,' he said, taking large spoonful after spoonful. 'What's in this – some kind of drug? It's really, really good. I love the sweet and the salty – sun and sea, like a day at the seaside.'

'I like that – the flavour could be called "A Day at the Seaside"?' I said.

'You could be onto something here. I mean the Caprioni ice cream van has been out of action for a year or so, and in the past few years it only sold packaged ice cream. But this reminds me of the stuff they used to make at the café when I was a kid, tastes of real cream, not sickly-sweet or fake tasting, just – real.'

I was delighted at his reaction and planned to experiment with more flavours over the next few days. Ben had a mechanic friend who'd offered to look over the van for me and said I could pay him once I'd earned some money, which was brilliant. He said he'd let me have it by the weekend, so I had time to practise before I headed out on my first day.

'Call me any time day or night if you need a taster,' he smiled when he left an hour later. And I said goodbye and closed the door with a great big smile on my face while heading into the kitchen to pulverise some frozen strawberries.

Ben was someone who could be a really good friend – he was so kind, and he made me laugh and he also inspired me. He didn't live by the rules; he worked in his father's office in order to do what he really wanted to do – dive in exotic locations. He made it happen, and I dared to think that perhaps I too could follow a dream that some may consider a flight of fancy. Could I really make a go of the rusty old van?

Only time would tell.

Chapter Eleven

Spilt Hot Coffee and Dog-Chewed Bacon

I spent the next few days walking along the beach with Delilah. It was an idyllic existence, but at the same time I was very much aware that I had limited money and time was moving on. The van was due back tomorrow and I couldn't afford to have it spray-painted so would have to do that myself.

'I just hope I don't make a pig's ear of it,' I'd said to Lucie on Skype one evening as I sat watching the tide come in, laptop on my knee. My daughter was looking well and happy and she'd asked for photos of the van and I'd managed to send them to her all the way in Thailand. She'd found a fancy app that showed me all the different combinations of colour I could paint it.

'I want it to be pale pink and white, just like Caprioni's used to be,' I said, and within seconds my brilliant daughter sent me a photo of the van exactly as I'd imagined it.

'Oh Lucie, you're amazing, the cleverest girl I ever gave birth to,' I sighed, longing to hug my little girl. She laughed and said it was easy and 'even you could do it, Mum'. But I doubted it.

Later I called Mum, who seemed quite flustered.

'Hello, who is that, I'm flower arranging,' she said. Mum had never arranged flowers in her life.

'Mum, is Frederick with you?' I said, knowing this was less about carnations and more like mother in flagrante delicto with Frederick on my pale cream sofa.

'No... no,' she said breathlessly.

'Mum, I'm not being a know-all, but to my knowledge flower arranging doesn't usually cause breathlessness. Are you sure Frederick isn't with you?'

'Yes,' she snapped, 'I'm flower arranging with... Leo.'

'Leo?' I said, presuming this was a new man and not the local florist.

'Oh I'm sorry I forgot you don't speak the lingo. It's LEON-ARDO,' she said this like it was a foreign word.

'I understand that, you don't have to speak Italian to understand your mother has a new boyfriend...' I said, thinking this must be the third in as many weeks, whereas I hadn't had a boyfriend for as many decades.

'Leo's not that new, dear, I've known him since Wednesday,' she said.

'Oh, you've been with him a whole two days, that must be getting stale,' I said, but she was saying something to Leo and didn't hear me. And just when it all seemed to be going so well and I had temporarily stopped worrying about her. My mother was now alone with a strange man in my living room. He could be a con man, a sex pest or a serial killer, but given the heavy breathing I wasn't sure what worried me most, my mother's safety or the condition of the soft furnishings.

'Oh Ella,' she sighed; 'Leo's a gentleman, he's from the old country.'

'Rochdale?'

'You know exactly what I mean, so don't be obtuse, Madam. He's a very nice man and I'm enjoying his company.'

'I'm glad to hear it, Mum, but I'm worried about you. There's a spare room here, you know. You could come to Appledore and I'm sure there are lots of eligible older men here too,' I added, knowing Appledore and the spare room wouldn't lure her, but the prospect of surplus single men might.

'Has *she* arrived yet?' she suddenly said, sounding like a frightened child.

'No.' I wasn't in the mood to hear my mother bitch about my cousin, so I told her about me. 'I'm taking the van out for the first time on Monday, it's back from the garage tomorrow and I'm going to paint it...'

'Come home, Ella, there's nothing there for you.'

My heart sank, she was back on this well-trodden path.

'No Mum, I'm going to give this a go.'

'Oh have it your own way. Look, I have to go, Leo's having trouble mounting...'

My heart almost stopped. 'What Mum... what is Leo mounting?'

'...the stairs. He has a stick, you see?'

Once we'd established Leo hadn't had a stroke, I told her I loved her and clicked off the phone. I didn't have too much time to worry about what Mum was up to because a few minutes later Josh Skyped and Delilah and I 'spoke' to Aarya. As luck would have it, Delilah was wearing lounging pyjamas in dove grey, of which Aarya approved. I tried to ask them about Nepal, the people and the mountains but all Aarya wanted was a minute by minute account of Delilah's moods, outfits and toilet times. Eventually I managed to get a few words in about my new van.

'I told you, Mum, you should vlog it all – the van, the place, the ice cream… even Delilah, people love a dog on YouTube.'

'Yeah I thought I might do that later in the summer,' I smiled into the webcam before we said our farewells and I turned off the connection wondering what the bloody hell vlogging was. Honestly, I'd only just got used to Facebook and now Josh wanted me to vlog… I had no intention of even googling it. Life was too short and I had ice cream to make.

Two days before my 'debut' on the beach, I moved into the café kitchens. I ordered all the ingredients to arrive there by late Saturday evening when the café would be closed and I'd have the place to myself.

I walked through the café now; the grumpy guy was sitting behind the counter and ignored me as I passed. Being the friendly type, I always liked to try to win people over so I smiled at him and said, 'I'm using the kitchens to make ice cream for the van.'

He looked up, 'Right.'

'I open up on Monday – it's my first day.'

'Right again.'

He really was quite rude.

'Do you have a problem with that?' I heard myself say. I wasn't the confrontational type, and I don't remember ever calling anyone out for just being off with me, but this was important. If I was going to work here in the kitchens, I needed a smile at least.

'I just think you're wasting your time. Sophia was the queen of ice cream. You can't just come in here and take over.'

'I'm not taking over the *café* – just the van,' I said. 'And for all you know, I might be the new queen of ice cream.'

'We'll see,' he sniffed and went back to his book.

So that was the feeling around here was it? People thought I wasn't up to the job and couldn't stick it. Well, I'd show them.

I could do this. After all, Sophia was my aunt, so I reckoned there must be some royal Caprioni blood passed down. I too could be the queen of ice cream – and I would!

So I whisked and tasted and froze and stirred and breathed in the sweet, cold sherbety air as I sang to myself. That evening in the kicthen I found an old radio under a table and they were playing Italian music, and I just knew Sophia was with me. She guided me as I juiced lemons, adding their tangy hit to creamy vanilla, the sugary air now spiky with the biting aromatic fruit. Then warm chocolate folded into cream, a slug of coffee-soaked sponge, and ice cream tiramisu was born. Salted caramel, pecans and berries all followed suit creating their own magical swirly iced concoction. I made lots of different flavours but in small portions so my customers – if I had any – could try them all out. The first few days would be essentially a straw poll of ice cream lovers; I would let people decide on the flavours I would make more of. Everyone had a favourite, but I recall Sophia saying chocolate, strawberry and vanilla were the Frank Sinatra, Dean Martin and Tony Bennett of her repertoire. So I made huge vats of these flavours, knowing

they'd also provide a base for other ice creams, along with cook-
ies, chocolate chips, cake crumbles and fresh fruit ripples. I finally
took off my apron at 4 a.m. and headed back for a few hours sleep
before I started the van 'makeover' later that day. I hadn't worked
this hard for years; it was physical, back-breaking stuff involving
lifting and being permanently on my feet. I was exhausted, but I
felt no pain, I finally had a purpose and a passion, and that was all
I needed to see me through.

After a mere four hours' sleep, I woke up more determined
than ever to make a success of the van 'makeover'. I'd pre-ordered
all the pink and white paint and early Sunday morning headed off
along the beach to collect the van from the garage on the other
side of Appledore. On the way past Ben's office, I glanced in and
saw he was inside. He was sitting on the desk, eating a large bacon
sandwich. I waved and he beckoned me in.

He was wearing overalls and looked even more dishevelled than
usual, and I noticed he had two paper cups of coffee and another
sandwich on his desk.

'Oh I'm sorry, I didn't realise you had company,' I said, directing my eyes at the sandwich.

'I haven't, but I thought you might need it,' he said. 'I knew
you were coming for the van and so I bought you breakfast.' By
now Delilah, who was permanently at my side, had smelled the
bacon and was becoming quite agitated, so I moved her slightly
away. This happened just as Ben got off the table to hand me the
coffee and sandwich, but Delilah's lead was now wound around
his leg and the coffee was about to hit the ceiling. I lunged to
catch it, but this alarmed and excited Delilah (I didn't lunge of-

ten, well, ever) who was now running round in circles, entwining both Ben and I in her diamanté-encrusted lead, which caused me to fall onto him in a rather compromising way. It lasted only seconds, but it was during all this that his father appeared in the office doorway.

'Working on a Sunday, Ben?' was all he said, like this was something he came upon often. He clearly thought we were about to have sex on the mahogany desk and I didn't know where to look as Delilah leapt up and took the sandwich straight from Ben's hand.

'Dad, this is Ella... Sophia's niece, she's come about the trading licence,' Ben was saying while trying to extricate himself from Delilah, the lead, the spilt coffee, the dog-chewed bacon and me.

'Ah, so this is Ella Watkins?' he gave a sort of smile and grudgingly shook my hand, once I'd escaped from the human/dog tangle. God alone knows what he must have thought of me, Sophia's niece, mounting his son on the office desk – on a Sunday too!

He nodded curtly at both of us before disappearing into an office and shutting the door. We both laughed silently.

'Are you going to explain?' I asked, my face scarlet from embarrassment.

'Explain what?'

'Exactly what happened... that *nothing* happened.'

'Why would I deny something happened with a beautiful woman?' He winked and I rolled my eyes, but I couldn't help smiling. He was definitely flirting.

'I'd better get off, and collect the van – it won't paint itself,' I said, feeling slightly overwhelmed. It wasn't that he was coming onto me, it was more to do with the fact that I hadn't had much male contact for a very long time and the slightest thing made me blush.

'Have you driven the van before?' he asked and I shook my head.

'I can drive it home for you if you like?'

'Thanks, but I think I can handle old Reginaldo,' I smiled.

'No – I wasn't suggesting you couldn't, it's just that…'

'It's very kind of you, Ben, but I'm not some helpless little woman.' I couldn't help but feel slightly prickly at the implication. I ran a house, brought up two children largely single-handedly and looked after a wilful OAP, I was sure I could manage driving a little ice cream van. How hard could it be?

'Fair enough, just take it easy,' he said.

'I intend to,' I gave him a wave and was feeling quite sassy as I sashayed out of the office and closed the door with a flourish. I was a switched on, independent woman who could take care of business. It was only when I walked on down the road feeling like I'd made quite the cool exit that I realised I'd left Delilah inside.

Chapter Twelve

Reginaldo Hits the Road!

Of course the van was a nightmare and having struggled to open the door, I sat in the driver's seat unable to work out how to pull it forward so I wasn't sitting ten feet away from the bloody pedals. Then when I'd finally mastered that, I couldn't find the indicator, wasn't sure where the horn was and the accelerator had what can only be described as bite! I discovered this as I shot out of the garage at a rather bracing nought to forty.

Mine and Delilah's maiden voyage along the front towards the apartment was equally surprising when I almost killed three tourists and a paper boy. I finally managed to find both the horn and the ice cream jingle at exactly the same time, causing quite a cacophony in the middle of Appledore. It was fairly busy with Sunday visitors, all of whom were either staring in horror at the crazy ice cream van or running for safety.

Then, in the middle of the madness, I received a call, and managed to pull over without giving either me or Delilah whiplash or further endangering any tourists

'Hey, it's me! I'm only a man but would you like some… company at least?'

'Er, thanks Ben, yes please – but not because you're a man – in *spite* of it,' I said.

Within seconds he was climbing into the passenger seat and had turned off the horn and the jingle.

'That was quite a show,' he said, settling Delilah down as I slowly drove on. The poor little mite was traumatised, her beret at an even jauntier angle than when I'd dressed her earlier in a Parisian look. I made a mental note not to mention this minor kerfuffle to Aarya when she next Skyped for updates on Delilah.

'I meant to do that,' I said to Ben. 'Making a big impact on the roads of Appledore is all part of my marketing strategy for the grand opening on Monday. Now everyone knows I'm here. And anyway, how did you know where to turn off all the noise,' I said, slightly annoyed because he seemed to know exactly how to operate everything. 'And don't tell me it's because you're a man!'

He laughed. 'You were ranting so much about being a strong independent woman I didn't get the chance to explain. I offered to help because I've driven this van before.'

I was surprised, so surprised in fact I nearly ran an old lady over.

'Look out!' he shouted in mock-horror, covering his face with his hands.

'Stop that,' I laughed, waving apologetically at the old lady. 'So when did you drive the van?'

'I helped your aunt out for a few summers; I spent quite a bit of time along this beach selling Caprioni's ice cream.'

I liked that Ben had spent time with Sophia; I had my own memories, but it was nice to hear his too.

'Was she lovely to work for?' I asked.

'She was great, when it came to ice cream making, serving and driving the van out to the beach, she allowed the staff the freedom to learn. She wasn't the kind of boss who breathed down your neck; I can imagine you'll be pretty much the same.'

I was flattered by this and turned to smile at him, momentarily losing concentration and Ben had to grab the steering wheel.

'As much as I'd like to let you learn how to drive the van without breathing down your neck, I am keen to get home tonight alive,' he said, before I could complain.

'Now tips for taking the van out. Let's begin with the horn; if you press it too hard it sticks.'

'So I gathered… anything else?'

'Yeah sure… my other tip is to have a blast. I did. And the women loved it – I had quite a few hot dates those summers after they'd tasted Sophia's strawberry dream.'

'I bet they tasted yours as well,' I laughed, feeling a sting of ir-rational jealousy at the thought of Ben and other women. After all we were only friends.

Having managed to get back to the apartment without any further mishaps of note, Ben offered to help me paint the van and I gratefully accepted.

'You've been a real friend, Ben, I can't thank you enough, I don't know how I can ever repay you.'

'How about free ice cream for life?' he said, which I reckoned was a pretty good deal and also added that I'd cook him dinner that evening as an extra thank you.

'Sorry I ranted earlier about you trying to show me how to drive because I'm a woman…' I started. 'I think I'm just a bit sensitive. Richard, my ex, was the kind of man... well, he'd talk about "women drivers", and refer to me as "the missus", I think you get the picture.'

'How long were you married?'

'Too long; we married very young. The woman he left me for has apparently said she's finally found a man who treats her like a woman. And if that's what she wants she's welcome to it – in my book he's a sexist pig. I never really saw it when we were together. Sometimes you only really see the truth about someone after they've gone.'

'Sounds like you're better off without him.'

'Yes, I think I finally realised that when I saw a picture of him on Facebook with his thumbs up at her new plastic boobs, says it all really.'

He laughed in horror, and in that instant I knew he was my kind of person.

I hadn't been able to share too much about Richard with the kids, he was still their dad after all and I didn't want to betray them. I also couldn't say anything to Mum because if she thought he'd really upset me I ran the risk of her saying something on his Facebook page. I hadn't even been comfortable discussing it with Sue, because she was likely to tell everyone that came into the shop. But this was my neutral space. Ben didn't know any of the people in my Manchester life and he didn't judge. He also listened, he didn't talk over me and he gave me his full attention, which made me feel more confident about what I had to say.

It was a pleasant change and I found myself really enjoying his company, which was a blessing as the van turned out to be a mammoth job! We began by scrubbing the outside, which took several bucket changes, a couple of bottles of washing-up liquid and a few awkward sponge incidents. This was followed by sanding down the peeled bits and filling in holes, of which there were many. Eventually we got around to the best bit – the pink and white paint. Several hours of back-breaking work later we were standing in the sunshine surveying our 'art' and it looked delicious.

'Good enough to eat,' I said, 'I'm thinking strawberry and white chocolate mint ice cream will be the signature cone to match the van.'

'That sounds unusual, but I like it,' he said, wiping the sweat from his brow. 'The Caprioni's Signature Cone?'

I nodded, liking the sound of that. I was coming up with names all the time for my new creations, my current favourite was an idea to have banana and peanut butter ice cream with chocolate chips and I was going to call it 'Elvis" Peanut Butter and Banana Blitz'. Aunt Sophia loved Elvis Presley and she once told me his favourite flavours were peanut butter and banana. 'If it's good enough for Elvis it's good enough for the folk round here,' she'd said.

As we'd completed each section of the makeover, Ben had taken lots of pictures, including many of Delilah who happened to have a ra-ra skirt with pompoms in the same shade of pink as the van. I knew Aarya would be delighted and I emailed the photos to the kids. As always, I sent them to Mum too, working on the theory that if I bombarded her with pictures of lovely Appledore and my new ice-cream-coloured life, she may come to accept it and even decide to spend some time with me here. Surely, when she saw how wonderful it was here, she'd have no reason to stay away. I lived in hope.

That evening I made us a huge bowl of pasta, topped with everything Italian, from tasty prosciutto to sour goat's cheese and sweet, tangy sun-dried tomatoes and pesto. The pesto was aromatic and oily and the tomatoes chewy like caramel, it was bliss. The dessert was the prototype for the planned 'Caprioni Signature Cone', home-made strawberry and white chocolate ice cream with fresh mint syrup – and I think it worked. Ben said it was delicious. We ate on the balcony and talked for a long time, just enjoying each other's company and swapping life stories. Ben explained that his mother had died when he was fifteen and as the only child he'd always felt guilty that his father had been left alone. He'd gone on to take a degree in law to please his father – until he realised he'd never please him and at thirty-two he began to travel.

'I come home as much for him as for me. He's a grumpy old sod, but I know he misses me and after a while away I need to come back. I just have this need – I can't explain it. I suppose it comes from being born here by the sea, I'm drawn back yet at the same time I'm restless. Wherever I go, I never stay in one place for long.'

As he pointed out, this had caused no end of conflict with his father who wanted a son who would stay around and continue the family business.

'Can't you do both?' I asked.

'I guess that's what I'm doing now. I work during the week, with a few hours off here and there to dive – and the weekends I usually spend practising, then I take off for a few months. It's like an addiction, Ella. You only have to ask other divers, once you're hooked, that's it.'

'It sounds like you've got the balance right, but could you ever make a living from just diving?'

'There's the rub. Sometimes I'm lucky and when I'm away I find work teaching people to dive, or taking groups of people on guided dives. Back here I have to work as a lawyer so I can go diving somewhere else. Crazy eh?'

I agreed, but I admired his passion; 'And you said the other day that girlfriends say you find it hard to commit, is that about your "diving addiction"?' I asked, keen to know his romantic history.

'I've never hung out with anyone long enough to find out,' he said. 'I guess people expect something more from you after a while, and I'm not sure I can do that. I never have.' He seemed emotionally self-sufficient – nothing got to him, so he never really needed anyone to come home to. Then there was the fact that he didn't stay in one place for too long – part of me envied him and part of me pitied him, but he seemed happy enough.

The meal was over, the stars were out and though the evening was cool I think we both wanted to sit a while. He poured wine into our glasses and our eyes caught in the semi-darkness.

'Are you happy? Have you been happy on your own all this time?' I asked.

'As happy as anyone. I don't feel I've missed out on anything. Sometimes I think it would be nice to have a partner to share things with, maybe some kids, but you don't miss what you've never had. And all that comes with a mortgage and a car in the drive and staying put. And those aren't the things I need in life. The minute you start to make plans and rely on other people, it all goes to pot in my experience.'

'I can't decide if I like what you're saying or if it scares me,' I said. 'I want the now too, but I have to make a life for myself, and my family, and that involves plans.'

'I guess it's just like being in the sea, like diving. You just hold your breath, dive in and let the water take the weight, give yourself up to the universe and know she has your back.'

Was he this wonderful, worldly guy sitting in front of me now in a T-shirt with a tan, his blue eyes vivid in candlelight? Or was he the shambolic solicitor, running away from his father, responsibility and life? Perhaps he was a little of both?

Because other people relied on me I'd had to live a life of planning and worrying about the future. But what Ben said made me wonder if I could ease- off, because despite all my talk about adventures and finding myself – the letting go scared me.

'I think it's time I went to bed,' I said. 'I have to be up at dawn.' I needed to regroup. It had been great fun painting the van and getting it ready for the next day and I'd enjoyed the evening with Ben. But now it was time for me to clear my head and concentrate on tomorrow and what was about to be the first day of the rest of my life.

He got up from his chair and smiled, then began fumbling about in his pockets, the calm, eloquent diver and dining companion replaced by the bumbling solicitor.

'I have all the keys,' I said, in case that was what he was looking for. 'And the trading licences…'

'No, I…' he tried to retrieve whatever it was in his pocket and in doing so managed to wobble the little table and knock over a half-empty glass of wine and the candle. The glass smashed into a million pieces and the candle caught a paper napkin which flew up in the air like a Chinese lantern. Then Delilah set off barking and twirling, and as chaos reigned around us he stood before me, holding out his hand, oblivious to the circus around him. He looked like a proud little boy.

'It's for you, a good luck thing for tomorrow,' he said, as I took the paper packet from his outstretched hand and carefully opened it. Inside was a silver ice cream cone necklace, I held it up and it twinkled in the darkness.

'Oh Ben, it's so kind of you. I feel like I shouldn't accept a gift, you've already done so much – but thank you, I love it.' I was so touched, I really loved the necklace and the fact that he'd thought about me. This was the first time anyone had bought me jewellery for a very long time and I felt a lump in my throat.

'Shame I had to create fire and flood to give it to you,' he pulled an 'awkward' face.

'I wouldn't expect anything less,' I laughed, looking around at the mess, the napkin had burnt out and the glass lay there twinkling in the candlelight.

'Wear it tomorrow, it'll bring you luck, Ella… I hope.'

'I will,' I sighed, putting it on my neck and trying to fasten it.

He moved around behind me to help, moving my shoulder-length hair away and brushing his hand on my neck for a moment too long. I could feel his breath behind me, on me, and I inhaled the salt, aftershave and sun cream that was Ben. It was intoxicating, and I couldn't help myself, I just leaned back into him.

His arms instinctively enveloped me from behind and I felt like I was sailing on a warm, beautiful boat at sunset. We stayed there for a little while, both facing out to sea, the stars above and the sea silvery and calm, and he gently turned me round, which made my heart thud so loud I could hear it.

Wordlessly he lifted my chin with his hand and, looking into my eyes, he reached down and kissed me full on the lips. His mouth was soft and warm and I wanted more, but he pulled away saying gently, 'Night Ella… I'll see you tomorrow – I'll buy your first ice cream.'

'Don't go…' I heard myself say. For once I wasn't planning or worrying about what might happen, I was going with 'now'. He was attractive, I liked him and it seemed he liked me too. I wasn't looking for love and marriage and neither was he, so who said I couldn't have a brief summer fling. It may only last for tonight, but who cared?

He immediately took both my hands and we started to kiss again and he led me into the living room. Slowly we sat on the sofa, still kissing, and we were soon lying down, and I felt his hands on my skin. He lifted my T-shirt and together we pulled off my jeans and soon we were naked in my apartment by the sea.

Only a few weeks before I wouldn't have believed something like this could happen in my life and here it was, soft kisses, stars outside the window and strawberry ice cream in my heart. And as the kissing became more urgent, I melted into him, our bodies swirling together, legs and arms wrapping around each other, his kisses hot on my shoulder, my chest, working their way down. I remembered this – or something like it – but it had never been as gentle or as beautiful. This was special, Ben was special, he wanted me, made me feel desired, and held me in his arms telling me I was beautiful, and I couldn't help it, I cried.

Chapter Thirteeen

Salty Pistachios and Strawberry Ice Cream

The next day when I woke I felt Ben beside me and opened my eyes to see one big brown eye looking back at me. Delilah was lying between us, happily snuggled in her little pink-striped pyjamas. Ben's hand appeared over her and caught mine.

'It's nice to wake up next to someone… and I don't mean Delilah,' I laughed, as she heard her name and licked my face. 'Have I done the right thing?' I sighed.

'You mean last night or the van?'

'Both,' I giggled.

'There isn't a right thing,' he said as he moved closer, taking me in his arms. 'We're all faced with crossroads at different times in our lives – and whichever road we take there are days when it feels like the wrong decision and days when it feels right. You've got to do what you want to do – and if it feels good, keep doing it. Oh, and I'm talking about the van *and* last night,' he said, with a smile on his face.

I put my hand to his stubbly cheek and took him in, his eyes reaching into me, his hands warm on my body. 'I can't decide if you're a wise philosopher or a confused dreamer,' I smiled.

'I like the first one.'

'I like both.'

I raked my fingers through his hair and went downstairs to make coffee. It was very early and I had a lot to do, but I also wanted to be on my own for a little while to let things sink in. What had happened last night? Was it a one-night stand? Or was it more than that; was this the beginning of something? Did he want that? Did I? And why was I agonising about it anyway? This was my summer of letting go, of barefoot Bohemia, it didn't matter what happened tomorrow or next week, this was now. Already my feelings were being whipped up like a vat of cloudy pink ice cream. Everything was swirling in my head, my heart felt very full and happy, but I had to learn to trust my heart – just because it had let me down before didn't mean I had to keep it locked up.

Then instantly back in 'mum' mode, I thought about what the kids might say about me having a fling with a diving lawyer, before immediately reminding myself that they didn't have to know. Unlike Delilah's outfits and the renovation of the van, I didn't need to send them photos of my burgeoning love affair/one-night stand. Thank God. Mind you if my mother had found out, she'd have had a field day – I'd been warning her about casual sex for a long time and there I was sleeping with the family solicitor/local diver boy within the first week of my arrival. No I wouldn't be telling anyone any time soon, this was my lovely secret, just for me and I'd just see where it went.

Back upstairs, we ate breakfast together and made small talk. I went on far too much about strawberry ice cream, but that was because I suddenly felt uncomfortable. When I'd considered him a friend, I'd been able to laugh with Ben, tell him all kinds of stuff, but suddenly sex had come between us and changed our dynamic. He was exactly the same, still teasing and warm and easy – but I felt a little vulnerable now.

I had only had sex with a few people in my life and when I was single in my teens an encounter like last night would have been scandalous, but times had changed. I just hoped that I could change enough to let go and embrace the carefree summer the universe was now laying before me. It was scary and exciting, and despite the tang of fear in the pit of my stomach, I wouldn't have changed this feeling for anything.

It was soon time to head to the kitchens to collect the ice cream and Ben kindly offered to come with me and help. This made me feel a bit better about whatever had happened between us, but I still felt I needed to clear the air.

'So, last night was fun, but I don't want it to change our friendship,' I said as he helped me put the ice cream in the van.

'It won't, we're still friends aren't we?' he looked up from behind the freezer.

'It's just that I've only known you a few weeks and I really value your friendship.'

'What is this?' he said, a puzzled smile on his face.

'I don't know... I just feel mixed up that's all.'

What I wanted to ask was what's in this for you? But I thought that would be rude.

'Ella, relax. It's fun and I like being with you, I find you attractive and amusing and I enjoy talking to you... and last night I enjoyed... what happened. Do we need any more than that?'

'No, it's just a bit new to me and I'm not sure what it is.'

He shuffled a bit and became the ungainly, awkward Ben who spilled his coffee and tripped over dog leads. 'It doesn't matter, but whatever it is or isn't, let's enjoy it – who knows what's going to happen tomorrow, it's about the now remember?'

He was saying exactly what I tried to tell myself. No ties, no more commitments just free spirits… so why did I feel a little let down?

We continued to take the ice creams from the kitchens to the van and I gave myself a talking to about what this summer was about. This was my adventure, no one else's and if Ben came along for some of the ride that was great, but I had to prove to myself I could do this. Carrying the tubs we passed each other and our eyes met. I felt a little shimmer run through me and just knew whatever this was, we both felt good about it. When we'd finally moved all the ice cream I needed and everything was ready, he kissed me on the cheek.

'Go get 'em, Ella,' he smiled.

'Thanks, for everything,' I said.

'Please don't feel like you have to keep thanking me, because when you get to know me better you'll realise I only do what I want to do. And I want to help, and if it makes you feel better I'm helping Sophia too… with the van and stuff.'

'That's kind of you.'

'Not really, I feel like I owe Sophia big time.'

'Really?'

'Yeah, she was my mum's friend, and I don't know what we'd have done without her when Mum was ill, so it's my chance to repay her – through you.'

'Sophia was a special lady, wasn't she?'

'Yes she was, when my mum was ill Sophia really looked after her. My dad had the business and me to take care of and Sophia just seemed to always be at our house, holding Mum's hand, reading to her, bringing her ice cream. My mum died of cancer; she didn't eat much in those last few weeks, but she always ate Sophia's ice cream, said it reminded her of when she was a child. We had tried to take her to the café, but she was too weak and she'd said: "Just bring me that strawberry ice cream and I'll imagine I'm looking out of the café window onto the beach." And every day Sophia would turn up with a bowl of strawberry ice cream for Mum.'

He had tears in his eyes and I touched his arm, unable to say anything, just reassuring him that I felt for him.

'Today when I sell my first strawberry ice cream I'll think of your mother,' I said, climbing into the van and starting up the engine. I looked at his face and saw the child who'd lost his parent – and how all these years and all this life later her death still brought tears to his eyes.

He smiled at me and I felt the tension lift between us. I wish I could have stayed there with Ben and talked some more, but I couldn't put it off any longer; it was time to go.

'Well, Reginaldo, we are off on our first day,' I said, feeling nervous.

'I think you might need to rethink the name,' Ben said. 'He's pink and white… shouldn't he have a girl's name?'

'You might be right… though my daughter would say we mustn't gender stereotype with colour.'

'Yeah, but it looks like a princess and sounds like a football team – the Reginaldos.'

'OMG, stop being so hetero,' I said in a mock lilting teenage voice.

He laughed and touched my cheek and I thought about how much I'd miss him today.

'Hey, before you go…' he said, he was now fumbling in his pockets. 'I promised to buy your first ice cream, but I have to be at the office so can I buy one now?'

I laughed, 'Of course,' and climbed into the back of the van, opened up the hatch and served my very first ice cream. It was quite a moment and when he offered me the cone to try somehow it felt intimate and delicious. Eventually he finished the ice cream and seemed as reluctant as I did to part; 'That was the best ice cream I ever tasted,' he said.

'That was the best ice cream I ever sold.'

We both laughed and then he helped me pull down the hatch and I moved into the driving seat and we said our goodbyes.

After he'd gone I tried to concentrate on the morning ahead, but my mind was on his mouth. My head took me to the night before and what we did and how it felt. I thought about everything he'd said about 'us' – whatever we were – and after I'd processed it all, it made a sort of sense. I mustn't see Ben and this 'thing' between us through the prism of my old life, because it wouldn't fit – this was about here and now. And I didn't need a relationship any more than Ben did at this time in my life. He was off to Hawaii in September and I'd be going back to Manchester soon after. I had to be free and uncomplicated, I mustn't get my heart hurt again and a 'no strings' approach was perfect. I could enjoy being with him but at the same time I was also able to stop myself from falling into something with this man, something that might hurt me. Wasn't I?

The air was laced with salty promise as I drove onto the beach that first morning and wound down the window, breathing in the freshness. Like eucalyptus it tingled in my nostrils, clearing my head and all my worries, I felt open, able to embrace whatever the day was going to bring.

On this beach leading out to this vast ocean, my life was small, I was a middle-aged woman with a little van full of ice cream. Today I was going to find out if I could make it on my own, just me and my van and Delilah of course. This was a new beginning – and if it worked, and I could make enough to live on then I might even be able to pursue this dream beyond September. It was the first time I'd considered this, until now I'd seen it as a summer job to tide me over and do something different for once. Was I being foolish to think it might be more? Had I been spending too much time with Ben who was putting all these ideas in my head? But he reckoned you could do anything you wanted to. So why couldn't I believe that too?

By 9 a.m. that morning I was in situ, aware that this was early in the day for ice cream, but as it was only the beginning of July, this was essentially a dress rehearsal. My customers would be old-age pensioners, students finished early from university, men walking their dogs and kids skipping school.

The first hour proved to be very quiet – I sold nothing – so to stop myself worrying about lack of customers I decided to make some plans. I was determined to make a go of this little business, but like any budding empire-builder I needed to work out how things were going to be. If the van was a success over the summer, that was great – but what if I decided not to go back in September, what if I did decide to stay?

When autumn came no one would be buying ice cream. The van wasn't an all-year-round option, but ice cream eaten indoors could be, especially if Gina had plans to keep the café. I could perhaps manage it for her in the winter months? I knew she had a big, exciting life in LA and probably wanted to sell, but what if I talked to her and convinced her to let me run the café?

I kept telling myself I had to stop trying to run before I could walk. Here I was sitting in the van having sold precisely nothing and I was wondering about taking over the bloody world, starting with the café. I needed to see if people even liked my ice cream first.

I'd made the ice creams as faithful to Aunt Sophia's as I could remember, but not all had turned out as I'd hoped. The lemon ice cream wasn't as tangy and the chocolate didn't have the depth, but without her recipes I'd just have to make the best I could. My own invention – salty pistachio, or 'A Day at the Seaside' – was wonderful, and the strawberry was sweet and fruity. It was a simple recipe but like magic to me as a child, and Sophia and I always made it together when I visited.

Looking at my prices, it was clear my ice creams would cost a little more than those at the supermarket. But I was hoping that just by tasting them people would realise how special they were and be happy to pay a little extra. Ben had said that when he'd taken the van out for Sophia, people had paid well for good quality products. But that had been Sophia Caprioni's ice cream – and this was Ella Watkins's version.

So on that first day I sat on a little stool behind the counter, the hatch opened, hope in my heart, waiting for my first customer.

Delilah was sitting on her throne in the passenger seat; she wasn't allowed inside the van for hygiene reasons but was dressed in a rather fetching floral playsuit. She was keen to make friends with other dogs along the beach and would bark and wag her tail at every passing mutt. An old man wandered past with a beautiful chocolate Labrador and smiled when he saw Delilah jumping up and down in the window. We chatted a while and he told me his name was Peter and his dog's name was Cocoa.

'She's very excited,' he laughed, nodding at Delilah.

'Yes I think she likes the look of Cocoa,' I said, 'she wants to make friends. She probably thinks she's a great big Labrador too!'

'Your little one can always come walking with us. Me and Cocoa don't mind if she wants to be a Labrador, she can be anything she wants to be, can't she, girl?' His beautiful, brown eyed dog looked up and wagged her tail in agreement.

I thanked him and said I was sure she'd love to. Having a dog certainly helped make friends.

'Does she always wear clothes?' he asked.

'It's got to the stage where I feel like a bad parent if she goes out naked,' I said and explained about Aarya and the extensive wardrobe.

Peter laughed and wandered off, throwing a ball for Cocoa to chase at a hundred miles along the sand.

'You might have a bit of catching up to do there, Delilah,' I said, as we watched the huge dog race along the beach. She panted and wagged her tail happily.

Everyone was so friendly here and though there weren't many people on the beach, most of them said 'good morning' as they passed. But as the morning breeze gave way to a milder midday, still no one had bought anything. By 12.30 I wondered if I should cut my losses, sell up and move back to Manchester. What the hell had I been thinking? I'd left my mother looking after my house while she entertained ageing lotharios on the sofa and here I was in a van in the middle of an empty beach hoping someone would buy an ice cream.

I couldn't really make any plans until I'd spoken to Gina to find out what she was doing with the café, so thought this was a good time to try to find a contact number for her. I felt a pang of guilt wondering how Mum would feel if she knew I was trying to contact Gina, but told myself that just because Mum was holding onto some Italian grievance from the bloody 1970s didn't mean I had to. My friendship with my cousin didn't have to be connected to my mother, I was a grown-up now and if I wanted to re-establish our relationship then surely it was up to me?

I googled Gina and eventually found her agent's number, quickly dialling it before I could change my mind. My mouth was dry, my heart beating high in my throat when eventually a woman answered.

'I'm trying to contact Gina…' I said, and explained who I was and where I was calling from. She was American and sounded like a big film star agent and proudly told me Gina was working on 'a big movie in LA darling'. I gave her my number and she said she'd ask her to call me when she had time.

'Can I ask what the movie is?' I ventured, before putting the phone down.

'Sorry, it's top secret, honey,' the woman said. 'She's working with Leonardo and he likes discretion.'

Wow, I thought as I clicked off the phone. My famous cousin! I thought she'd 'retired' from films, married her millionaire and was enjoying the good life in Bel Air, but this was exciting. I couldn't wait for her call, I was dying to hear all the Hollywood gossip. I desperately hoped she'd come to Appledore soon and we could just start again where we left off, me and my beautiful blonde cousin.

Eventually, I had a customer – but it was Ben; smiling, happy, laid-back Ben peering at me from the other side of the hatch.

'You open?'

'Yes of course I'm open – I just don't have any customers.'

'Well don't sweat it – early July isn't exactly crazy busy here, even last wills and testaments are thin on the ground this time of year.'

'Now he tells me,' I said. 'I thought you said this was a thriving hub of business potential?'

'Yeah, during July and August – you know, summer?'

'I just feel a bit adrift, literally – like I'm a little boat bobbing about in the middle of this beach. I'm not waving but drowning and no one's noticed.'

'You aren't doing anything wrong, it's just different now…' he said, looking around the beach at an older couple walking their dog.

'What do you mean?'

'Well, Sophia had advantages you don't – she had the café and she sold ice cream long before any of the big brands.'

'Yes, she had the ice cream monopoly around here. I guess I need to do a bit of blue-sky thinking.'

'Well, we've got the sky for it,' he said, gesturing above to the endless blanket of blue.

'Exactly, it's sunny, but chilly, and too early in the season for ice cream, I'm so stupid. People want to be out under this big blue sky, but not necessarily eating ice cream, right?' I said, an idea forming.

'Yeah... so you could also serve hot drinks?' he suggested.

'Yes I could, that's a good idea, but what about branching out even more? Okay, so I haven't sold a single bloody cone yet... and I'm offering this amazing ice cream, but until they taste it they don't know it's amazing.' I remembered something I'd read recently in a food magazine. 'What about ice cream sandwiches, made with croissants, or brioche... they're the new black, or the new breakfast – or something.'

'That's a brilliant idea,' Ben said. 'Okay... hang on, don't go anywhere.'

And he was off up the beach, I wasn't sure if he was running away from me or running towards something else. I had to giggle because he almost fell over a dog and a small child as he threw himself Ben-like up the beach and into the deli on the front. After a few minutes he came out carrying a large brown paper bag and ran back to the van even faster than he'd left, only just avoiding a large hole in the sand.

He plonked the bag on the counter while trying to get his breath. 'Those... in there... brioche.'

'Thanks,' I said, taking the bag gratefully, he was so supportive, so enthusiastic on my behalf I wanted to hug him. 'Perhaps people are more likely to buy something any time of the day if it's called a sandwich,' I said, opening up the bag and breathing in the warm, sweet, bready fragrance. 'Yum, these smell delicious,' I took one out and gently prised it apart with a short knife as curls of sugary, buttery steam exuded from the soft dough. I reached in with my scoop and squidged in a blob of butterscotch, sweet and crunchy with an echo of salty caramel. I took a bite and Ben's hand reached in, seizing the warm brioche from my hand and taking a bite too.

'Wow that is delicious,' he said.

The combination of the warm, buttery sweet bread and the cold crunchy ice cream was sublime and we playfully fought each other to finish it.

'Yeah, the ice cream needs something to sell it at the moment – and I reckon this is one way,' I said. 'It's a sort of brunch sandwich. I could even add maple syrup… or bacon, yes crunchy little niblets of salty bacon in maple syrup ice cream. I'll make posters to stick on the van advertising ice cream sandwiches; I can just pop the bread in the microwave.'

'But you don't have a microwave in the van…'

I shook my head, I was so excited about my idea, for once I was forgetting about the basics. It wasn't like me to get carried away like this – but it felt good.

'I'll get a microwave next week,' I said, feeling like a creative entrepreneur. I wanted to lean out of the hatch and kiss him but I resisted, thank God, business was bad enough without me doing that!

'Yeah – this is the gateway drug to Ella's ice cream,' he said, holding up the half-eaten sandwich.

'I'll be back in a minute,' he said, as he scampered back up the beach like an overgrown puppy. He was shouting, turning round to see me and running backwards. 'We'll have them crazy for it,' he yelled as he fell down the hole he'd narrowly missed earlier and disappeared for a moment. Emerging a few seconds later with his thumbs up like nothing had happened.

I laughed aloud, and watched him go, loving his enthusiasm, his optimism in the face of an empty beach and a lonely ice cream seller. Perhaps he was a mentor, an idiot, a dreamer? I didn't care – I was enjoying now, with him, and nothing else mattered.

Eventually he returned with a small microwave from his office, and a couple of large sheets of paper. God only knows what his father thought of him stealing all this office equipment for an ice cream van. Together, like two little kids, we created a picture of the brioche and ice cream with the wording: 'Ice Cream Sandwiches, a delicious anytime snack'.

We proudly stuck the poster on the side of the hatch where it could be seen by anyone passing by. Within a few minutes a woman had read the sign, bought a brioche, and walked away eating it from the paper napkin. She waved and shouted 'This is delicious!' and I glowed. It wasn't much, but to me it was everything and I almost wept with gratitude. Ben was the only person who'd tasted my ice cream and as my friend and supporter was always going to tell me how good it tasted. My idea had worked, this was a good feeling, and here was a total stranger who also thought it was delicious – I just hoped she'd tell her friends.

I don't think 'brioche woman' got the word out because the rest of the day was quiet, except for the time when I was drinking a cup of coffee and someone asked if they could buy one too. In my new entrepreneurial way, I thought a sale is a sale, and immediately boiled the kettle and added 'hot drinks' to the poster on the side of the van.

But by the time 5 p.m. arrived I was feeling quite low and was just about to close up when a whole load of school kids appeared – there must have been about twenty. They all clamoured at the van and I was suddenly overcome with customers; they were loud and rude and fighting among themselves, but I didn't care – they were customers. I sold seven strawberry cones, four vanilla, six chocolate and several fruity ice lollies I'd made from puréed fruit. Again, it wasn't much, but it was a sign that perhaps it was worth sitting here all day every day, and for kids it didn't matter what time of year it was they loved ice cream.

I had to have patience, so gave it another couple of hours and eventually saw a gaggle of women jostling across the sands. 'Hey… hey you're not closed yet are you, we need ice cream,' they chorused, as they staggered across the beach.

There were at least ten ladies, all keen to know the flavours and discuss and decide on toppings, and all excited.

'We've just been to our slimming club, you see,' one of them explained, 'and we go a bit mad when we get out – we've got a whole week to weigh-in so tonight anything goes – can I have double chocolate sauce and nuts on mine please?'

I was delighted. These ladies would appreciate the different flavours, the fresh ingredients, the lovingly made sauces. I opened the freezer, waffle cones in hand to start making their orders, but on opening the lid of the chocolate ice cream I could see it had melted and gone to liquid. My heart was in my mouth as I opened the butterscotch, the fresh raspberry, the rich and creamy vanilla… all melted! I couldn't bear to look any further, and when I checked the freezer temperature it was clear the freezer had completely broken down. I wanted to cry, and with my back to them, all I could hear were their excited voices discussing exactly what they were going to have. Slowly I had to turn round, swallow hard and explain what had happened.

'Look, I'm so sorry but I don't have any ice cream left,' I said.

They stood there open-mouthed, the deep disappointment clear on their faces. I looked back at the contents of the freezer and back at the faces in front of the van, what could I do?

'Perhaps… you'd like to come back next week… and I'll make sure the freezer is working,' I tried, but they weren't impressed. They wanted it now and I couldn't turn customers away, they might never come back again. Then I recalled watching an episode of *The Apprentice* with Mum some weeks before when they'd made a fortune selling smoothies and suddenly an idea came into my head.

'But what about a thick shake instead?' I offered, because the melted ice cream was now looking just like a thick shake.

The disappointment didn't move from their faces, so I offered free toppings and squirty cream, which seemed to soften them slightly.

'And… if you come back next week and show me your slimming club badges I will give you an ice cream for half price… with free toppings.'

They seemed almost happy with this and as I handed them various flavoured milkshakes crowned with squirty cream, nuts, sugar strands and syrupy sauces in every flavour, I did my market research.

'As you're all slimming ladies perhaps you might be interested in my pure fruit lollies next week?' I suggested.

At this they all laughed loudly like I'd just told the best joke ever, then there was a blanket of silence.

'On a Monday night we come straight out of slimming club and head for something far naughtier than fruit lollies,' one of them explained.

They all giggled and another lady pointed out that the ice cream van was actually a stopover on the way to the chip shop.

'Then we go to the pub for cocktails,' another said and they all laughed as the first one added, 'When you've been dieting all week a fruit lolly is the last thing any of us wants.'

I said I understood and happily promised them all kinds of fabulous, fattening ice creams the following week and made a note to stay late every Monday evening for the 'slimming' girls.

And half an hour later as I closed the van, and they headed for the chip shop, I waved them off, pleased with my quick thinking, knowing I had guaranteed customers for Monday and also that I had to think outside the box to make this a success. Ben was right, things were certainly different from when Sophia had been the queen of ice cream. All hail the new queen, I thought, with a smile.

Chapter Fourteen

Strawberry Shakes and Sex on the Stairs

'When life gives you melted ice cream, you make milkshakes!' I said to Ben later, when I bumped into him in the deli, buying myself a bottle of wine and some olives.

'You're bound to have a few teething problems,' he said.

I appreciated his upbeat energy most of the time, but I was angry at myself. I still had a lot of melted ice cream to shift and though I'd not actually lost any sales, it was a textbook error. 'I hadn't checked the freezer properly – I'd been so busy making ice creams and planning a summer of flavours I hadn't actually done a test run on the van. I'm so bloody stupid,' I was saying, shaking my head.

'You're not stupid,' Ben put his arm around me. 'You're clever and funny and I like the way you put your finger to your mouth when you're thinking hard. It's cute.'

I laughed. 'I am not cute. I'm this savvy, creative businesswoman coming up with plans and ideas and forecasts… until her ice cream melts.'

We both smiled at this, I couldn't stay down for long with Ben around and he asked if I wanted to 'hang out'.

I said, 'That's what my kids do, but if it means you want to take a look at the van freezer while I make ice cream, then I'll "hang out" with you.'

Eventually, when Ben had mended the freezer we put a couple of small containers of ice cream inside and sat in the van with the freezer on to see if it was working. An hour later, and the ice cream was as cold as it had been when we put it in, and Ben gave a little cheer as we closed up the freezer again.

We then took all the frozen ice cream to the café and drove back to my apartment. I wanted Ben to try the 'milkshakes' from the remainder of the melted ice cream and he sampled them while I cooked a late supper.

Ben was so supportive, so enthusiastic, I couldn't help but think he'd make a great husband or partner for someone, it was a shame he couldn't settle down. Mind you, his clumsiness could drive someone mad, the amount of milk on the floor when he'd finished adding toppings to his various milkshakes was ridiculous.

I was wiping up the milk he'd spilled when I spotted an old carrier bag lying on the floor, with the word 'Coin' emblazoned across. This rang a bell and I remembered this was an Italian department store – Mum often talked of going to Coin in Naples with Grandma and Aunt Sophia years ago.

'Do you know where this has come from?' I asked Ben as I reached for it. He was still 'experimenting' with melted ice cream and not really listening, but eventually managed to answer.

'When I pulled out the freezer in the van to check the connection, it was stuck in there. I meant to tell you, but forgot. Funny place to put a bag, behind a freezer, there's loads of old papers in there, it's probably rubbish.'

I was grateful Ben hadn't just thrown it away, but in case there were any important documents in there I moved it out of the way – I didn't feel it would be safe to leave paper anywhere near a 'milk-shake-sampling' Ben. I stuffed the bag in a drawer and got back to cooking the marinara sauce, a rich, tomato seafood concoction of my grandma's – a recipe my mum had taught me.

When the sauce was ready, I filled a huge bowl with steaming tagliatelli and poured it on. We ate outside, overlooking the sea as we had the previous evening, but this time the air was sparkly. After sharing a kiss, I wondered if we might last the summer – and as I tasted the rich, tangy tomato and sipped on warm Italian red I tried not to look too far into the future.

There were already many x factors in this new life and I wondered again if I was doing the right thing? Could I stop myself if I began to fall for this man?

Before we'd even finished our pasta, he'd reached out and touched the tips of my fingers with his and my stomach was filled with electricity. I could think of nothing else but his lips on mine and I could tell by his face and the urgent touch of his fingers that he felt the same.

I stood up from my chair and moved towards him. It was like a dance; he knew exactly what I was doing and where I was going and despite being the clumsiest person I knew he moved back in his chair. I sat on his lap, we started to kiss and the world stopped and so did I. The sea was still under a silent blanket of stars with no yesterday, no tomorrow – just now.

We kissed each other gently at first, just like the night before, but now more slow and meaningful, exploring each other with our lips and eyes. His hand moved under my T-shirt and he took my breath away as he touched my breasts, my own hands now cupping his bristly face. In his kisses I tasted the sea, and felt the swirling waves beneath us as he lifted me and carried me inside and up the wooden slatted stairs. Before we even reached the bedroom he put me down on a step, it was strange and uncomfortable but exhilarating as he climbed onto me and still kissing we tore each other's clothes off. As he moved into me I felt an explosion of stars in my head and I cried out in ecstasy. I felt uninhibited, as wild as the sea, unable to stop until the tidal wave of pleasure licked over me.

I didn't know where this was going, but the uncertainty only heightened the excitement. I'd thought I might never love again after Richard, not that this was love – but here, now in this new life I felt different, more alive than I had for years.

Afterwards, we lay together on the bed, naked, his hand on my tummy, mine on his chest, breathing together and thinking apart. Having felt wonderful, I suddenly felt vulnerable again, like a shadow coming over me.

'Ben, I'm scared,' I heard myself say into the darkness.

'There's nothing to be scared of… this is good, we're good together, you and me.'

'Yes, we are aren't we? But it's not just this… you and me. I've made this big decision to move my life in a different direction… but sometimes I wake up in the night and think what have I done? I still have my home but now I have here too, and I'm scared to stay and scared to go back. I feel like I'm in no-man's-land – terrified of the unknown and what might happen.'

'I know, and I understand, I feel it too sometimes, but it's life. It doesn't matter if you're scared or not, you're on the ride – so just enjoy it,' he leaned over, gently touching my arm.

'I like that, and it's so true, we think we have choices but we're all just at the mercy of whatever's next.'

'Exactly, we're in control to a point, but there comes a time when if you're wise you'll accept that we have little influence over the big stuff in our lives. It's all about the universe. "Like flies to wanton boys are we to the gods," he said, '"they kill us for their sport."'

I recognised the line from *King Lear*, a play I'd studied at school a hundred years ago. 'Funny I always liked that line, it spoke to me somehow,' I said.

'Me too, because it's reminding us that we have little say in what happens and we really aren't the architects of our own lives,' he sighed. 'But there's a certain freedom in realising that. That's why I dive, I let the water take the pressure; the feeling of letting go, deep into that ocean and becoming weightless is like saying "world, you've got this". Some people have religion – but I have the sea,' he smiled.

I kissed him, tipsy from the wine and his wisdom, and I felt so lucky to have him in my life, like he was sent to me just when I needed him.

Later as we lay together, we talked about more earthly things. He told me about his family, how he resented his father but understood him. I said I had my own struggles with my mother, and my advice was to never let his father near the internet, or near a teenager who could provide access to the internet.

'My mother's dangerous with a mouse,' I laughed, after regaling him with more of Mum's dating exploits. I'd rung her the day before and she told me her and Leo had progressed from flower arranging to line dancing; I told myself that at least this accounted for the breathlessness.

'So what about you?' he said, sitting up in bed, pulling the sheets over both of us. 'What's the story with you and Richard?'

'Dick.'

'I'm not,' he joked.

'I prefer to call him Dick, it makes me feel better to get the insult out first if ever I'm forced to refer to him, and it provides endless opportunities for jokes too. His story isn't new and different, it's as old as the Bible. He left me for someone with bigger breasts.'

He sighed, turning to lie on his arm so he was looking into my eyes and listening. 'Are you over him?'

'Oh God yes. I still miss the guy I married, and I still feel a pang for the family we once were – but then I guess that's life. We all move on in some way – even families and now I'm saying the long goodbye to my kids.'

'That's why I never married; it's not worth all the pain. Like you say, everyone leaves in the end.'

'I meant life moves on, Ben... people don't always leave.'

'In my experience they do,' he sighed.

My heart tore a little for him, his inability to rely on others, assuming they would leave, could probably be traced back to his mother's death. He had loved her very much, but it wasn't enough, she left him.

'But we're talking about you,' he said. 'Dick's affair, how did it happen?'

'Oh he'd been having trouble at work and I'd suggested he make his life easier and stop railing against the management. I told him he needed to charm his new female boss, who'd just bought the company. "Tell her how great she is," I said. And he took my advice – he did it so well she fell for him, he dumped me and now lives an idyllic life in an exquisitely furnished villa in Marbella.'

'Oh that must hurt.'

'It did… still does, but not from a thwarted love perspective – more as the embittered ex-wife who doesn't have her own villa in Marbella. He's making me sell the family home while he sends the kids the minimum allowance with cheques he writes by his sun-drenched pool – I've seen it on Facebook,' I added with a rueful smile.

'That's not easy.'

'No, it's one thing to be deserted by the father of your children for someone younger, prettier and richer – it's another to have to sit and watch their perfect life from the shabbiness of your own cold living room.'

I waited for the familiar sting of resentment as I said this, but for the first time I didn't feel a pang of anything. For the past few years his smug red face and her smug brown boobs had been all over bloody Facebook every time I clicked on and it had driven me wild with anger. I was only prepared to put up with the sheer masochism of being confronted with their fabulous lives because

I hoped if I waited long enough I'd live to see the day her boobs dropped and he went bald in my timeline.

'You okay,' Ben asked, moving my hair gently from my face.

'I'm fine,' I laughed, realising it was true, I was fine – then added, 'Now... here with you in this lovely place – I finally don't care how pert Dick's wife's boobs are,' I said.

'Dick's wife's boobs – that sounds like a bad porn film,' he laughed.

'Not one I'd like to see,' I smiled.

'It's all over now,' he whispered, 'no more dastardly Dick.'

I giggled and he kissed me before slowly rolling on top of me and I saw the stars, felt the waves beneath us all over again.

Later that night, as Ben slept, I tiptoed out of the bedroom and downstairs. In the back of my mind I'd been waiting for a call back from Gina all day and though I kept checking my phone, there was nothing. I was surprised how much this hurt me, it was like I was her little cousin all over again, just waiting for her to shine her light on me. I suddenly remembered all those times we'd made plans to paint our nails and have 'a girlie night', only for them to fall through at the last minute when her boyfriend appeared. A much talked about shopping trip abandoned by Gina because a friend asked her to go to the matinee at the cinema instead. As I rewound the girlhood slights that I'd pushed to the back of my memory, I was surprised how each one still pinched all these years later. I'd really hoped that the minute she'd got my message she'd be on the phone shouting, 'Ella, Ella how are you, where've you *been?'* Delighted to hear from me and making me feel like I was the most amazing person in the world for phoning her. Perhaps she hadn't got the message? Didn't have a signal? I could make a million excuses for Gina, but she just hadn't called. After all, a woman too busy for her own mother's funeral wasn't going to drop everything to call her long-lost kid cousin.

I made myself a cup of chamomile tea and as I'd gone to the cupboard to get a mug, I spotted the old Italian carrier bag, so I took it out, made my tea and carried both into the living room. Wrapping a throw around me, I snuggled up on the sofa and looked at the bag, remembering my mum going back to Italy with Sophia when I was very young. Their mother had died and was being buried 'back home', and I'd stayed in Manchester with my dad. When Mum had returned she'd brought with her the most beautiful doll all the way from Naples. I wanted to call the doll Gina, but Mum wouldn't let me, she said I should call her Roberta, which was of course her name. I remember Roberta came in a bag just like this one. And deep down I had a feeling that whatever was inside this dusty old bag was more than just bits of old paper and bills – it was something important – a message from the past.

Looking inside as I reached in, I was amazed at how much was in there. The bag was quite heavy, and there were stacks of letters and what looked like postcards and photographs. There was also a smell – I couldn't quite place it at first, it reminded me of being very young, sea salt, strawberries and perfume, my aunt's perfume, Rive Gauche. It was the same perfume my mother wore but seemed so different on each woman – on Aunt Sophia it smelled sweet, on Mum it smelled citrusy.

Inhaling the echo of this scent, I knew this bag had belonged to Aunt Sophia. I wondered if perhaps her recipes might be inside, so I delved deep, picking up the odd letter, a list of appointments, a shopping list. I even found photos of Gina, blonde, glamorous, sitting on a sunlounger by her pool in LA. Photos of her lying on a huge, circular bed in the mansion, and other photos of her with famous film stars, singers, at parties, glass in hand, a sparkle in her eyes. What a life she must have, I thought, laying the photos on the coffee table and admiring them. I spent a few minutes escaping into her life, how far she'd come since this sleepy little seaside village. You had to admire her courage, just upping and leaving – and now this, a life of luxury in Bel Air. Eventually, I dragged myself away from the past, and from Gina's wonderful starry life – I hoped she would tell me all about it herself soon enough.

It was already late and I had to be up early, so now wasn't the time for the full excavation, but I allowed myself to take a look at a small bundle of letters. They were tied with a pink ribbon, and as I undid it I knew they were probably personal, possibly love letters, and I shouldn't be doing this.

Looking back, I sometimes wonder if I should have just burned the bag with all its secrets, rather than prying into other people's lives and opening a door into a past that should have remained there. But that was later – on that first night I read letters from 'Old Italy' from Sophia's friends, telling her of engagements, marriages and babies, back home in Italy. And so many letters from my great-grandmother writing to her own daughter, my grandmother. These letters had probably taken weeks to arrive in a world so different from today, yet she was asking the same questions of her daughter that I asked Lucie on Skype: she wanted to know they were eating and keeping warm and that they were safe and happy.

It's all we ever want as mums, to know our kids are safe and happy, I thought, as I put the letters back in the bag. And even though it was after midnight and God knows what time in Nepal and Thailand, I called Josh and Lucie to make sure they were safe and happy… and eating well.

After a few days in Appledore, I had soon settled into a routine. Business was slow, but promising, and Gina had finally texted to say she was coming over – but I wasn't holding my breath. Best of all, I woke most mornings to find a gorgeous man in my bed, and after a breakfast of brioche, ice cream and kisses, I'd set off for work, heading for the beach, with the wind in my hair and happiness in my heart. I'd drive down the narrow streets onto the front, waving at random kids on their way to school, the van's jingle playing loudly, unable to take the smile from my face. I could now put names to some faces, and my fourth day, I spotted Beryl, one of the slimming ladies, rushing from the bakery with a bag of doughnuts. She gave me the thumbs up and shouted something about 'salted caramel…' and I knew she'd be arriving at my hatch well before next Monday's after class treat time.

Pulling up on the sands that morning, I saw Peter with his Labrador Cocoa and he gave me a wave – and I felt inexplicably happy. This lovely beach with the seagulls above and the blue skies meeting the sea was now my workplace. I finally felt a real sense of freedom. This feeling of being totally alone, not having anyone depend on you and not worrying about anyone (for a little while anyway) was what I'd needed. This is what a gap year must be like minus the backpacks, bungee jumping and obligatory tattoos.

Just at that moment, as I looked up to take in my surroundings, I suddenly saw a figure walking along the promenade and I just knew it was her. So she'd decided to come to Appledore after all.

Chapter Fifteen

Jelly Sandals and Gina's Tears

I noticed her shoes first. Black patent high heels with a flash of scarlet sole. Looking up, I saw her cream, fitted skirt, short, boxy jacket, probably Chanel, and her hair, a cloud of creamy gold around her face. Gina had arrived and she was walking from the car park, dark glasses on, film star stroll, heading down onto the front. All the time she was looking into her phone, unaware of the stir she was causing around her.

I quickly closed the van and headed across the beach to greet her, my legs carrying me there; jelly sandals on my feet, a bucket and spade in my hand I was running to Gina. Just like when I was a kid, any little niggles and doubts were swiftly replaced by the familiar bloom of pride filling my chest as I neared the promenade to greet my cousin, the film star.

The sun was behind her like a halo, full red lips, golden, sun-kissed face, the sea breeze ruffling her hair. I remembered the last time I saw her, saying goodbye at the end of a holiday, hugs at the car, Mum telling me to hurry up and get in, and Gina's tears, always the tears saying goodbye to her little cousin.

It was the closest either of us had ever got to having a sister, and I worried what she'd make of me now, thirty years later. Gina a successful movie star with a mansion in Bel Air; Ella a wannabe ice cream seller with half a house in Manchester. I was just a child when we knew each other back then, and she a young woman, so much had gone on through the years; could we ever hope to reach each other again?

Gina was almost sixty, yet still she was turning heads in Appledore just as she had in her twenties. As I ran, I watched her go into the Seagate pub on the front, disappointed she hadn't looked out for the van and come to find me. But that was Gina, she did her own thing and she probably fancied a drink first (even though it was only 9 a.m.), so I headed to the pub and opened the door. I walked in, and I didn't need to look around for her, she was there, leaning on the bar, making the surroundings look old, the furniture shabby. I was aware the pub was quite busy with people breakfasting, but Gina had this light that seemed to follow her around and everything and everyone else dimmed in her presence. I stood in the doorway unsure of how to approach her, what to say.

'Gina?' I said, breathlessly. Unable to hold back, I was suddenly standing in front of her and for a moment I wondered if she'd recognise me. But as soon as she looked up from her drink, pulled down her sunglasses and peered over them she squealed loudly.

'Darling… darling Ella, I was just about to phone you.'

I doubted that, but in an instant I forgave her for the little white lie. She just wanted to make me feel special – Gina always made people feel special, and there was no doubt she was genuinely delighted to see me. As we embraced, I breathed in that familiar citrusy perfume, the same one Mum and Sophia always wore, but Gina's was sweeter, laced with French vanilla and first-class travel.

'Darling, oh darling, I have missed you! It's just so wonderful to see you,' she said into my ear, both arms tightly around me like she would never let me go. I was reminded how much taller than me she was as she kissed my head and squeezed me for what felt like forever.

I was delighted at her sincere warmth and affection after all these years – clearly our relationship would be as strong as before. This was good for both of us, as Mum, me and the kids were probably the only family she had left now. We could all regroup as a family; it was time. In those few seconds as we hugged I had visions of us sitting together on those fabulous sun loungers by her pool, sipping martinis with Leonardo DiCaprio and clearing up all the stupid pain that had hung around us for all these years.

'I so wanted to be at the funeral, but I was caught up in filming,' she said, climbing onto a bar stool and patting the one next to her. It wasn't my place to judge, my mother did enough of that for all of us. I had felt resentment about Gina's no-show on Sophia's behalf, but I didn't know Gina's life and commitments. And I certainly wasn't going to ruin this wonderful reunion by reprimanding her or trying to make her feel guilty.

'It was a sad day, but your mum had a good send-off.'

She nodded and ordered two large vodkas, looked like she'd already polished the first one off. I wanted to protest, to tell her it was too early and I had a business to run on the beach, but I didn't because this was my wonderful cousin who'd come thousands of miles to see me. I also didn't want to seem boring and straight in the presence of my fabulous, high flying cousin. My business was important, but so was family, and after all these years I could finally sit and have a drink with her.

'I'm sure Mum would understand that I couldn't be there on the day,' she said.

'Yes, I'm sure, I mean you can't just walk off a film set, whatever happens,' I added. 'I spoke to your agent.'

'Yes, she told me. She said you sounded upset, so I dumped Leonardo and jumped on a plane.'

'Oh Gina, you didn't?' I was surprised, and flattered, she hadn't left filming for her mother's funeral, but she'd done it for me, which seemed strange. 'But what about Leonardo... did he mind?'

'He understood. "Leonardo," I said, "I have a very special cousin who needs me." "Then you must go to her," he said, and I hopped on the red eye from LAX,' she said, like she'd simply jumped on a bus.

'Wow! I didn't mean for you to change your plans, I was just calling to thank you for the accommodation and to talk to you about the business.'

'Oh it was no trouble, I wanted to come and see you and sort out mother's estate at the same time.'

'Oh?' I was torn between asking about Leonardo's understanding nature and the burning question about what she planned to do with the café, 'is everything okay, with the café?'

'It will be,' she said enigmatically.

'Will you sell?' I asked.

'It depends,' she replied, rummaging in her bag. 'Do you mind if we sit outside, I need a...' she waved a box of cigarettes in the air and I dutifully grabbed my drink to follow her. 'I started vaping, but the flavours in the UK make me gag… and anyway, I bought a million dollars' worth of duty-free ciggies so I'm damn well gonna smoke them,' she laughed.

Once we were seated on wooden benches at a table outside I continued the conversation about the café. 'It might be nice to keep the café? If you were wondering about a manager, I could… I would love to be involved.'

'Ella, my darling, I won't do anything without discussing it with you first, but give me a break. My ass has only just landed and I haven't seen you for thirty years.'

I smiled, she hadn't changed in those thirty years. The beautiful, sophisticated older cousin was still there, she was still as loud, but now with a slight American accent. And I laughed at the way she said 'ass', it sounded funny coming from Gina.

'So let's not talk about boring old business decisions, let's talk and talk and drink and drink,' she laughed. 'I'm going to keep drinking vodka until everyone looks pretty,' she said too loudly, causing some disgruntlement on the next table. I'd forgotten, but Gina had always loved a floor show – she was always the centre of attention, and if she wasn't she would make it so.

'Hey Ella, I remember the last time we said goodbye, you were in a red T-shirt, white shorts, honey, you looked so cute!'

I was flattered she'd remembered. She was so flaky, in a lovely way, I almost doubted she'd recall much about me at all, especially with Mum's comments about her being fickle, telling fibs and forgetting about everyone when she left Appledore. I knew now, this just wasn't true.

'So, tell me everything. I want to know *all* about grown-up Ella,' she said, uncrossing her long legs, as slim as they'd always been. Her eyes were sparkling and she was leaning forward, excited and eager to hear all about my life.

'There's not much to tell...' I started, suddenly feeling daunted about sharing the disaster I called my life with Gina.

'Oh honey, don't say that. You're young and beautiful and...'

'I'm forty-four, Gina...'

'You're still young, trust me, babe, when you get to my age anything under fifty is YOUNG,' she laughed. 'So tell me about the kids, you have one of each right?'

'Yes, Josh and Lucie. They are both fine, travelling the world,' I was glad to at least offer something exotic to my worldly cousin, even if it was by proxy.

'Fabulous. Are they gorgeous? Please tell me they're both rich, beautiful doctors?'

I laughed, 'They're students.'

'Good – so one day they'll be rich, beautiful doctors,' she stubbed out her cigarette and picked up her Chanel handbag. I took that as our cue to go back inside the pub and followed her as she mounted the bar stool elegantly.

'So, what about you, Ella?' she said, sipping her drink. 'You were always the clever one in the family – my clever cousin,' she reached over and rubbed my knee. 'I've often imagined you in a big boardroom working for a huge company...'

'No, no, I didn't do anything like that,' I was almost tempted to make something up. I had nothing to wow her with, her life had been so exciting and I'd done nothing.

She was looking at me expectantly, waiting to hear about my brilliant life and I felt a crush of embarrassment, shame even. What was she expecting? 'I'm starring in a musical in the West End', or 'I'm working on a cure for cancer.'

'I'm… er currently trying to build up the ice cream business here – with Reginaldo, the van.'

'Oh God, I heard about that,' she said, looking into my eyes with deep pity, as if I'd been given six months to live. 'Poor old Reginaldo,' she continued; 'I said to Chad, my husband, God knows why she left it to you. He said it's because I'd never move it off the drive my driving's so SHIT,' she shouted this a little too loudly and people turned to look. Again. Then she laughed loudly for too long and suddenly stopped. 'I don't drive.'

'Oh,' I smiled, and spoke in a low voice, hoping she'd catch on, 'I always imagined you in an open-topped car driving through palm-tree-lined Beverly Hills.'

'No… why drive when you have a driver?' She giggled and I instinctively giggled back. This was the Gina I remembered, ir-reverent, charming, outrageous and funny. Gina always seemed to be in control of her life and of all situations, an alpha female who other women could only look at in awe – my wonderful cousin. And as we giggled together and flicked our hair in the same way, I realised I still wanted to be just like her.

'But you're not seriously just working the dirty old van are you?' she asked now.

'Erm, yes it's just a summer fling, a vacation from real life…' I said, liking the way that sounded.

'Thank GOD!' She leaned forward expectantly, 'So what do you *really* do?'

'Yes, well I lost my… I gave up a career in… fashion to take this vacation from life. Of course it's only a summer job, but I might stay on.'

'Fashion? How wonderful. You were a model, weren't you? Ah, I knew it! You've got the cheekbones, doll.'

'God no,' I laughed; 'I wasn't a model, I just… I worked in a dress shop,' there was no point in telling fibs, my life just wasn't as spectacular as hers and we both had to face it.

She seemed a little deflated. 'A dress shop, my ass! You never modelled? Do you sing? Act?'

I had to smile, she really had no idea about real life, she lived in a fantasy world unaware that people spent their lives changing nappies and making ends meet.

'No, I'm afraid I'm very boring. I'm not like you, working with Leonardo DiCaprio and sitting by my pool.'

'You're not boring, Ella, so please don't say you are,' then she touched my arm. 'Leonardo's a hoot, and the pool's divine, but it isn't everything, honey…' For a moment her glamorous, smiling mask dropped and she looked like she might cry.

'You okay, Gina?' I asked, concerned.

She immediately composed herself and I saw the mask slip back on. 'Of course. I am bloody FABULOUS,' she said loudly. And she was back – beautiful, fun and flirting with the barman as she ordered yet another two large vodkas. I couldn't possibly have any more, it was midday and I had to get back to the van, not only was I in danger of losing custom, I'd also be too pissed to drive it home.

'Oh one more little one won't do you any harm,' she said when I protested. 'Don't be a bloody bore,' she winked at me.

I felt a frisson of irritation then. It was okay for Gina who could afford to go swanning around Malibu all day, but some of us had work to do.

'If you'd told me about your plans to come here I'd have tried to arrange cover and had some time off with you,' I said, a little pointedly.

'Oh babes, don't get all over my ass, I didn't mean it. Oh you are SO cute! Go on... have another little drinkie...'

'No, and I'm not being boring – just imagine the shame if I'm stopped for drinking and driving an ice cream van,' I said smiling, but pushing my vodka gently in her direction. She shrugged and knocked hers back, long, red nails clutching at the glass, eyes closed as the rim touched her lips, revealing flawless, smoky eye make-up and long, long lashes. Up close her skin was lined, her neck crěpey, her hands old – but she still had that special something. In a dim English pub on a Wednesday afternoon, she sprinkled little flakes of Hollywood glitter.

'So what's it like, living in Bel Air?' I asked, aware I was staring and sounding like a twelve-year-old fan girl.

'Fabulous, babe,' she smiled, drinking the second glass of vodka. 'I see Victoria and David in town, and of course there's Heff and his Playboy bunnies down the road. Simon Cowell's home is beautiful, I went to a party there – oh it goes on and on. But I want to know about you. I can't believe you never modelled,' she said, throwing the focus back to me again, when I wanted to know all about her.

'I was never model material,' I said.

'Bullshit,' she said, a little too loudly, as everyone seemed to do a double take once more. 'Is that what Roberta told you? Don't let her dampen your sparkle, you were and are absolutely stunning. You may be forty-four but you're still gorgeous.'

I smiled, she was being kind. 'No, you're the beauty in the family,' I said.

She kept looking at me, just staring.

'What?' I asked.

'It's just… I don't know, I always thought you'd be blonde, that you'd bite the bullet and bleach your hair. I bet Roberta told you it was tarty.'

I laughed, a little awkwardly. I didn't like the way she kept referring to Mum in slightly derogatory tones. 'I'm dark-haired and dark-skinned like Mum; I don't think blonde would suit me.'

'You're nothing like Roberta, you're gorgeous, you'd rock blonde hair.'

'I don't think so, but you do. You seemed to have missed that Italian gene with your pale skin and blonde hair.'

'No, I'm as Italian as you, girl. The answer is bleach, bleach, and more bleach, and the lightest shade of foundation known to woman, oh and sun avoidance,' she said. 'I always wanted to be Marilyn, not Sophia Loren. You could be Marilyn too.' She was slightly tipsy by now, but she even managed this with her customary elegance, and her giggles were still very cute fifties starlet.

'You should let me do your hair, Ella… you'd be a gorgeous blonde,' she was saying.

'Oh when I was younger maybe, but it's too late to go blonde now.'

'MY ASS,' she said, which made me laugh, despite feeling a little uncomfortable about the volume and the attention we were getting from other customers. 'It's never too late to be blonde,' then she looked at me directly and asked: 'I bet Roberta would hate you being blonde. She's always been a bit controlling, hasn't she?'

I was a little surprised at this comment and again out of loyalty to Mum, I shook my head. 'Mum's just… Mum,' I said. 'She's always been very protective. When I was a teenager she didn't want me to go blonde in case I had unsuitable boys chasing me. She feared I might get into bad company.' I was recounting this in a light-hearted way, another of my 'mum' stories, until I realised the implications of what I'd just said.

'Because you might end up like your no-good cousin Gina?'

Bingo, she got it in one.

'No,' I lied. 'Look, if being blonde means living the high life in Beverly Hills with the Beckhams for neighbours, then I'd do it in an instant,' I said, desperately trying to rescue the situation.

This seemed to placate Gina who offered me yet another drink, which I again declined. I was surprised at how much she was putting away, and despite her loudness and apparent confidence, I wondered if coming back here had made her nervous. Unfortunately, I really needed to get going, so I went to make my leave.

'But I haven't seen you in years and now you're off,' she said, dropping her lower lip in a mock sulk.

'I'm so sorry; it's just that I'm trying to build the business. I've only been here a few days and I'm not busy yet, but I need to…'

'Okay, okay, you just abandon your old cousin,' she said. I didn't want to leave, but I had no choice.

'I'll call you this evening, we'll meet up, I'll take you for dinner?' she said, and I agreed, delighted at this prospect. We hugged and she kissed me on the cheek, holding my chin in her hand and looking into my eyes. 'I missed you, Ella,' she sighed.

I'd forgotten how affectionate Gina could be. She swept you up in her compliments and kisses, told you how wonderful you were and made you feel a million dollars. And I wondered, as I walked out of the pub if Mum's feelings about Gina were because she had this 'gift' of making everyone fall for her. Looking back at my perfectly beautiful cousin charming the considerably younger barman, I thought, that's quite a gift – and a lot to be jealous of.

Chapter Sixteen

Fun, Frappuccinos and
a Frantic French Farce

As I walked from the pub back onto the beach, a warm breeze was blowing and I felt happy, complete almost. Gina was back where she belonged, it might be a short visit, but while she was here there'd be some fun – and the chance for us to heal the family rift that had cleaved us all apart for too long. I was feeling so buoyed up I decided to pop into Caprioni's and see how things were ticking over, but just approaching the building filled me with darkness. The place seemed deserted, no one was coming here any more, and walking in to see Marco at the counter didn't help.

'Hi is all okay with you?' I said, trying to be friendly, after all it can't have been much fun for him sitting here day in, day out. 'Now Gina my cousin's back you should know your fate soon,' I said, referring to his job at the café.

'Wow thanks for the heads up,' he muttered sarcastically.

'I just thought you might want to know about what's going to happen with the café – I know I do.'

'This isn't a café, it's hell with fluorescent lighting,' he said, and with that, took his phone from his pocket and ended the conversation. So I said goodbye, which wasn't returned, and I left the café to walk back into the sunshine, feeling so happy that even Marco couldn't bring me down.

To add to my happiness, by the time I'd arrived at the van there were several people waiting to buy something. I soon started serving, aware that there was almost a queue forming – something I hadn't experienced so far. As I slowly worked through the orders, I was delighted – dare I hope things were finally starting to take off? But turning around to hand someone their two large cones of chocolate ice cream, I looked behind to see the last person in the queue and almost dropped the cones. There in my queue on Appledore beach was my mother standing bold as brass.

'It's me, it's Mum,' she said, pointing to her chest, like she needed to introduce herself.

'I can see that, Mum,' I laughed. My first thought was oh God, not now, not just as Gina has arrived, and this wasn't the time to tell her, so I smiled bravely and climbed down from the van. I gave her a big hug and then helped her inside. 'Come and see my new office.'

She explained that Sue had dropped her off at the station in Manchester and she'd wanted her visit to be a surprise.

'Well it's a lovely one,' I said, grimacing. This was completely unexpected, and the timing was horrific. Just as I was about to build bridges with Gina, my mother was here – and she wasn't in the business of building any bridges. It seemed Gina wasn't too keen on Mum either and now I had to entertain both of them without offending either. It looked like my new life of fun and freedom was about to turn into a frantic French farce.

I made us a cup of coffee while she sat on the little stool inside the van looking round. I didn't want to question her too much at this stage about why she'd suddenly decided to turn up, I was just glad she was okay and she seemed happy to be here – which was a bonus. I just wondered how long her happiness would last.

'You don't do frappuccinos then?'

'No, Mum.'

'Not very big is it?' she said, twisting her head round awkwardly, like it was so cramped she couldn't even turn her head.

'Well it has to be driven around, Mum, it can't be too big – I couldn't get a juggernaut down the narrow streets round here.'

It would have been so much easier if she'd arrived a month later, in the height of summer when I had a huge queue of people at the van, and everything was sorted with Gina. We drank our coffee and I made her an ice cream brioche 'sandwich' which she accepted graciously, and ate without criticism – a new look for Mum.

'So have you seen anyone?' she asked.

She was presumably wondering if I'd met up with 'that bad influence', Gina.

'If you mean Gina, yes she's here – and honestly Mum, I don't know what your problem is. The woman is lovely, and at almost sixty I doubt she'll be leading me astray. I wish!'

'You'd be surprised, a leopard doesn't change its spots,' she said, raising her eyebrows.

'Anyway, she's well, thank you for asking.'

'Oh I don't doubt it. Gina's always well; it's everyone around her that gets caught up in the drama that suffers. She tells such fibs, Ella.'

'No she doesn't, you mustn't say things like that, Mum.'

'Has she told you what she's doing with the café?'

'No, but she says she won't do anything without talking it over with me first. I imagine she'll get offers.'

'Oh I'm sure she'll get offers – girls like her always do.'

I ignored this remark, the very fact she was referring to Gina as a girl showed me that Mum was still firmly stuck in the past.

'I was thinking, Mum… if the van does well, I might ask if she'd let me rent the café, or run it for her.'

'Don't get involved, that's my advice.'

'Well she's family, we have to get involved with family,' I tried.

'Never once got in touch with me to find out how we were. She forgot us all once she'd gone to America… and I'm her aunt, you know?'

'Yes I know, Mum.'

'Family – it's supposed to be about family, but she was very selfish – a fickle girl…'I nodded because that's what Mum wanted me to do and I didn't want an argument; it wasn't worth it. This diatribe of Mum's would continue, on a loop repeating various key points for some time, but this van was my business and not the place for a full-on argument. Thankfully realising it was all falling on deaf ears and I wasn't going to bite, Mum continued to sip her coffee and looked around asking questions about the fridges, eventually abandoning the subject of Gina. So I took the opportunity to move to safe ground.

'How's Leo?' I asked.

Mum looked at me blankly. 'The boy I was at school with? Haven't seen him for over sixty years, Ella, what are you going on about?'

It was going to be one of those conversations.

'Leo, the man you were, apparently, flower arranging and line dancing with?'

'Oh you mean Leo?'

I nodded.

'He had a roving eye – what a Casanova. He sent photographs of his bits to Doris… while he was dating me! I said, "Doris, it's like bloody *Dynasty*, I'm Alexis, you're Crystal and he's JR." But Doris said he was nothing like JR because Leo had a very small one and JR was known for his prowess.' She sat back on this final word, the emphasis firmly on the 'ss', her handbag clutched to her knee.

I moved swiftly on… 'So where's your luggage?'

'At the hotel. I'm in that big one on the front, won't stay too long – just wanted to see you, make sure you were safe and hadn't been ravished by a local fisherman,' she laughed at that and so did I.

I hoped she wasn't spending all her pension on the fancy hotel, but the alternative was to stay with me in Sophia's apartment and she wouldn't want that.

'Mum, are you here because you were you worried I might become best friends with Gina and she'd introduce me to the fisherman who would ravish me?'

She looked sheepish – ah so that was it.

'I'm a divorced mum of two, not an impressionable teen – Gina can't turn me into a lady of the night… not that she ever would.

And have you seen the fishermen round here? They're less Jack Sparrow and more Captain Birdseye.'

'You just keep yourself to yourself while you're here and ignore *her*.'

I sighed, we were back on the Gina loop.

'She's my cousin! Why must I ignore her?'

'Because I said so.'

'You can't say *that* to me, Mum,' I laughed. When was Mum going to realise that I wasn't a child and that Gina wasn't the devil.

'Mum, while you're here let's forget about long-held family feuds, let's use your family knowledge for good, not evil. So, what about Sophia's recipes – any idea where they might be? Any idea *what* they might be?'

'It was a long time ago, Ella, I can't remember my own name some days – so I'm sure I can't remember what my sister put in her sodding ice cream,' she snapped.

'Stay classy, Mother,' I said, and leaned into the hatch to see if there was a single soul out there who might want something from my van, anything: directions to the local pub, a bag for their dog mess, a seventy-eight-year-old mother with a grudge. But naturally there was no one there in my time of need.

'You're not very busy are you?' she said into the silence. As perceptive as ever, finding the wound and sprinkling in lashings of salt.

'No I'm not busy because my ice cream is awful and I'm rude to the customers… oh but it's okay because Gina's here to show me how to lap dance so I won't need this old van. I can get work as a stripper… even better, we can turn the van into a mobile lap dancing club.'

'Oh may God forgive you.'

'Oh don't bring him into it. You always bring in the big guns when you're losing,' I said. 'Anyway, what did you and God think about that brioche?'

'Not that bad…'

'Stop, Mum, you're making my head swell.'

'It was a bit bready now you ask… you're not seeing Gina again are you?'

Oh not again! 'Yes, I am. She's my cousin and she owns the café that my van belongs to. So not only is she family – she's a fun, interesting and glamorous friend, and a work colleague.'

'I know why you're not busy.'

'Let me guess,' I sighed, 'it's Gina's fault?' I was now waiting for the pearls of wisdom and venom that would both enlighten and crush me at the same time.

'You're quiet because no one knows you're here.' So she was now criticising my business marketing, an unexpected move, but it bore my mother's hallmark of taking one by surprise with her insults.

I continued to lean on the hatch looking out, while Mum sat on the little stool. We were both lost in our own thoughts, two women who'd known each other forever and knew each other too well.

'Trouble is they can't see your van from the hotel,' she continued. 'There's some kind of yuppie conference on there and they're all on their iPhones. They don't look up from their devices… that's what they call them, devices.'

She should talk, I thought – but she had a point. I'd watched people walking the front gazing into their phones and thought what a waste of all this lovely scenery.

'Yes, imagine staying here and not taking this in,' I said, gesturing around me. 'Before them is the most stunning view and they're missing it to stare into a tiny screen.'

'That's what you should do, Ella. Put fancy pictures of your ice cream on the screen so they can see it and increase sales.' She said this like she was pitching to Lord Sugar on *The Apprentice*.

'Oh Mum, advertising a business isn't like online dating, you know,' I could only imagine the weirdos that would turn up.

'Yes it is – it's exactly like online dating. You dress it up, take its photo and put it on the internet – and if people like what they see… then you've got a date.'

I smiled and patted her knee in what was perhaps a rather patronising gesture, but wondered if what she was saying made some kind of weird sense.

'So how… exactly how would you advertise this business?' I asked.

'I told you, take photographs…'

'No I mean, literally, what would you do, put them on Facebook or what?'

How to confess to your seventy-eight-year-old mother that you needed her help online, that you used words like Twitter and Instagram, but you hadn't a clue how they worked. Thanks to having time on her hands and teenage grandkids, Mum knew far more about it all than I did. But I absolutely couldn't admit this to her – if she knew she was in the driving seat she'd try to take over.

And as we'd learned, mother could get a little ahead of herself and make mistakes (I give you, Gay and Gorgeous and 'sextgate' with the vicar).

'Well you make an Instagram and a Twitter account,' she said, looking up for inspiration. 'Oh that reminds me, have you seen Josh and Lucie's photos on Instagram?'

I was a little embarrassed to admit I hadn't because I didn't know how to work the mysteries she spoke of.

'Well it's a good job one of us knows what we're doing and can keep an eye on them, isn't it?' she said, making me feel like a complete Luddite.

She took out her phone, clicked a few times, then turned the screen towards me. And there was my handsome son, standing on rough terrain, a spade in his hand, a smile on his face. Another one of him building a brick wall, then holding a little child, with Aarya by his side beaming. Then Mum scrolled along and we found Lucie in Thailand on a beach, sunbathing in a very small bikini.

'I thought she was seeing the sights?' I sighed.

'I think she's making her own sights,' Mum smiled. Funny how she was so accepting of her granddaughter in a bikini, but she'd once spotted my photos of her niece Gina in a bathing suit when I'd holidayed here and she was horrified. 'I don't want to see you following her example,' she'd said. I suppose times were different, but I couldn't help but feel that Mum had it in for Gina simply because she was Sophia's daughter.

'Oh Mum, the kids look so grown-up don't they?' I said, grateful for what felt like an illicit peep into my children's world. I could speak to them on Skype, but this was 'mummy stalker' paradise – I would get Instagram now so I could look at them when-ever I missed them. Young people didn't seem to use Facebook any more whereas Instagram was a chronicle of every minute of their lives in picture format. On a still photo I could really study their facial expressions to make sure those smiles were real and they were genuinely safe and happy. Sue and I used to do that in 'Fashion Passion' with copies of *Hello*; we'd worked out the truth behind many a WAG's smile and therefore the real state of her marriage that way. And here I was now with a whole album of my kids' photos for me to go through with the tenacity of a good forensic analyst.

'Be careful not to let the kids know you're checking their social media every four minutes,' Mum said, reading my mind. 'They call that creeping… and you don't want to be a creeper, Ella.'

'No, I don't,' I sighed, as she scrolled onto a photo of Lucie with a man I'd never seen before. 'Who's that?' I said.

Mum looked closer through her glasses. 'Oh that's Pang, don't worry about him, he's gay,' she said knowingly. 'Always difficult when you see something or someone and you want to know about it but can't ask, because then they'll know you were creeping,' she said, with a warning look.

'Oh yes, I can see how that would be a problem. Sometimes ignorance is bliss?' I said, trying to swipe onto the next picture but Mum snatched the phone off me.

'I'll say, love. I remember when you were their age and I caught a phone conversation you had with your boyfriend. I remember you came off the phone in tears and I wanted to go round and punch him, until you explained his dog had died.'

'I remember that, and I also remember resenting you for trying to get it out of me. I can hear the same tone in the kids' voices when I try and find out what's going on in their lives,' I smiled. 'Sorry I gave you a hard time, Mum,' I reached out and touched her arm.

'Oh I'm sure I did the same to my mother. My parents wanted us to be good church-going housewives; sex wasn't on the agenda before marriage. I think they were hoping for at least one nun for a daughter, but no chance of that with our Sophia,' she laughed. There were times, like now, when Mum talked about the past and Sophia in a light-hearted, nostalgic way and I'd realised this was usually when she was thinking about the distant past. Memories of their childhood and when they were young women still made her smile, and I wondered again what had happened later to change everything?

'No chance of you becoming a nun either – given your recent activities, Mother,' I said in an affectionate reprimand.

'Yes but it's not about sex, Ella…'

'Enough information, Mum,' I said, sounding like Josh or Lucie.

'No, what I mean is everyone talks about it and the young ones are using all kinds of orifices… but it's not for me.'

'I'm glad to hear it,' I said, desperate to change the subject and adding the word orifice to the growing list I didn't want to hear my mother say again.

'I just want someone to be there for me, everyone wants someone for them, don't they? Sometimes I think no one would notice if I wasn't here, because I just get in the way.'

I looked at her and suddenly felt such sadness; 'Mum, you're not in anyone's way, it's just that the kids are gone now and I'm trying to make a living and… a life I suppose. I'm trying to make a grab at something before it's too late.' But in my selfish pursuit of happiness, I'd forgotten about Mum – she also wanted something before it was too late: she wanted to be loved again. We lost Dad many years before, and even though Mum had me and the kids it wasn't the same as having that companionship. Sometimes she could be a little critical, sometimes a little crazy, difficult even – but I could see now that she was trying to readjust to being older while still searching for her own happiness.

'I think we both need to find our "happy" don't we, Mum?' I said.

'Oh as long as you and the kids find your happy, I'll be okay,' she said, then she looked at me and I knew that familiar question was about to be asked. 'I've been a good mother, haven't I?'

And I answered the same answer as always, 'The best, Mum, the best.'

She seemed reassured by that and began scrolling through her phone again. Another picture of my lovely son.

'He's rebuilding Nepal, love,' she said, 'one brick at a time. Have you read his blog?'

'I didn't realise he had one.' I wasn't completely sure what a blog was, and I worried if I looked I might be caught out as 'a creeper'.

'Oh love – you need to get with the programme. You're no one without a blog,' Mum was saying. 'Mind you it all moves so fast – Doris says vlogging is the new black, whatever the bugger that means.'

For someone who couldn't remember her name, the woman could retain amazing facts.

'Mum, you amaze me the way you know all this internet stuff.'

'Well, I dated that internet billionaire for a while…'

'Did you?' I was surprised.

'Did I? Bill Green, he volunteered at the library. Oh that's right, he wasn't an internet billionaire, I got mixed up with Bill Gates.'

'Easy mistake to make,' I said, and we both laughed.

Later, I took Mum back to her hotel. I invited her to look at my apartment, but she said she didn't want to see too much of Appledore and the surrounding areas because it brought back happy memories.

'But that's good isn't it?' I asked.

'No, because we used to drop you off here when you were little and you're not little any more and that makes me sad.'

I felt for her. I thought of my own kids and understood what she meant; 'I know, it's hard isn't it? You have your kids for such a short time – and all the while we're preparing them for life without us, but it's still a shock when they leave and your little family's spread or gone.'

She smiled and patted my hand; 'You're so precious, Ella, thought I might lose you once or twice along the way.'

'What do you mean you thought you might lose me, was I ill?'

'I don't want to talk about it,' she said, suddenly closing up again like a stroppy child.

'You can't just say that and expect me to leave it alone,' I said.

'You were, are, so precious and I worried… I worried you'd leave.' She was either confused or had decided not to tell me something, but either way she seemed to need my reassurance.

'All children leave eventually, it's part of the process, but I'm still here, Mum, we're still together, you and me.'

Her mood had changed completely and once more I was puzzled. Was this Mum's age confusing her, or was it something more?

'Will you be okay here tonight, Mum, you could come with me and stay at the apartment?'

'*She's* not there, is she?'

'No, I think Gina's in a hotel,' I said, praying it was a different one to my mother's.

'No, I won't come to the apartment – there's chicken cacciatore on the menu, and as it's my speciality, I thought I might have a word with the chef so he doesn't make any mistakes.'

I smiled, thinking that would go down well. Then we hugged and she said she'd come and see me at the van the next day.

'I'll just be glad when you're back home safe and sound, love,' she called after me as I walked from the hotel.

It seemed Mum had been worrying about me in Appledore while I was worrying about my kids on the other side of the world. Once you're a mum that's it – they can be a million miles away, but they take a little chink of your heart with them until they're back again.

'Ella, there was something I had to tell you,' she called as I headed back to the van. So I turned round and walked back.

'What?'

'I can't bloody remember.'

'Tonight's cacciatore?' I suggested.

'That might be it,' she said, 'too much oregano and it's buggered...' and with that she wandered into the hotel.

I walked back, got into the van, and was just starting it when I saw her face at the window. She looked frantic and I was immediately concerned; 'Mum, are you okay?'

'Yes... I just remembered what it is. That Dick you were married to?'

'Yes, yes... what, Mum?' I asked, hoping something terrible had happened to him, or that his wife's breasts had finally popped.

'He sent a man round, said the house is sold. But worse than that, he wants the telly! That's why I came here. Oh damn, I was looking for my room key and I just found it in my bloody handbag, look!' She thrust a thick brown envelope at me and my heart began to thud.

I opened it with trepidation and, as I'd expected, it was from Richard's solicitor – the house had been sold and we had to move out before the end of the month. The Dick couldn't wait to get his hands on the money from the house and it made me livid. When he left he'd felt guilty about the affair and said he'd never see me or the kids without a roof. Then he'd changed his mind and we were now all homeless – it was bad enough for me and the kids, but I also had a homeless mother too.

I sat in the driver's seat of the van, my face crumpled along with the papers in my hand. It wasn't a huge surprise, I just didn't think the house would sell so quickly, especially with my mother in it when people were being shown round.

I was vaguely aware of my mother now opening the passenger side door, but I was in shock and just concentrating on the immediate problem. I would receive a small amount of money for the sale of the house, but if the kids wanted to come home and live with me again I'd need at least three bedrooms.

I had the apartment for the summer, and I had time to think about this, but I was still responsible for three other people despite my new-found freedom. It was more important than ever that I make a go of this business so I could at least earn enough for a deposit on a small house.

I was suddenly jolted back to the here and now by Delilah's barking, alerting me to a drama going on at the passenger door. There I was worrying about the weight of responsibility for my mother, not realising she was now dangling in the open door, clinging to the side, being nipped and barked at by a dog in a stripey jumpsuit and jaunty beret!

Unable to lift herself onto the seat, Mum was yelping and Delilah was barking and they were creating quite a scene.

'Mum, oh Mum, I'm sorry,' I said, abandoning my seat and running round to help her, arriving after Ben, who happened to be walking along the front, had seen the kerfuffle and come over to help. He was now offering my mother a push up.

'I'm all right dear, this nice young man is helping,' she said to me. Given his track record for spills, falls and general catastrophe this was more of a concern than relief.

'Meet my mother,' I said as she handed me her handbag like the queen to one of her courtiers.

'Hello,' Ben said to me while hoisting her up. I had been right about the French farce, I was officially living it. My mother's bottom was now in Ben's face and Delilah was yapping at his heels, it wasn't the introduction I'd imagined – or perhaps it was. Between us we eventually calmed Delilah and settled Mum into the passenger seat.

'So you changed your mind, you're coming back with me to-night after all?' I said to her.

'Well, you're upset, I don't want you going back on your own, I'll get a taxi back later.'

'I'll be fine, Mum, Ben's... a friend and he'll... probably pop over later won't you, Ben?' Now that Mum had dropped the 'Dick' bombshell I needed some thinking time, and an evening of my mother wasn't going to provide mental sanctuary. Besides, I'd said I'd see Gina later and I didn't want to tell Mum I was standing her up for the woman she hated second most in the world. More urgently, I had a deep desire to call Dick up and scream vile things loudly down the phone – things a mother should never hear from her daughter's lips.

'Oh,' she said, looking hurt. 'Well if you'd rather I wasn't here...'

'No Mum I didn't say that...' There was no point trying to convince her when she wanted to play the martyr. I'd have to put Dick on hold, along with thinking time – and Gina. 'By the way, Mum, this is Ben Shaw, he's the family solicitor,' I said.

'Oh...' her face dropped and without smiling she scrutinised him openly. 'Are you Ronald's son?'

Ben nodded, 'You know my dad?'

'Mmm he was more a friend of my sister. Is he dead yet?'

Ben laughed (thank God) and told her his father was alive and well.

'He's not still soliciting, is he? He's far too old to still be doing that... I bet he's lost all his marbles.'

'Mum!' I gasped, surprised at this outburst, she was getting worse. 'You're talking about Ben's father…' I started, embarrassed at her outburst. I wasn't even aware she knew Sophia's solicitor, but then sometimes I forgot how much history they shared.

'Oh no your mum's right, Dad probably should have retired years ago, but as far as I know he's still got all his marbles, Mrs…'

'Call me Roberta,' she said, a glimmer of a smile forming as we both melted in Ben's easy warmth.

Eventually we said our goodbyes, Mum firmly entrenched in the passenger seat now and ready to come back with me to the apartment. I felt a pang of longing as I watched Ben wander off in my rear-view mirror. I'd just discovered a place where I wasn't responsible for anyone's happiness but my own, and now I suddenly felt the weight again. It hadn't taken long. And on a more superficial note – it occurred to me that having Mum around might just mean an end to mine and Ben's sex on the stairs.

'Can't believe he's Ronald's boy,' Mum was muttering. 'He's quite a nice-looking lad, but his father…'

'I get the feeling you didn't really like Ben's dad,' I said, making this understatement while negotiating a tight bend.

'I never trusted him, that Ronald… don't believe anything he tells you, Ella.'

I didn't answer her. I was wondering why she'd say this. And what it was about Ronald Shaw that upset her so much.

When we arrived at the apartment, Mum seemed to go out of her way to be unimpressed. I showed her round and pointed out the lovely Italian plates and the rugs on the walls. But she stood there tight-lipped, refusing to like any of Sophia's ornaments or wall hangings, just because they were Sophia's.

'Mum, is there something wrong? I know you don't like me being here – but I love this place, this apartment. Please be happy for me.'

Her face softened slightly; 'I just want everything to be back to normal, Ella, I'm too old for all this upheaval.'

'I know Mum, but you have to let me do this. And now, with the house sold I think you're going to have to join me, at least for a little while until we work out what to do.'

She shrugged and looked away and I went into the kitchen to make coffee, reminding myself that I didn't need my mother's approval, but I did need her support. I knew she had her reasons to not want to be here, but as long as she refused to tell me I couldn't address the problem, so I would just have to keep going and try to make a success out of this summer, while I planned what to do next.

Mum stood at the window gazing out. 'I used to know the rhythm of the tides as a girl,' she said, absently. 'My mum would ask me, "Can we take the van out today, Roberta?" And I'd check in my little diary, it was all written down. Me and Sophia both had our diaries, filled them in every night,' she was smiling – and I wondered if perhaps the sea was welcoming her home and Appledore was beginning to work its magic.

Chapter Seventeen

The Prodigal Returns – with Sushi

Later, as the sun went down, we ate pizza and drank citrusy sweet limoncello. We talked about ice cream and I wondered if this lovely sharp drink would make a good ripple through sweet lemon curd ice cream.

'I've been thinking about making cocktail ice creams,' I said.

'You can't let the children have them…' Mum said, stating the obvious. 'Just for grown-ups.'

'Ooh I like that, we could call them Grown-up Ices?' I said.

'Adults Only,' she smiled, 'and you could put some of that nice chocolate liqueur in ice cream too… ooh and what about amaretto?'

'Imagine an Italian Sunrise ice cream, made with limoncello and orange juice?' I said. 'What a lovely thing to have on a summer's evening, the sharpness of lemons with the sweet creaminess of the ice cream would be delicious. Did Sophia ever make that?' I tried, knowing if Sophia was involved Mum wouldn't want anything to do with that idea.

'I don't think Sophia made alcohol ice creams, but our mother made the most delicious chocolate liqueur ice cream with vodka,' she smiled.

'That sounds lovely,' I said, reaching for my notebook to jot the ideas down. 'Oh Mum, wouldn't it be wonderful if the café opened again?'

'Yes, but not with Gina.'

'She might sell, I'd love to buy or rent it from her – I'm just waiting to hear what she's going to do. She said she won't make any decisions without discussing it with me first, and I was thinking that perhaps the house might sell and I could make her an offer with the house money?'

'Would there be enough money from the house sale?'

'I don't know – because even if we managed to sell the house in time I have no idea how much Gina would want for the café.'

'Yes don't run before you can walk, love,' she said.

She then rather astutely moved onto a subject she'd guessed was also on my mind. I think I must have mentioned him quite a lot during the evening.

'So how well have you got to know Ronald's son, you seem to like him?'

'Ben? Oh, he's lovely, but just a friend… well, he's a bit more than that, we're just enjoying time together – nothing heavy.'

'Are you exclusive?'

'What do you mean?'

'Well… I remember Lucie telling us that her last boyfriend wasn't, but he didn't bother telling her.'

I remembered that long weekend, when she dumped him because he thought they'd had an open relationship and didn't realise they were 'exclusive'.

'So he's only sleeping with you and are you only sleeping with him?'

'Of course,' I looked at her incredulously.

'Has he said you're exclusive?'

'He doesn't need to.'

But suddenly it made me wonder if I'd perhaps been taking too much for granted regarding Ben, I hadn't actually asked the question, and he might have very different ideas about us.

'Oh, well you're a lucky girl, you get him exclusively. And you do a bit of what the kids call "Netflix and chill", do you?'

'I don't have Netflix.'

'Neither do I.'

'So what are you saying, Mum. What's Netflix and chill?'

'I'm not sure, you made me lose my thread. Look, if you do one thing, Ella, just ignore his father.'

'Okay, I will Mum,' I said, reaching out and patting her hand. I didn't want to get into all that again so I got up and went into the kitchen.

I made coffee from the cappuccino machine, and Mum said it was like the coffee she used to have when she visited Italy, which was magnificent praise. Encouraged by her admiration for the cappuccino, I thought it might be worth sounding her out about what would happen once the house was sold.

'The quick house sale has thrown me a bit,' I started, as I cleared away the coffee things. 'I'm not sure what to do, but perhaps for now you could come and live here too, Mum?'

She shook her head vigorously. 'I don't know… I don't want to, Ella…'

'But where else can you go? I don't want you going back to Manchester and living in a little flat all on your own, Mum.'

She didn't either, I could tell by her face.

'It's just… being here reminds me …'

And in that moment I really thought she was going to spill the beans and tell me why she didn't want to be here and why she hated her sister.

'Of Sophia? Does it remind you of…'

'The past, that's all. It reminds me of the past and I don't like to think about it.'

'You can tell me, Mum, whatever it is, you can tell me…'

'I can't…'

'Yes you can. Mum?'

'I don't want to talk about it.'

That was it, she was refusing to say any more and I could see how much it was hurting her, so I had to let it go. Perhaps I had to try and find out the truth myself, perhaps Gina might know?

Later, after I'd called Mum a taxi, I glanced at the clock on the wall surprised to see it was almost eleven o'clock. Then I panicked: in all the madness I'd forgotten that Gina and I were supposed to be meeting for supper. Of course I wouldn't have been able to with Mum here – but the plan was that Gina would call me – oh God, she must have been calling me all night, I thought, frantically searching for my phone. Eventually I found it under the cushion where I'd been sitting, expecting lots of missed calls and texts. But nothing, Gina hadn't called. She was probably jet-lagged and had collapsed into bed and would wake up later, horrified that she hadn't been in touch. I was sure we'd meet up again another day, so it was no big issue.

When Gina hadn't called by six o'clock the following evening, I decided to check in with her. The phone rang for ages but eventually she picked up sounding groggy and surprised.

'Oh honey, what can I say… I didn't call.'

'It's okay, Gina, I knew you were probably jet-lagged…'

'Yeah, I was jet-lagged, exhausted. But let's do tonight?'

I was about to say that Mum was in town and it might be difficult but then I reminded myself I was a grown-up and I could see whom I liked. I'd tell Gina that Mum was here when we met up, I didn't want to come over as some simpering mummy's girl over the phone, so we arranged to meet at the pub at eight and take it from there.

I was just putting the phone down and planning to call it a day when I saw Mum trundling across the beach – with her suitcase. I hoped this didn't mean…

'Oh Mum, let me help you with that,' I called and rushed out of the van to take the heavy case from her. 'Are you going home?' I said, I was worried about where she would go. 'No, I've decided I'm going to come and live with you, there's a spare room and you could do with the company.'

'Oh, okay,' I said. I knew this would happen at some point – but had a sneaking suspicion that the reason for her sudden decision had more to do with the fact she thought Gina might beat her to that spare room.

So I packed up the van and we headed back to the apartment together, singing along to Dean Martin's CD of old Italian songs.

'Oh it makes me want to go there now, Sorrento, the sparkling sea, Vesuvius covered in clouds. And the lemons, Ella… the lemons…'

'As big as your head!' we both said together, laughing.

'One day we'll go, Mum, we'll get into Reginaldo and we'll set off for Italy.'

'Ooh I'd love that.'

Once inside the apartment, Mum opened up her overnight bag and produced a bag of fresh pasta, some tomatoes and onions and a bunch of basil. 'I thought I'd make us a lovely meal tonight, just me and you,' she said.

I was just working up to how to tell Mum I had already made plans with Gina, when she took out a pan and began boiling water, still singing 'Volare' in an Italian accent. She seemed so happy, I hadn't seen her like this for a while and there was no way I could burst her bubble – so when she went upstairs to unpack I quietly called Gina, explaining Mum was here unexpectedly and that I couldn't come out and meet her. I suggested we meet the following evening, but Gina wanted to see me that night, and as my mother had often warned me, what Gina wants, Gina gets.

'Then the mountain shall come to Mohammed,' she said. 'I'll bring supper, I'll be there about 8.30.'

Before I could say, 'No please GOD NO,' she'd put the phone down. I wandered into the kitchen where Mum was now serving up two large plates of pasta and I groaned inwardly.

'Come on then, get that bottle of wine opened, we shall dine like Italian countesses,' she said, taking the plates out onto the balcony.

I followed her through with the wine and once seated I took several large gulps, but still couldn't summon up the courage to tell her Gina was coming over. I didn't want to upset her or spoil this lovely mother and daughter moment, sipping wine and eating pasta on a beautiful blue evening overlooking the sea.

I almost choked on my linguine when she asked, 'Are we expecting any guests this evening?'

'No. Of course not. Why would you think that?' I said, a little too defensively.

'Oh, I just wondered,' she said, sipping slowly from her wine and watching me over her glass.

'Mum…' I started, about to tell her.

'I knew it. I bloody knew it,' she was smiling. 'Ben's coming over, isn't he? I know you two have a thing going on, I can tell by the way he looks at you.'

That surprised me, 'Really?'

'Oh yes… he definitely has a thing for you, love.'

I glowed as she piled up the plates and took them back to the kitchen and then I remembered that I still had to tell her about Gina.

I went upstairs and washed my face, anything to prolong the moment, and when I came downstairs Mum was engrossed in *The Apprentice*. I wasn't sure what would annoy her the most, that Gina was coming to see me or that she would arrive before someone was fired.

'Ella, I don't like this TV,' she was saying. 'It's not as big as our one at home – I won't be able to see Lord Sugar's face when he says "you're fired!"' She pointed her finger like a gun, she seemed happy, and I hated all over again that I was about to spoil her evening.

'It's an old episode, you've seen it before haven't you?'

'Yes – but I still enjoy the moment... you're fired,' she said in a cockney voice.

'Mum, I don't want you to overreact and turn this into a drama... but erm... we're having a visitor... not Ben.' I felt like I'd thrown a grenade and was just waiting for it to blow.

She sat up, and tore her eyes away from the TV, 'Not *her*?'

'Yes, Gina's coming over, to see us,' I said slowly and calmly. 'She's bringing... a snack.' I don't know why I felt the need to say this, I just felt that I had to let Mum know that more food was on its way, and there was nothing I could do about it. 'I'm sorry, Mum, but Gina just offered and I...'

'Well, just pretend I'm not here. You two carry on and have your *snacks*,' (she said the last word with venom, the emphasis being on the s at the beginning and the end as if the snacks themselves were grotesque). 'Whatever you do, I won't be speaking... or *snacking*!'

'Oh Mum, you're being silly...'

'Silly? You and I were going to have an evening together, I haven't seen you for weeks, I make a lovely meal and then you invite her over... with sodding snacks.'

'Mum, before I could explain that you'd cooked, she'd offered to come over and bring...'

'*Snacks.*'

'Snacks,' I repeated.

'Well isn't that just like her? She disappears for the best part of thirty years then turns up like the bloody snack fairy.'

I knew it wasn't the prospect of snacks causing such vitriol, it was the source of those snacks. I knew damn well that if instead of snacks Gina was bringing diamonds, kittens or orphans my mother's bitter hatred would have been just the same.

'Mum… please be civil. It'll be embarrassing if you don't speak to her.'

'Gina's dead to me,' she said, in full mafia moll mode, and turned straight back to the TV, a sign that the conversation was over. I stared at the screen too, for a while, wondering where I could take this, but I couldn't think of anything to say so just kept staring, dreading the knock on the door.

Mum and Gina hadn't seen each other for over thirty years and I'd always assumed Mum's main gripe had been with Sophia. After all it was so long ago Gina would have been a teenager when the sisters had fallen out, and though I knew Mum had never approved of Gina, I didn't expect this anger from her.

Surely now after all this time, Gina's lifestyle and choices weren't upsetting my mother. Whatever it was, it seemed my mother disliked her niece as much as she'd disliked her sister, and any minute now Gina would be arriving with supper. For the three of us. To eat together. I didn't know how it would go but I had an idea – and quite frankly was amazed my mother hadn't already flounced off to her room the minute Gina's name was mentioned.

Eventually, the doorbell rang and I felt like throwing up; 'That'll be Gina,' I said, but Mum didn't acknowledge me. 'Mum… I'll make it up to you, we'll have dinner again tomorrow night, just you and me,' I added, before heading for the door. I stood there just wishing it was Ben at the door, with Mum and Gina safely tucked up in their respective beds.

Would I ever have an evening free for Ben with my mother and cousin now in town? What had happened to that lovely space I'd found, in my home, my heart and my life, not to mention my bed?

The doorbell rang again so I swept past the wall of hate emanating from my mother and opened the door. I put on my best smile and there she was, blonde and beautiful, a bottle of champagne in one hand, a bag of food in the other and a huge bunch of flowers clutched to her chest. She was peering over them and smiling, her lips glossy, French perfume wafting over me. And I thought, not for the first time, how I wished I could be like Gina, always glamorous, full of confidence and life, her actions uncomplicated by others.

'Are these for Mum?' I asked hopefully, as I admired the enormous bouquet stuffed with huge headed hydrangeas and white roses.

'No they're for you,' she said, looking slightly affronted.

'They're beautiful, thank you,' I said, no one had ever bought me flowers.

'Oh it's good to see the old place,' she smiled, wandering through to the kitchen without going into the living room to say hello first. This simple action/oversight on Gina's part would give Mum yet another reason to hate her. But Gina wouldn't understand, she lived on a different planet from my mother where you did what you wanted to do – not what everyone else expected.

'Mum's through here,' I said brightly, grabbing a bottle of wine from the fridge and guiding Gina through. But when we walked in, the room was empty – no mother. I had a feeling she'd do this.

'Mum's tired, she's probably gone to bed…' I started, assuming she was hiding upstairs. I have to say this was a slight relief – though I wanted to spend time with both of them it wouldn't be ideal at this juncture. I hoped one day I could bring them together, but it was evidently still raw, and tonight would have been less about mediating and more refereeing.

'Good, it's just you and me,' Gina said, squeezing my arm not the least bit upset by Mum's absence in fact seemingly glad of it. 'I bought this, I'm going to do your hair,' she was holding a pack of blonde hair colour and, before I could say anything, we were both distracted by a creak on the stairs.

It seemed Mother had made a reappearance, standing there like bloody Bette Davis in full make-up and my earrings.

I looked from one to the other, my mouth probably open, unable to say anything, unsure what would happen next. The two women eyed each other wordlessly, no smile or glimmer of recognition while Mum stood on the top stair like the queen of everything.

After what seemed like hours of icy silence, I was about to cut in when mother spoke.

'So, Gina – you're back.'

Mum steadily began walking down the stairs, while I held my breath, you could hear a pin drop but Gina didn't flinch. I half expected Mum to stop mid-flight and instruct us to fasten our seat belts and was relieved when she arrived at the foot of the stairs and swept over to Gina with a perfunctory peck in the air. Gina returned the air kiss façade and they wordlessly sat down on chairs opposite each other, both cautious, like the other might attack at any time. What the hell was going on here? I'd hoped Sophia's death had brought an end to this nonsense, but it looked like Gina was carrying it on in her name.

I plonked myself down and we all sat there in a triangle of deafening silence, as I waited for a volcanic eruption of Italian tempers.

Eventually Gina started talking – and I so wished she hadn't. 'So Ella, I bought supper, and some bleach for your hair,' she said, picking up the bloody packet again – she might as well have stuck two fingers up in Mum's face.

Mum twitched and I honestly thought for a moment she was going to just take a run at Gina, but she remained seated and restrained herself, though her scarlet face told another story.

Oh God, I didn't want Mum to think I'd been planning this with Gina. I felt like I was walking a tightrope: I wanted to be Gina's friend, but I felt Mum didn't approve. Why did the two of them together make me feel like this? I was back on that beach in 1984, shivering and covered in a towel while Mum and Gina had their stand-off. I was stuck between these two women once more; it was uncomfortable, embarrassing and bloody stressful, I felt like I was treading on eggshells.

'My hair?' I said, surprised for Mum's benefit. Yes I know I was forty-four and should have been able to dye my hair or not as I chose, but this was about control, and both of them wanted it. 'Oh thanks Gina, that's kind of you, but… I don't know about…'

'Oh Ella, we talked about it yesterday,' Gina said, the lower lip dropping in potential sulk. 'You said you'd always wanted to be blonde like me.'

Damn she made it sound like something we'd cooked up in Mum's absence, which just wasn't true. I didn't even want my hair dyed, and I'd said as much, Gina obviously hadn't got the message. I was aware Mum was watching us like a game of bloody tennis. I felt so awkward because I didn't want to hurt anyone – especially my mum.

'Yes perhaps when I was younger I might have enjoyed being blonde,' I said, not meeting my mother's eyes, 'but as I said, it's a bit late now…'

'Nonsense. I've bought everything and we're going to have a lovely girlie evening doing your hair – I bought nail varnish too. I noticed yours were a bit chipped. I'm going to give you a fabulous makeover, don't you just LOVE a makeover?'

Nail varnish? Yes, my nails were chipped because I was so bloody busy working I hadn't had chance to think about them.

'Gorgeous colours I've got,' she was saying, holding up a couple of Chanel varnishes in the latest shades.

I nodded uncertainly and my mother began making weird snorting noises like a geyser about to blow. I didn't know which way to turn. But Gina was still going.

'You'll be gorgeous and blonde and…'

'She's already gorgeous. You heard the lady,' my mother started, puffing out her chest and making like an Italian matriarch. I knew I should never have bought her that box set of *Mob Wives*. 'She *does not* want to be blonde.'

'I think she's old enough to make her own mind up, don't you, Roberta?' Gina said, with a sickly-sweet smile.

'Exactly, she's old enough to know that it's too late to suddenly go blonde.' Oh God, this was getting out of hand. Who would have thought a packet of bloody L'Oréal could have caused such a diplomatic incident but I didn't have time to get a word in as the crisis escalated.

'It's never too late, Roberta,' Gina said, and I got the feeling we weren't talking about hair dye any more. They were staring at each other with such hatred I couldn't bear it, and I finally said what I thought, at the risk of causing even more anger.

'What is it? Why does everyone seem to have fallen out in this family?' I asked. 'It's like a scene from *The Godfather* in here to-night. I thought the two of you would be okay, I know Mum had a misunderstanding with your mother (that was putting it lightly), but why are *you* angry, Gina?'

'It's nothing,' Gina said.

So I poured a very large glass of wine and drank it, while Mum went back to Lord Sugar and Gina sulked as silence descended.

After a while I opened up the food she'd brought, but when I looked inside, I knew I couldn't take it into the living room and present it to my mother under the title 'snack'. This was so much more than a snack, and God knows where she'd found platters of sushi in a sleepy Devon village on a Wednesday night. There were all kinds of delicate flowers of raw fish with salty scarlet centres, oblong pale pink morsels of salmon, deeper pink tuna wrapped around seaweed and pinwheels of rice sitting in liquorice black nori. Mum would hate it, on every level, and as lovely as it looked I really didn't have room after the pasta.

'Open the champagne honey,' Gina said, as she came into the kitchen and grabbed a large platter of raw fish, taking it through to the living room before I could stop her. I wanted to cover my face, Mother was still embroiled in a boardroom bloodbath and one false move from Gina and her wasabi pickle and we were likely to have our very own bloodbath in the living room.

Mum looked up from the TV begrudgingly, determined not to like whatever Gina was offering. 'We've already eaten,' she said.

'Mum, Gina kindly brought this for our supper,' I said, mock politely.

'I eat this all the time when I'm in Malibu,' Gina was saying over her shoulder to me. 'We get it from Nobu… it's the best Japanese restaurant in the world.'

Mum glanced at the sushi with a curled lip like it was a bushtucker trial and Gina was brandishing a plate of kangaroo testicles under her nose, before turning back to the TV.

Gina winked at me and sat back down, nibbling on raw salmon while finishing off her glass of wine.

The next twenty minutes was spent on raw fish and superficial conversation, between Gina and I, which was punctuated by Mum's complaints that she couldn't hear the TV over 'the chatter'.

Two hours later, at the end of an incredibly tense evening, Mum decided to go to bed. I thought she might be thawing when she offered to call a taxi for Gina, but realised this was just a ruse to get her away from me before she could dye my hair blonde and turn me into a lady of the night. I was surprised and slightly angry with Mum, I'd pointed out a million times that I was my own woman and that she had nothing to fear from Gina influencing me.

So I was actually glad when Gina told Mum she wasn't leaving yet and I could enjoy a quiet evening with my cousin without my mum watching on as if I couldn't take care of myself.

Wind on half an hour and I'm sitting on the sofa, drunk on champagne, wearing a headful of bright blue bleach. Even now I'm not sure how I came to give in to Gina's insistence I go blonde. Perhaps it was too much champagne, or the fact that I have always been putty in Gina's hands?

Chapter Eighteen

Limoncello, Sweet Sorrento and a Bag Full of Secrets

The next morning I awoke to a lovely text from Ben asking if I was free later. I said yes, but explained that my life was turning into a 1970s sit com and I may have to spend the evening placating my mother after the Gina situation the previous evening, especially as she had yet to see my 'Iced Nordic Blonde' hair.

I got out of bed and looked in the mirror – I was like a different person, my shoulder-length hair, always dark, unremarkable and recently sprinkled with grey, was a bright, bubbly blonde. I'd had a few drinks when I finally agreed to Gina bleaching it, but I liked the new me – maybe it wasn't too late after all.

I rummaged in my make-up bag and found an old red lipstick, like the kind Gina wore, and when I applied it I was transformed further. I posed a while in front of the mirror like Lucie always did when she was taking selfies and I laughed at how silly I'd become. A few weeks ago I wouldn't have dreamed of dying my hair and posing in a mirror, I was too busy worrying about everyone else to have any fun, and it felt good. Then I remembered Mum, she'd probably hate it simply because Gina was involved, but as she wasn't up yet, I did what any self-respecting, mature sophisticated forty-something would do and made a run for it. I'd leave before she had a chance to tell me how awful it looked – that way I could enjoy my hair for a little while at least.

Later when Ben popped down to the beach in his lunch hour he seemed stunned at my transformation.

'You look seriously hot,' he whistled, making my face burn.

He was standing outside the van, his arms on the counter and he reached for my hand as I stood in front of him. It felt good to be back with Ben, here was someone I could be myself with, and completely at ease rather than a referee treading on eggshells with Mum and Gina.

'So, are you still not free tonight?' he asked.

I longed to spend time with him, I knew he'd be going away soon, so we were on borrowed time, but what could I do? I explained more fully about Mum and Gina and how Mum would now be expecting me to dine with her after the previous night's debacle.

'It's fine,' he said. 'I'll catch up with some old mates, you should spend time with your mum, she came all this way to see you.'

'Mmm all this way to keep an eye on me,' I sighed, feeling thirteen again, and not in a good way. 'Don't get me wrong, I'm glad she's here, because I worried about her alone in Manchester – but I just know she's going to take over my life like she always has.'

'Then give her something to do… you'll be busy once the season starts and I bet you'll be glad of some help on the van. And if that doesn't work, what about Delilah? She needs walking – let the doggie take the strain,' he laughed.

I thought about it and it wasn't such a bad idea; if Mum was doing the deli runs or taking Delilah down the beach, it meant she wouldn't be harassing me.

'There's the small matter of Mum driving me bonkers all day, but I reckon Delilah would be able to handle her,' I said. We both looked over at the cute, innocent little dog in polka dot sundress wagging her tail, unaware of the fate awaiting her as my mother's chaperone.

After a while he wandered back to work and I watched him leave, wishing I could be with him, but knowing it was more than my life's worth. Mum hadn't yet seen my hair and even if it did look fabulous and take ten years off me and make me 'hot' – she just wasn't going to like it. Not one bit.

'Oh my God what the hell have you done to your hair?' was Mum's opening gambit as I collected her outside her hotel after work. She'd packed and checked out and was now, officially, my 'roommate'.

'I've had so many compliments,' I said, refusing to allow her to bring me down. I knew this wasn't aimed at me; it was a direct hit at Gina.

'It's not you,' she said sniffily.

'I can assure you, Mum, it is,' I smiled as we pulled away. 'It's all me, but a different me – and I like it.'

She pursed her lips and raised her brows in a 'do what you like' face as she got out her phone and started bashing angrily at the keyboard.

When we arrived back at the apartment I ordered a pizza – I was too tired to cook. Though the July days were sunny, the evenings could still be quite fresh so we stayed inside to eat. The crispy crust and melted cheese appeared to soothe my mother's soul slightly and I asked her if at any time she'd ever consider going out for a meal with Gina.

'I just think we should be together,' I said. 'We're family and we're all each other's got now.'

'I know, love, but I'd rather poke my own eyes out.'

'Okay, thanks for being open to the idea…'

'She just makes me so angry… she walked out years ago and she comes back with her champagne and her sushis talking about Mabu in Nolibu…'

'*Nobu*… it's a Japanese restaurant, Mum, in *Malibu*.'

'I don't care, she can stick her Nolibu and her sushis.'

'Why don't you give her a chance? She's lovely.'

'Oh to you she might be. She comes sweeping in turning your head and making you think she's so special. Then before you know it she'll be off again.'

'But that's okay, she's got her own life, Mum.'

My mum paused as she looked at me. 'But every time she goes she takes something back with her. And I worry it might be you, Ella. I'm your mother, I've been here for you and yet you choose her over me, you let her dye your hair… you always choose her…'

'I'm not going anywhere with her. And last night you wanted to leave…' I said, trying to sound reasonable. Mum seemed to have this all out of perspective and I didn't want her running away with this and convincing herself she'd been thrown out of the apartment.

'Mum, you chose to leave.'

'And you chose to stay – with her.'

'I just enjoy her company, she's interesting and fun and…'

'More fun than me?'

'No one could be more fun than you, Mother,' I said, rolling my eyes.

She shot me a look; 'Just don't forget who loves you, I don't want Gina giving you any ideas and then upsetting you when she disappears again.'

'I'm not twelve, Mum.'

'No, but you'd have thought so last night, she was all over you – and you just let her manipulate you.'

'No I don't.'

'So when you said you didn't want her to bleach your hair, what happened?'

'Too much champagne?' I smiled. 'But you know what? I'm glad I let her do my hair, I love it and I don't care what you say, so bugger off,' I said this with affection and she knew I was teasing her, but she was like a dog with a bloody bone my mother.

'This is what happened when you were younger, you'd come home with a filthy mouth,' she said, 'just trashy, and it was all her doing…'

'Mum, you say bugger – I got it off you,' I teased.

'… laying down her poison and buggering off.'

'There, ha you said it – pure filth, Mother,' I laughed. But she didn't crack a smile.

After we'd eaten I suggested we talk to the kids. It was something we could share – something Gina wasn't part of. It would be late where they were but I had this need to speak with them, see that they were okay.

'I saw Lucie on Instagram this morning,' Mum said, apparently cheered up at the thought of calling the kids. 'She's still with Pang. He seems very nice, but I told you, he's gay – on the other side of the ballroom. My gaydar is glowing,' she added with a knowing nod.

I had to smile, I wasn't sure how Lucie would feel about her new friend causing Nan's gaydar to glow.

Within seconds, Lucie had been woken from her slumber and was on screen smiling sleepily. Despite it being the middle of the night where she was, my daughter seemed pleased to hear from us.

'Hey Mum, cool hair… it really suits you,' she said.

I beamed while Mum growled quietly at the side of me.

Lucie went on to tell us about the place she was staying, and sent us photos of a nearby temple she'd visited that day.

'And how's Pang?' Mum asked, unable to resist doing a Miss Marple and investigating the poor lad.

'He's lovely – so cute!' she said, and her little face lit up and my heart swelled.

'Has he had a girlfriend before?' Mum asked, and I just knew we were seconds away from Mum unfurling her theory on Pang's sexuality across the miles. I doubted it was true, mother's Gaydar wasn't, in my view, to be trusted, it hadn't even twitched throughout her online 'lesbian period'.

So I quickly changed the subject and told Lucie all about the ice cream van, my new flavours and the fact it was slowly but surely becoming busier.

'Mum, you should start using social media if you're going to be an ice cream entrepreneur,' Lucie offered.

'I keep telling her,' Mum said and I nodded in agreement.

'That photo you sent me the other day on that lovely beach, Delilah in her little dress, you serving up swirly cones,' Lucie said. 'That's all you need, Mum, just shots of the ice cream and the beach. Delilah's so gorgeous, she's pure click bait!'

'Click bait? That isn't doggie porn is it?' I asked, only half-joking, it certainly sounded a bit dubious and I doubted Aarya would approve.

'So get Nan to take the pictures and she can help set you up on Instagram and Twitter, Snapchat and all the rest,' she said.

I liked the idea, though I wasn't sure if Mum was the right operative given her online faux pas to date. But it could be fun and a lovely way to document my summer here. By September it would all have melted like the ice cream, so it would be nice to have a record that I could one day show my grandchildren – my ice cream summer.

'Who's the guy in the photo you sent to me?' Lucie said, referring to Ben. We'd taken a selfie outside the van a few days before and I think subconsciously I wanted to see the kids' reaction.

'Oh that's Ben… he's just a friend,' I said, still unsure how to classify Ben in my life, especially as Gina and my mother's arrivals had meant I hadn't seen him for a couple of days.

'Oh, thought you might be hooking up with someone,' she said.

'Hooking up?' I laughed, and wondered again if that's all it was. But I didn't dwell on it and Lucie looked sleepy so I suggested we let her go back to bed, and after a quick chat to a very sleepy Josh Mum retired for the night too.

With the apartment now quiet I delved into the old cocktail cabinet and brought out all the dusty spirit bottles and fancy liqueurs. Then I dug out my Dean Martin Italian love songs CD and whipped up a batch of cocktail ice creams with a taste of Italy. I'd found some Italian cocktail recipes in the old magazines I'd discovered in Sophia's carrier bag and gave one or two of them a go – making notes and tweaking the recipes along the way. I made lots of ice cream and even experimented with a cocktail float; it was delicious and made me feel quite tipsy.

The bag was proving to be quite a Pandora's box... filled with unexpected things, but I hadn't yet realised the full impact of its contents. For the time being I was simply delighted with the old magazines with ads and photo features of glamorous women and cigarette-smoking men. It was pure nostalgia, reminiscent of a past I could barely remember, and a 1950s Italy in black and white I'd only heard about. I'd wanted to share my carrier bag discoveries with Mum – she'd always painted such a vivid picture of Sorrento – but I also wanted to keep the carrier bag and everything it contained to myself for just a little longer.

I added the fresh peach purée to the ice cream and poured in a glug of frothing Prosecco to create a 'Bellini' ice cream, then ran my finger along the bowl. It was delicious. Fresh summer peaches with cream and a little background fizz, the perfect combination for a summer evening alfresco.

Next was 'Sweet Sorrento', limoncello, vodka, sugar and lemon zest combined with the base of eggs and cream, swirling into a tart, yet sweet and creamy ambrosial pillow. I immediately thought of my diet club ladies who had made me promise to stay open after 7 p.m. for them. I would make a batch of ice cream cocktails and see if they liked them, and if they went down well I may stay open a little longer as the nights stayed lighter. I really had to make this work, it had been a rocky start but I had to give it the whole summer and only then would I know if it was worth trying to make a life here.

Later, when all the ice cream was packed away safely in the freezer, I brewed a mug of chamomile tea and took the Italian carrier bag out of the drawer again. I waded through some boring paperwork, official forms, bills paid etc., but what I really wanted to read were Sophia's letters.

Although I hadn't read them yet, the beribboned and elasticated bundles of letters had been left in the van I'd inherited as though fate had meant for me to find them. This sounded a bit fanciful, but I would be their caretaker – Sophia's secrets were safe with me. I wouldn't be showing anyone, least of all Mum who might discover something else about Sophia to use against her. I was probably being slightly hypocritical keeping the bag to myself when even I shouldn't have been reading my aunt's private letters – but I ask you, if you found a bag of unread letters from a family member who'd died would you be able to turn away?

The first was a letter dated 4 September 1973 and I settled down to read. I couldn't imagine when Sophia had had the the time to write letters, Caprioni's had always been packed, Sophie red-faced and stressed as she had managed the customers. But looking at the beautiful handwriting I knew that she must have found the time from somewhere, though clearly she'd never actually sent them as they were still in her possession when she died. Around the edges of the tattered paper were little doodles of flowers and butterflies drawn here and there among the words. It began, '*To my darling*,' and I suddenly felt like a voyeur, an intruder on the past – was this a love letter between my aunt and uncle? I couldn't help it, I read on.

I want you to know that I tried hard for us to be together, but ultimately it wasn't to be. But I need you to know how much I love you…

For a moment I thought Sophia had perhaps had an affair, but I immediately looked down to the signature at the bottom of the letter, it said, '*all my love, mummy*', and I smiled. This was a letter from Sophia to Gina, who always called her mum 'mummy'. As a child, I'd found it quite endearing and had once called my mum 'mummy', wanting to play around with the word on my lips the way Gina did – but Mum said I sounded 'babyish', so that was the end of that.

I'd always been fascinated by the fiery Italian women in my family, perhaps that's because I was one too and I wanted to live like them. I also wanted to avoid their mistakes, get inside their relationship, try to figure out how it worked – and why ultimately it hadn't, so I picked up the next letter.

'*Take care of yourself while we're apart. Stay warm and safe and happy – and don't let anyone hurt you*,' it said. '*I will get my girl back, it may be a while before we see each other again, but one day.*' There was no date on this one, so it must have been when Gina had gone to America and Sophia was missing her.

Sophia's ice cream was also made with love and she put so much of herself in it I wondered now if perhaps she'd been pining for a young Gina. She was a working mum like me and she had to be strong and hope her daughter could be strong too, but somewhere along the way it had all gone wrong for Sophia and her daughter. Gina had left her mum behind, never to return.

I wondered if Mum had an old carrier bag somewhere containing letters she'd never sent telling me how amazing I was. I doubted it, and yet I knew she adored me. She loved me so much she couldn't let me go, even now she was scared I'd be kidnapped or something.

The contents of the carrier bag had reminded me of my own past and offered more questions than answers. So with everything swirling around my head I eventually put the bag away for another day; my heart was heavy, why did the past push so hard to be let in? I felt tormented by memories, and coming back here the pull was even stronger.

The following day I was quite busy. I'd been trying out some new flavours and the customers seemed to love them, from earl grey tea to white chocolate and ginger, they were going down well. I had all the basic flavours but wanted to expand – I had to offer something different if I was going to succeed. My new cocktail range (for adults only was) being 'sampled' by my slimming club ladies and going down very well. I had even thought about getting the café a drinks licence and making cocktail ice cream floats. It was all just dreams until I knew what Gina's plans were for the café. So, until then, I was determined to keep developing ideas to make the van a huge success. My smoky whisky pecan was going down very well with some of the dog walkers. Peter, the older man with the chocolate Labrador, said it was just like drinking whisky under the stars.

'You're quite the poet, Peter,' I said, delighted at his reaction to my new flavour.

'I used to write the odd bit of poetry,' he said, gazing off into the distance. 'I used to write it for my sweetheart, many years ago.'

'Oh how lovely,' I said, feeling gooey inside.

'She was... very lovely,' he said, and I thought I saw tears in his eyes. I wasn't sure what to say, I didn't want to upset him, but was intrigued.

'What happened... did you marry her?' I said.

He shook his head, 'No, I never married. And she's not here any more,' he sighed, 'oh, I do miss her.' He was obviously grieving for the love of his life who'd died, how tragic to lose someone like that.

'I'm sorry to hear that,' I said, which felt inadequate given the amount of pain he'd obviously suffered at the loss. I looked around at the walkers and the couples and the odd teenager kicking stones along the beach thinking how everyone had their own story. Looking at Peter I'd always imagined a settled, married man with grown-up kids and a dog – but it seems his story was different. Who knew the stories and secrets in this place, along this lovely coast of seagulls and foam and long, golden beaches.

I liked Peter, he was kind and gentle, but there was a sadness about him, and now I think I understood that. We'd bonded over the few weeks I'd been here; he'd always lived in Appledore and was happy to tell me the history, the good walks, the scenic drives. He also came from an Italian family – his parents were both from Sicily and, like my mother, he still sometimes used the odd Italian word.

'Today I've got a special cone combination just for you, Peter,' I said this morning, piling a ricotta strawberry scoop onto limoncello ice cream.

'Ah, a nod to our Italian heritage,' he said, tasting it. 'That's delicious, it's absolutely sublime! I think you should call it "Ciao Bello", which in Italian means, Hello Beautiful.'

'I love it… Ciao Bello it is!'

We chatted some more and when he'd finished his cone he offered to take Delilah for a walk with him and Cocoa. Delilah had spotted Peter, heard her name and was now twirling around in the front of the van.

'We love walking with Delilah, but last time her necklace got caught up in seaweed,' he said, wiping his ice cream hands on a napkin. I took the hint and relieved her of her tutu and tiara before she embarked on her playful run.

'Ciao Ella,' he called as he marched up the beach, Delilah and Cocoa racing each other on the sands, happy to be alive in the early summer sunshine. And I took a moment to inhale the salty air, gaze out onto the sea and count my blessings.

A little later, when things were quieter, Gina turned up at the van, smiling in the sunshine and telling me how gorgeous I looked with my new blonde hair.

'I'm sorry about the other night… about Mum, she has no filter,' I said, trying to make light of everything.

'It's okay, I suppose some things never change,' she said. 'They're written in the past like the sea – they are what they are and it doesn't matter how far we run. Everything that happened in the past shapes our lives now, doesn't it?'

I was surprised at this, Gina wasn't usually so profound, so philosophical. Her face had lost its sunshine now and I wondered where this was going. Was she trying to tell me something?

'What do you mean?' I asked.

'Oh your mother… my mother… it's all too late for people to change.'

I felt like a veil had been lifted briefly then dropped again. Like a detective, I was storing the clues and trying to fit them together. But I was thirsty to know the truth so pushed on. 'You mean the fallout? Do you know what happened?' I'd always assumed it was just between the two sisters, but Mum's reaction to Gina at the apartment had made me wonder.

'I can't talk about it… about anything. I chose to live with it, but please know I don't blame your mum for hating me, Ella…'

'Why?' was all I could muster. So many thoughts were in my head it felt like a washing machine on fast spin, the colours and thoughts and ideas all tumbling around too fast to isolate, too entwined in each other to see.

'I'm not ready to talk about it, please respect my feelings,' she said, back to the cool, sophisticated actress. I'd lost the honest Gina again.

What had happened between the two fiery Italian sisters had been about more than just pettiness coupled with pride, I realised now. But what could possibly be serious enough to keep two sisters apart for more than twenty years – and what role did Gina play in all this?

Chapter Nineteen

Sue, Sequins and a Threatening Storm

Later, after a busy day filled with sunshine, ice cream and smiling faces, I caught up with Ben on the beach.

He was leaning into the hatch of the van. The sun was behind him, his eyes were lovely and soft, his arms strong as he rested them on the counter, and I felt an overwhelming urge to kiss him, but managed to control myself.

'I'm sorry about last night – I just had to be with Mum, don't want you to feel like I'd stood you up.'

'No, you didn't. I mean, we're mates… no worries. I caught up with an old friend, we had a good night,' he said.

I kept smiling, but felt a little uneasy at his announcement that we were 'mates' and recalled the 'exclusive' comment Mum had made a couple of nights before. I wasn't looking for a husband, but I wasn't a one-night stand or a hook-up either. For me to sleep with someone was huge, I didn't do it lightly – this wasn't a 'friends with benefits' situation. Was it? Perhaps for Ben it was?

I went from feeling all gooey and calm to prickly, defensive even.

The sun had gone in, dark clouds were forming over the estuary and it felt like my world was tipping slightly. I missed the kids, was worried about my mother and Gina and the business and now it seemed as if Ben might have put me in the friend zone without me even realising.

He moved away from the hatch as a couple of young women wandered over, and I had to deal with the task in hand, although my mind was still whirring with what he'd just said.

I glanced at him as I squished the thick, creamy ice into cones and my tummy shimmered. He was so handsome, so dependable and yet he was going away soon and I knew I mustn't get hooked on him. I had to stay single in my head; I had to do this for me. Alone.

Now wasn't the time to get myself caught up in worries about what my relationship was with Ben, I needed to focus on other things. In the next couple of weeks the schools would break up and I had high hopes for a busy summer. I had to have hope – with the house being sold, a slow start to business, and Gina and Mum at loggerheads I had enough things to cope with. Then there was the tantalising prospect of the café… would Gina make her mind up soon?

'So… any news on the café?' I asked.

Ben shook his head; 'I don't have access to that stuff, it's Dad's side. I don't think he trusts me to deal with that.'

'Surely that's not the case,' I said annoyed on Ben's behalf, he might not be the most organised or typical of solicitors but surely his father would give him a chance?

'I can see his point,' he said, 'bit of a vicious circle really – he says I don't stick around long enough, so there's no point in handing stuff over. But one of the reasons I get itchy feet is because I don't get to work on more interesting stuff – there's absolutely nothing to keep me here.'

I felt another little sting. Was 'nothing to keep me here' another way of Ben telling me we were just friends?

'You around later?' I asked.

'Not sure,' he said, 'I'll text you.'

I nodded and he touched my hand, then walked away with a backward wave. And in that moment I realised that Ben was a visitor wherever he went, he was almost forty and so far he'd never settled anywhere. I wondered if he ever would, or if he'd always be on the verge of leaving?

My feelings about Ben had deepened, yet I knew I wasn't his final stop on life's journey. I loved being with him, but I had to make my own world, not just rely on being part of his. I didn't want to go through the devastation I had with Dick. This time I would be a strong, independent woman, not the whining, clinging mess I'd been when Dick had left.

The sun finally disappeared that afternoon, taking the remaining scraps of blue sky and replacing the whole canvas with grubby white clouds. The sea and sky were now etched in charcoal and a cool rain-threatening breeze flurried the air.

Peter was walking back past the van with Cocoa, they were on their late afternoon stroll – I could set my clock by him. 'A storm's coming,' he said and looking up at the heavy, swollen sky my heart sank.

I'd been lucky so far, but the weather wouldn't always be beautiful in my new life, there would be rain. This wasn't an ice cream day and standing in the little van on that wide expanse of sepia beach I suddenly felt very lonely.

The breeze soon became a stronger, swishing wind and I suddenly felt like I was in a boat cast adrift from life. The wind rippled the ocean into threatening waves and the infinite sky above made me feel very small. I drove inland, aware that even armed with tide times, the sea could sometimes take you by surprise.

Gazing out onto a beautiful, but rather bleak seascape, I decided to cheer myself up and give Sue a call. We'd kept in touch by text since I'd left 'Fashion Passion', and I knew she'd closed up and spent a couple of weeks at her place in Tenerife where she'd met a new man. She'd informed me by text the day before that she'd come to the 'illusion' that he wasn't the one for her. She was now back in Manchester, probably a bit down and needed to talk too, so I was looking forward to a catch-up.

'Oh Ella it's just wonderful to hear from you, love. I've had a hell of a time – Pablo turned out to be a wolf in cheap clothing so it's back to the dating scene for me.'

'Oh love, I'm so sorry to hear that,' I sighed, smiling to myself at the 'cheap clothing'.

'I was thinking of coming to stay with you for a few weeks,' she said. 'I can't come straight away so don't get too exhilarated.'

I wasn't.

'I'd pay my way – I could help serve when you're busy, I'd love to spend a few weeks in Devon, such a beautiful place – I miss you, El.'

'I miss you too,' I said, but all I could think was Oh God she said, 'stay with you' and, 'a few weeks'. She also offered to 'help serve when you're busy', and as much as I loved her, Sue was the last person you needed when you were busy. If 'Fashion Passion' was anything to go by, she'd turn Reginaldo into a party van. She'd be offering my slimming club girls free ice cream and regaling them with her latest love exploits. I already had a 'mother/cousin/management' situation, and a lovely but worrying love affair, I didn't want to add Sue and her madness to the mix.

But instead of trying to gently put her off I heard myself say, 'That would be lovely, Sue,' while my insides screamed a very loud, guttural NO!!! What else could I do? Sue had been there for me through the dark days and she was a true friend, I couldn't turn her away. On the other hand, the whole reason for me being here was the fact that I wanted to be on my own, and take a break from my real life. But however fast I ran, it seemed my real life was catching up with me – one person at a time.

Sue 'promised' to come and stay for a few weeks and spent the next couple of hours texting photos of various outfits she might wear. In between customers, I tactfully pointed out her 'beautiful' sequins and gold lamé trim may be wasted on the folk of Appledore. I wasn't sure if there was enough room in the van for all those sequins and frills, Delilah's outlandish outfits already filled that space.

'Jeans, T-shirts and jumpers are de rigueur here,' I replied, but still they came, endless photos of sparkly boleros, satin gowns and patent, decorated heels. I loved Sue, but my heart sank at the prospect of this circus turning up on top of everything else in my once quiet corner of the world.

'I think she's great,' Ben laughed when I showed him the pictures later. 'She'll bring some life down to the pub, the old fishermen and the boatyard workers will wonder what's hit them.'

'I think I'll wonder what's hit me too,' I sighed. 'Since I last saw her she's discovered karaoke – she has her own YouTube channel and her *Titanic* theme tune has to be heard… to be heard!'

'Celine Dion?'

'Not quite, though she makes a fist at it, arms spread out, a wind machine in her hair. Celine may sue.' We were sitting on the balcony of my apartment after another long day at the van. Mum had offered to spend the evening working on menus with the chef at the hotel she'd stayed at, I was sure he'd be thrilled. But for me it was a wonderful opportunity to see Ben, so I'd invited him over.

'Funny how we all communicate these days, isn't it?' I smiled, still scrolling through Sue's photo 'collection'.

'Yeah, makes you think… wouldn't it have been amazing if we'd had this kind of technology in the past?'

'Yes, imagine if we'd been able to film the café in its heyday…'

'You remember it in the YouTube channel in your head?' he said, looking into my eyes.

I sighed; 'Yeah, the pink and green interior, gorgeous ice cream, shakes, fizzy drinks with floats melting on top… Sophia whisking up wonderful flavours.'

'Good that you can remember it like it was, rather than it is now. The broken-down counter, smashed coffee machine, everything covered in dust.'

I nodded. 'I've told my kids about it, but they'll never know how magical it once was and if they saw it now they wouldn't believe me. Mind you, it isn't just the café, the Caprioni family are broken too.'

'Ella… I hope you don't mind me saying this… and tell me to shut up if you like, but you must try and let go of the past,' he said. 'I understand how you feel, you cared about Sophia and somehow you feel guilty because the family isn't together – but it isn't your fault. When my mother died the one consolation was that I had the chance to tell her how I felt and she with me. I was very young, and it kept me going over the years, that I had told her I loved her and was proud to be her son. But somewhere in my twenties, there came a point when I was crippled by grief and, though it hurt, I had to let her go. You have to do this now, you have to stop living through others and for others and feeling guilty about the past – because the past is holding you back.'

I sighed. 'I know, but I feel like I'm not complete, I can't explain it.'

I knew I had to forgive my mum for the past, for all the times she'd stopped me from living my life and doing as I pleased – as a mum myself I knew she did this out of love, but it was still hard to reconcile. Mum wasn't easy, she could be controlling, jealous and angry, and this had reached a climax now with Gina. The problem was that Gina represented the past for both of us – but it seemed we saw it differently, we saw Gina differently.

For me she was the amazing fun-loving beautiful cousin I looked up to, but for Mum she was a fickle girl with no morals who seemed to let people down. It said a lot for Mum that she'd allowed me to go and spend a fortnight every summer with Gina. She knew I loved spending time in Appledore and I'd often wondered why Mum agreed to it, given the animosity between the sisters. I suppose it was the Italian thing about 'family' that made her do it, but sending me off must have been torture for her.

Then the summer I was twelve the visits suddenly stopped. I remember Gina calling our house and Mum arguing with her – 'Gina I'm sorry, I just can't keep doing this,' she'd said. 'I know how you feel, I've been hearing for years how you and Sophia feel, but it's time everyone considered my feelings in this.' I didn't understand what they were talking about, it sounded too grown-up for me to even begin to comprehend, it was about adult feelings, something beyond my comprehension. But later, I noticed that Mum had been crying, and I decided then that even if I was invited the following year I wouldn't ever go to Appledore again, because it hurt Mum too much. And now it seemed history was repeating itself, and I had no idea what to do.

Chapter Twenty

Ice Cream I Do!

My ice cream summer continued slowly, undulating through warm air, a baby blue sky melting into strawberry ice cream and golden syrup each evening. Each day seemed to be a little busier, parents arrived with their children after school, couples wandered past and bought a large cone to share. The brioches were doing well, the kids had christened them ice cream burgers, and I was working on slices of ice cream cake too. I would watch the customers wander off down the beach together, a cherry frangipani piled on top of a pale green pistachio, cold and sweet and creamy with a nutty crunch. I was aware my small successes weren't going to make me a millionaire, in fact I was only covering costs and my own expenses, but I had goals, I was doing something, and it felt good. I also added bunting, some stripey deckchairs and a pale pink and white striped awning and imagined this was my café.

'You're beginning to fit,' Ben said one day as he joined me for lunch in the van.

'What do you mean?'

'Your life – you didn't fit into it at first. It felt like you were lost between oceans, you'd grown out of your old life but you had to settle in this one... and now you just fit.'

I hadn't really thought about it, but as each day became busier, the making and selling of ice cream and caring for Delilah had begun to fill the gaps my kids had left. Not that Josh and Lucie could be replaced by a tub of Ciao Bello and a tutu-wearing pooch, but I now knew I could survive without them. I also had Mum and Gina around which wasn't always easy, but I managed to make it work – even if only by keeping them apart, and as Gina was such a free spirit she wasn't around much anyway. Mum had decided to stay in Appledore with me while the house sale went through and she came out most mornings and walked Delilah on the sands for me. She also took pictures of everything and anything on her phone and for once I was glad of her mobile obsession, it kept her busy and meant I could get on with working. Sometimes she'd just wander up and down the queue chatting to the customers and often she'd take their photos with ice creams. All the children wanted their photos taken with Delilah, and with their parents' permission she put these on her blog. To my relief Mum took over Delilah's 'wardrobe management' because I apparently was choosing doggie outfits that weren't 'photogenic'. 'She needs ice cream colours,' Mum said, 'to match Reginaldo.'

Mum had become very positive about the whole project and she was always posting pictures of Reginaldo on her blog, 'Roberta and Reginaldo'. She had originally named it 'Netflix and Chill with Roberta', but we googled it and discovered this was basically a euphemism for having sex. This certainly explained some of the online requests Mum was receiving for various exotic sex acts. 'I mean could anyone physically do that,' she said, screwing up her face and pointing at a request she'd received from 'GobbleBox' via the website.

Each evening she'd sit on the balcony sewing various different doggie items, from tutus to hot-pants for the following day's activities. After each day's 'session', Mum would email or tweet the photos she'd taken and was gaining lots of followers. But most importantly, she was happy, and from behind a mountain of ice cream and a pleasingly growing queue I enjoyed watching her chat away and charm the customers, and hoped finally we were beginning to get past Mum's aversion to Appledore.

One day a young guy turned up at the van and asked me to place an engagement ring inside a Summertime Cooler Sundae (orange, melon and lemon sorbet). He'd read Mum's blog and followed her on Instagram and as his girlfriend loved ice cream so he thought it would be the perfect place to propose. So he got down on one knee by the van, declared his love to his girlfriend, and when she cried and said yes, Mum and I cried too! As luck would have it, a local newspaper journalist happened to be waiting for ice cream, took a picture and did a quick interview. The following week, we were splashed all over the local paper with the headline, 'Ice Cream I Do!'

It must have been a quiet news week because the story travelled beyond Devon and a Japanese TV company turned up asking for a proposal re-enactment. Unfortunately, and predictably, there was a language problem, but Mum said she understood exactly what was needed and would 'help' Akahito the TV director. He just thought she was being friendly so kept nodding in agreement and before we knew it Mum was in charge. Ben and I watched from inside the van as she swept across the sand like bloody Steven Spielberg telling them to 'feel it' and 'go one more time', while Akahito stood politely by.

Mum was so pleased with her shoot that she announced to all bystanders that she was going to give everyone 'a little treat'. I immediately worried she was going to start handing out free ice cream cones and ruin me in one afternoon. But no, Mum had something else in mind; 'I'm going to sing my Rihanna song,' she said. I wanted to die. And just when I thought it couldn't get any worse Akahito decides he's going to film the whole debacle. I was horrified to think Japan would be sitting down that night to the spectacle of a seventy-eight-year-old Englishwoman singing tunelessly and twerking along to Rihanna.

'What's her Rihanna song?' Ben asked under his breath.

'God knows. Does it matter? My mother's not a twenty-four-year-old woman with a voice and body to die for, so it's going to be mortifying whatever it is.' I wasn't familiar with Mum's Rihanna repertoire but vowed I would never forgive her if she sang 'Bitch Better Have My Money'. What sort of message would that send to the holidaymakers of Appledore?

But then I heard this voice, it didn't sound like my mother, and everyone around seemed surprised too at the sound coming from this little old lady, powerful and strong with such a beautiful tone. She was singing Rihanna's 'Diamonds' ballad, and I was amazed how beautiful she made it sound. I recalled her telling me about her thwarted career in the opera and how she once was invited to audition for La Scala but had married my dad instead. I'd assumed she'd been teasing, but as I heard her voice ring out, I guessed that this was probably true. I'd never heard Mum sing like this before, and it made me wonder at the hidden depths there were to this woman I thought I knew.

Mum and I were both living a new life happy, spending each day together under a blue sky, drinking hot tea from a shared teapot. I knew it was what I wanted, but now she seemed to want it too – the sun on her face, the sea lapping at her toes – and as she raised her voice to the heavens my heart swelled with happiness and pride.

When Mum finished singing everyone around cheered and clapped and she took huge bows with great flourish, her face flushed with pleasure, her smile lighting up her face. Later as the evening drew in and we began to fold up the deckchairs and close the van for the day I told her how proud I was and she glowed again.

'Mum, you could have been a singer... opera, ballads, I don't know, but you could have sung to huge audiences, travelled the world... been rich?'

'I am rich, I have you and two perfect grandchildren and my only regret is that your dad can't be here now, with us.' She carried on wiping down the little tables and folding them, then she looked up at me; 'Ella, I would have swapped you for all the opera houses in all the world. You know that don't you?'

I nodded and carried on wiping down the inside of the van, my eyes brimming with tears.

I loved those summer days on the van, they stretched out before me and behind me in a golden light. Seagulls flocked, the tide came and went and the sun kept on, through fluttery breezes and sparkly little showers leaving rainbows in their wake – but I knew it had to end.

'I really want to stay here,' I said to Ben one evening as we sat on the beach watching the sun go down. 'I know it sounds crazy but I have this affinity with the café... and this ridiculous idea keeps coming back that I'll be able to get enough business from the van to create new customers and reopen the café. I reckon Gina might sell it to me – or perhaps let me rent it from her.'

'Have you spoken to her about this?' he said, he was doodling in the sand. He'd seemed a little quiet and I wondered why.

'Yes, she knows it's what I'd like. She said she'll talk to me before she makes any decisions, but I haven't seen her for days. Someone said she was in Westward Ho!... she's always been like that, never stays around. A bit like you,' I smiled.

He looked at me and paused; 'Ella, I'm sorry, I shouldn't say anything, but you asked me about the café the other day, and what was happening, so I had a root around and...'

'What?' I thought my heart had stopped.

'I'm sorry – but Gina's about to sign the papers to hand the café over – looks like she's sold it.'

I felt the breath taken from me like I'd been punched in the chest. I was devastated, how could she do this without even telling me.

'But she promised... she said she wouldn't do anything without speaking to me first,' I said, my voice catching with emotion. Is that why she'd gone AWOL because she didn't want to tell me what she'd done, she knew it would devastate me and possibly ruin any chance I had for a future here. 'I thought that she genuinely hadn't made up her mind and... all the time she's been planning to sell but hasn't had the balls to tell me.'

I was angry, but then my chin wobbled and I had to stop myself from crying. I could tell from Ben's expression that he knew what this meant to me and he'd hated giving me this news.

'When?' I asked, my voice breaking.

'I'm so sorry, Ella... I don't know the timeline, but I know it's imminent.'

I gathered myself together and thought through my options, I was hurt and angry with Gina, but that wasn't going to help.

'I should try and talk to her before she signs...' I said. 'If she knows how much I want to keep the café in the family, she might let me rent the property. I could give her some of the money from the house sale if that helps, it won't be much but...'

He was shaking his head; 'Ella, it's too late.'

'No... no,' I said, my voice breaking into a sob.

I knew I was being stupid and naïve and that it was an impossible situation that I couldn't change. I felt like I did when Dick had left, with no control of my own life and once again someone else pulling the strings and wrecking everything. But I'd never have expected it of Gina.

'Mum was right,' I said, a spark of anger mingling with the well of hurt. 'Gina's all about compliments and kisses, but she doesn't really care. She's always telling me how much I mean to her, but she knows how important this is to me... and she didn't even have the guts to tell me.'

'Yeah, she should have told you. But look at it from her perspective, she probably needs the money.'

'No she doesn't, she's rich, she has a big house in bloody Bel Air,' I said, my face wet with tears, my voice rough with hurt and anger. 'Without the prospect of the café – even a portion of it – there's little point in me working the van. I'm slowly building customers but it can only make so much money even if I'm really busy.' I realised then that for me this had always been about the café, and now I felt I had nothing to aim for.

'It was always going to come to an end in September, wasn't it?'

'Maybe, but the goalposts have changed, I don't have a home up North any more and… I love it here. I wanted to make it my home. I wanted a business that could at least pay me enough to live on and support me and Mum. I wanted to make a go of this, Ben, it was important to me.'

'So don't give up now, Ella, you've got all these ideas and plans, don't just walk away. Stop longing for what you can't have, and make the most of what you do have…'

He hugged me and I could see that in the great scheme of things I was bloody lucky. I had two lovely kids, my mum was there for me in her own way, I had Gina (though the jury was currently out on that one) and I had Ben (though I still wasn't quite sure how to categorise him). I also had the van, and perhaps I should try to see the van as an entity on its own and not part of something else?

'I have to think of a million ways with ice cream now, I can make a living from the van,' I said, rallying, inspired by Ben's enthusiasm and faith.

'Yes of course you can,' he smiled.

'Thanks Ben,' I said, 'you're a good friend.' I quickly glanced at his face, wondering if he might react to this 'friendship' comment. Would he contradict my remark and say he was more? Might he confess he had feelings for me as I did for him? But after a few seconds I let it go, perhaps me and Ben were just friends after all? And perhaps that was okay?

Chapter Twenty-One

A Tsunami of Happiness and Trouble over Teabags

I saw Gina the next morning, she'd obviously returned from West-ward Ho!, but hadn't thought to let me know. She was sitting over-looking the sea smoking a cigarette. It was early and unusual for her to have risen before ten so I parked up on the beach, locked the van and took the opportunity to go and talk to her. If I could broach the subject of the café, I hoped I might be able to convince her not to sign it away. I headed up the beach, waiting for her to wave, but she was looking far out beyond me, and seemed sur-prised when I joined her on the bench.

'You're up early,' I said.

'Yes I couldn't sleep.' She looked a little tired around the eyes, but it was hard to tell because as always she was in full make-up.

'You were miles away,' I said, sitting down next to her.

'Dreaming, just dreaming,' she smiled and, taking my hand, continued to look out at the ocean.

'It seems so bleak on a grey day when the tide's out,' I said.

'Mmm the sea goes so far. I used to know the rhythm of the tides, when the sea would be here and when we'd have this endless emptiness,' she said, without taking her eyes off the horizon.

I wasn't sure how to broach the sale of the café – obviously Ben shouldn't have told me and I didn't want to cause problems for him, but I needed to find out. I'd lay awake the night before thinking it through and going from hope to despair; perhaps the café had been bought by someone who wanted to keep it as a café? Perhaps they'd be interested in a business partner who would, in the summer, take the café 'on the road' in the van while they worked the cafe? Or perhaps it had been bought by a conglomerate who wanted to tear it down and build holiday flats? I tried not to think about that possibility.

'We're having a great summer – with the van,' I said. I turned on my phone and showed her photos of the van, the different ice creams, Delilah and Mum in their matching pink dresses, hoping it might inspire her to rethink the sale.

She scrolled through; Delilah's extensive wardrobe made her smile. 'She's such a cutie,' she said, 'and I *don't* mean Roberta,' she rolled her eyes and she took a long drag. I'd hoped the time apart might have cooled tensions but it seemed the feelings were as strong as ever, it was down to me to try to smooth things over.

'Mum's okay you know, I think she just feels a bit left out, you and I get on so well and…'

'We do, don't we?' she said, flicking her ash and looking at me. 'I value our relationship, Ella…'

'Me too,' I said. And we both stared ahead, me thinking about the café and Gina probably thinking about the filming she'd abandoned to come here. 'Are you missing LA?' I asked. 'It must be a different world here.'

'Yes, I miss my friends, and the sunshine... it isn't the same since Whitney passed.'

'Whitney Houston?'

'Yes.'

'You knew her?'

'Sort of... we were at some of the same parties.'

She seemed almost reluctant to talk about her LA life. She'd offer a tantalising glimpse then immediately take it away before I had a chance to ask any more. I'd expected the old Gina to be gossiping constantly about everyone she'd met or worked with, but more often than not I'd have to tease it out.

'And your husband? Chad? Are you missing him?' She hadn't talked about her husband much since she arrived.

'Chad? Oh yes... of course.'

And she closed the door again, making it difficult for me to take the conversation any further. I left it a few minutes watching the beach slowly come to life and eventually I said, 'What are your plans, Gina?'

'Plans?'

'Yes, are you staying here a while – or leaving for LA soon? You've been here a while, what about the filming? Is Leonardo okay with you being here – and the director too? I don't want you to lose the role...'

'No... I won't.' She was silent, I could see it must have hurt to leave the fiming, it could be her big break, she still had time to be the next Helen Mirren. She obviously didn't want to talk about this which I understood, so I changed the subject, staying on her possible departure, but shifting slightly.

'Mum seems to think you'll just take off one day and I won't know you've gone.'

'Your mother…' she looked at me awkwardly, like she was about to say something meaningful, and finally reveal herself, but then she looked away and I knew the moment had passed and what she was about to say was not what she'd wanted to. 'Your mother doesn't like me very much, she has this… opinion of me and I don't know if that will ever change.'

'Mum can be judgemental… give her time and I'm sure she'll realise how lovely you are and how kind and that you wouldn't just leave without letting me know. You wouldn't, would you?'

She seemed uncertain. 'I will try not to, Ella. Look I have to go… I have an appointment.'

I suddenly realised this was my chance to try to find out about the café.

'Is it with Mr Shaw? Is it about the café? I hope you're not selling, Gina – I know it might make financial sense – but it would mean so much to me…' I said, my words rolling after each other in my anticipation to find out.

'I'm sorry, Ella, I really am running late. Perhaps we could get together this evening?'

Before I could say anything else she was already off down the road. But what could I do? The café wasn't mine and never would be, and if Gina wanted to sell I just had to hope the buyers wanted it to stay as a café and might be persuaded to let me help restore it to its former ice cream glory – but somehow I doubted it. I was beginning to realise that miracles didn't happen in my life.

And I didn't see Gina that night as she'd suggested, she never called and when I texted she didn't respond. She seemed to have gone off the radar as Mum had said she would.

'I hope you understand now why I've kept her at arm's length and advised you to do the same,' Mum said. 'Gina always comes first and she doesn't care who she hurts along the way.'

She was probably right, though I found it hard to give up on my cousin, she'd brought a little bit of sparkle into my life – always had. I wanted to believe in her, but I hadn't been able to get in contact with her and when I'd been to the hotel where she was staying they said she'd checked out. My worst fear was that she'd sold the café and felt she couldn't tell me so had gone back to LA without saying goodbye. As much as the café meant to me, losing Gina like that after all these years would hurt terribly. I called her agent to see if she knew where she was but there was no answer – and despite leaving several messages, she never got back to me. Ben was equally flummoxed and when he asked his father he said he had no idea where she was, he was her solicitor not her keeper.

There was nothing I could do, so I took Ben's advice, to let the water take my weight and try to let go. It was tough, but as the busy bright days segued into soft amber evenings I began to feel a kind of acceptance. I wasn't sure if it was the beach, Ben or something in the ice cream, but my heart felt lighter and my mind was free. There was nothing I could do about Gina and the café, so I just had to concentrate on the van and let the universe decide.

Ben would come over to the van during the day and tease Mum, telling her Simon Cowell was looking for her, and she'd whack him over the head playfully (which he said actually hurt). We were so busy some days I could barely speak, and mother seemed to spend most of the time with Delilah entertaining the queue. Meanwhile, Ben had been helping a lot, lifting boxes, moving fridges, and as grateful as I was, I hoped this wasn't taking him away from work at his father's firm.

'Does your dad expect you to be in the office?' I asked one evening when he'd been around most of the day.

'Dad knows what I'm like, he doesn't approve, but he's given up trying to turn me into his mini-me. I want to wear flip-flops and be here... on the beach... with you.'

I melted, and rested my head against his warm T-shirt smelling of salt, fresh air and strawberry ice cream. I was lost in his smell, breathing him in deeply, and yes, I'll admit I may have lingered a little too long against his chest. But I was at work, and as the boss I wasn't going to put up with unfitting behaviour from anyone, including myself.

'You okay?' he murmured into my hair as I reluctantly pulled away.

'Yes, I didn't want to be inappropriate around the sorbets – I may have to terminate my own employment,' I smiled.

'I on the other hand don't work for you, so I could be inappropriate, without contravening any sorbet rules,' he sighed, snaking his arm discreetly round my waist and under my T-shirt. Just the feel of his warm hand on my bare flesh made me go weak at the knees, and I wanted so much to give in to my feelings. However, being arrested for outraging public decency wasn't going to help my business, so I pulled myself together.

Later that day we dropped Mum back at the house and Ben and I drove up around the coast road, alone at last. The sun was setting as I drove along, his hand on my knee, my heart racing. We hadn't been able to spend as much time together and glancing over at his dark eyelashes, his strong, wiry arms I realised how much I'd missed him, and by the look on his face, I guessed he felt the same.

'Keep going, then turn right,' he said, directing me to the mouth of the Taw-Torridge estuary, a grassy coastal plain fronted by salt marsh and sand dunes. I pulled up and we climbed out of the car and began walking towards the dunes.

'I read another letter last night,' I said, looking out to the sea. 'It was returned unopened from LA, I shouldn't have read it – but I feel like there are secrets I should know.'

'And what did you find out?' he asked.

'Nothing really – it was from Sophia to Gina telling her about her father, that he loved her and forgave her at the end, before he died. I've been thinking about it – I wonder what he had to forgive her for?'

'Probably her leaving?'

'I don't know, but much of the correspondence seems to refer obliquely to one "event", something that happened years ago, before I was born. But no one ever talks about it, or explains what caused this terrible rift – and don't tell me it's all about a teabag feud.'

'Who knows?' he sighed. 'Tea can be such a catalyst – many families have perished from a disagreement over teabags.'

We both smiled at each other and I linked arms with him, two people standing in a vast expanse of sand dunes. Our lives were so big to us, yet here they were as insignificant as those teabags, and I finally felt myself letting go, allowing the troubles of my family to fade as I took in the here and now. Ben's hand gently caught mine and I looked up at him; we didn't need words.

We were completely alone in this golden paradise of silence, sand and setting sun and I felt the echo of the past impacting on the present in this small place, holding so many secrets.

Ben put both arms round my waist, leaning down to kiss me softly on the lips, causing time to stand still. He tasted delicious, his tongue moving gently into my mouth, a prelude of what was to come as we both melted into each other, slowly lying down on the bottle-top and cigarette-butt remains of the warm day. I lay back as his hands explored under my T-shirt, gently pulling down his jeans and then mine, our hips now together, undulating. I cried out as he entered me, his lips on my breasts, my hands on his warm back reaching down to his buttocks. We were outside, I could feel the fresh evening air on my face and thighs, I felt exposed and ex-cited, this was wild and wicked and I'd never done anything like it before. And I experienced such intense pleasure as he gasped and we came together, breathing hard, molten in the sunset.

I lay in the warm sand, my arm across Ben as the night came in, bringing with it a million scattered stars. We didn't speak, we didn't need to, there was so much world to contemplate as the evening breeze ruffled the sea and danced across us. I couldn't have been happier and I pressed my face into Ben's neck, savouring him, the moment and the deep, deep peace I felt inside.

'You were right about not taking on the future – there's nothing we can do is there?' I said, thinking about the café. 'I've never been able to let go before, thank you for making me realise that I can.'

He kissed the top of my head and I knew whatever happened with us I would always be grateful to him. He would always have a special place in my heart.

'You know the saying "the journey of a thousand miles starts with one step"?' I said, lifting my head so I could see his eyes. He seemed miles away, and I was again reminded that this wasn't a man who stayed, he was probably thinking of other seas, other lives, other journeys yet to take. I knew this, it came with the package, and I'd accepted it – but still it made me uneasy.

'Yeah... I know the saying,' he answered eventually.

'Well you were that first step for me... I wouldn't be here if you hadn't casually suggested I start working with the van,' I said, pushing thoughts of him ever leaving out of my head. 'I'd have put the van in storage – a little flake of hope locked away...'

He smiled, turning to me with a kiss. And we made love again on the sand and I'm sure the stars exploded above us as huge waves broke, crashing onto the beach below.

Yes, I was intoxicated, a tsunami of happiness and relief, and a little bit... just a little bit, in love, with Ben, and with Appledore. Little did I know this was a moment I had to truly cherish, because what came later was to test everything, especially me.

Chapter Twenty-Two

Fresh Raspberry Purée and
Dick's Pics on Facebook

The following morning, I set off for the beach down the little streets through Appledore. Ben had left at dawn so Mum wouldn't be aware of what was going on. I wasn't ready to share my relationship with Mum, it was a corner of my life I was keeping just for me, and besides, I worried if she knew she might be tempted to appear in my bedroom and serenade us from the bottom of my bed.

I was happy. I'd become so much stronger and more in control of my life, I could even look at 'The Dick pics' of my ex on Facebook without snarling. I now laughed at his red face and ridiculous shorts as he sat by a large swimming pool – I wasn't eaten away with envy and hate. I hadn't been left behind; I now had a brand new life, a burgeoning business and spent my days on a beach looking out to sea. I missed my kids, but they Skyped and tweeted and thanks to Instagram I saw Josh in the Himalayas and Lucie in Thailand. Life was good.

And yet... I was trying to fathom out what to do next. I didn't want to just sit on the minor success of my burgeoning ice cream van business which could mean lots of money over the summer, but would dribble to nothing by October. As I poured fresh raspberry purée on velvety vanilla and handed out bountiful cones of pure fruity and creamy pleasure, I knew I wanted more.

If I'd learned nothing else that summer I now knew I didn't have to 'accept' anything – even my own life. I had a choice, opportunities, and sometimes they didn't present themselves with a label on and it was easy to miss them. But they were there. The van that had disappointed me at first had turned out to be a great opportunity and I marvelled daily at the way it had changed my life. It was a rusty old vehicle with unusable equipment and dodgy brakes and on the surface it offered me nothing, but it was taking me to places I'd only ever dreamed of. It had given me my own business, a new and exciting (and scary) future. The van had literally been my ride away from a life that didn't fit me any more. Whether I liked it or not, the future of the ice cream café and my future in Appledore were linked and however hard I tried to be laid-back about it I needed to give it one last go with Gina and try to change her mind about selling the café.

It was about seven that evening and Ben was waiting for me to finish up on the van, so we could eat together before I started making more ice cream for the following day. It had been busy and fun and I'd decided to share my plan with Ben.

'I'm going to talk to Gina, confront her about the café and see if there's any way I can change her mind,' I said.

He just looked at me.

'What? She doesn't *have* to sell it, she can let me run it for a while and when I get some money together I'll buy it off her. It's not like she's desperate for the cash, she's loaded, well her husband is – she married a really rich guy… she's…'

'No, she divorced… didn't you know?'

'No, she never said.' I was shocked.

'My dad mentioned it earlier. I don't know any details but it seems she's single.'

I was upset she hadn't told me this, especially as she knew I was divorced – we could surely have bonded over this. Gina had probably always been this way, secretive, hard to pin down, but now I felt like I was constantly being surprised by her. Despite the declarations of love, the animated flurry of hugs and kisses, I was beginning to see that she never really gave anything of herself. I was sad for her and wondered what had happened for her marriage to end. I hoped it had just fizzled out and there wasn't some horrible betrayal, but that's the only reason I could think of as to why she hadn't mentioned it.

'Okay so she's divorced, but she's still got the house in Bel Air and she's working with Leonardo DiCaprio, I'm sure she doesn't need to worry about money,' I said, still unable to hide the pride in my voice.

'Dad never mentioned that. Mind you, Dad probably wouldn't know who Leonardo DiCaprio was anyway.'

'Well even if she's lost money through the divorce, she'll be making mega bucks starring in a film alongside Leonardo – she could still afford to keep the café.'

'Who knows? Have you told your mum about Leonardo?'

'Yes, but she's determined not to be impressed,' I smiled.

'Give her time; she'll be so star-struck she'll forget all about the family feud. Dad mentioned something the other day about there being "long-held trouble in the family".'

I was intrigued, perhaps he knew? 'Did he say what?'

'No, I did ask but he's their solicitor and I might be his son but he can't discuss stuff like that.'

'It sounds like he may be involved, or has been in the past. Do you think it might be something… legal?'

'Money… it's usually money,' Ben sighed, as he piled a Fruit Salad Sundae into a cone and dribbled apricot and raspberry purées on top.

'No, if it was money Mum would have said, but she told me not to listen to anything your dad told me anyway. Which makes it all the more intriguing.'

He shrugged and I decided to give it a rest.

I watched the fruity syrup drip onto his forearm and had to stop myself from licking it off.

'You're getting good at that,' I indicated the sundae. 'I might even take you on.'

'I don't mix business with pleasure, even with a gorgeous blonde,' he winked as he handed the cone over to an excited little girl who only had eyes for the ice cream; the same couldn't be said of her mother as she handed the money over to Ben!

'I'm not the gorgeous blonde, that's my cousin's territory,' I smiled.

'Yeah but now you're blonde you look like her, only younger.'

I felt all warm inside, I loved being compared to Gina and despite telling myself constantly that this guy might leave at any time and not to get too attached, I really did like him. Perhaps the idea that this might not be forever was part of the attraction? He'd never be a slippers by the fire kind of man and in a way that made me want him more. Just being close made me tingly and warm and I couldn't stand near him without finding an excuse to touch him; I'd slap his arm in jest, or pull a non-existent hair from his shoulder. Sometimes I'd pretend I needed to hold his forearm for steadiness while walking along the beach together. We did this often, Delilah dancing ahead like a little show pony. I was, at last, beginning to feel this was part of my adventure and I wasn't sure how it was going to end yet but I was staying along for the ride.

I was thinking about Ben the next day while blobbing blueberry ice cream onto lavender and topping it with creamy honey and ginger. It was a lovely pastel-hued cone and I was enjoying the thought of his lips savouring this latest concoction. Ben and ice cream – my two favourite things. I was handing the large cone to the customer when I was rudely awoken from my daydreams by my phone ringing. I took the money and quickly answered. It was a number I didn't recognise and I waited for a few seconds – there was nothing but silence. I said 'hello' a few times, but there was no reply. I was just about to click off when I heard her voice.

'Ella... is that you?' It was Gina, I hadn't seen or heard from her for several days.

'Where the hell are you?' I started. I'd never spoken to her like this before, I'd always been respectful, in awe, but she'd let me down. 'You said you wouldn't just go off and leave without telling us,' I felt tearful, like a child abandoned. 'And... I miss you,' I heard myself say, and a wave of guilt engulfed me thinking of Mum and how this would make her feel.

'Oh darling, I miss you too. I know it's been difficult, but I've had a lot of thinking to do.'

'Why didn't you say? And I just heard you're divorced… you never told me. What else haven't you told me? Mum always that you can't be trusted, but *I* trusted you, Gina.'

'I didn't want this to be about my problems,' she sounded upset. 'My divorce is just another thing on the list of my failures.' There was a silence and then she brightened, typical Gina, unable to cope with real life, she had to plaster make-up and gloss over everything. 'I wanted this time together to be happy and carefree like it used to be when we were younger.'

'And it has been, it can be. Gina, being happy doesn't mean hiding things from people who love you.'

'Sometimes it does,' she said.

'I wanted to believe in you, Gina, I really did – but Mum said you'd come in and shake everything up and leave again… and that's exactly what you've done.'

'I haven't. I've not left, I'm in Barnstaple – I just needed some time to think everything through. Mum's estate has been complicated.'

My heart lifted at this, so Gina hadn't left after all.

'And the café?'

'We need to talk about that…'

I wasn't sure that I wanted to. She'd probably just tell me that she'd sold the café and was going back to LA with the money. Perhaps that was the only reason she came here in the first place?

Against my better judgement, I agreed to meet her the following day and I put down the phone, unsure if she'd even turn up.

Later, Ben and I sat together on a bench overlooking the beach and ate fish and chips from paper. It was late, the stars were out and the night was slightly chilly. I was tired, talking to Gina had upset me, and I'd called Ben from the beach, he'd said a bag of salty chips was just what I needed. He was right. In fact, it seemed he was always right. We ate as we looked out to sea and I told him all about the phone call.

'I don't know what makes her tick, she's an enigma,' I sighed.

'Perhaps she's like that for a reason?' he suggested. 'She doesn't want to be pinned down emotionally or physically.'

The irony of this statement wasn't lost on me – he was describing himself.

'She's always been that way,' I sighed. 'I'm beginning to wonder if something happened that made her crave freedom and head to LA. It can't have been easy growing up in a small town, where everyone knows your business, especially with Mum here, poking her nose in.

'Yeah, one Italian matriarch would be bad enough, but two?' Ben rolled his eyes. 'Yeah, perhaps Gina's boyfriend came up against the Italian matriarchs and went off and married someone else? Or perhaps he was already married, which would explain why she ran away.'

'And would also explain my mother's feelings towards her,' I added, imagining my mother's reaction to that bit of news.

So many permutations, and somehow they all led back to my mother. 'I wonder if Mum tried to stop Gina from doing what she wanted to do? I'd resented it as a child, my mother always wanting to know where I was, who I was with…'

'I imagine that must have been difficult for you as a teenager,' he sighed, 'but I'd have given anything for my mum to be around at that age. Dad wasn't the most sensitive – and I conformed to the stereotype, staying out late, smoking pot and smirking in adults' faces… oh and sleeping with unsuitable women.'

'You're still doing that,' I winked.

He laughed, 'No, I don't think you're an unsuitable woman.'

For a moment I wondered if I was 'suitable' for Ben, but doubted someone like him could ever relax into a life with someone, however well they were suited.

'I can see why you've never settled; you lost your mum as a young kid and you've never really had anyone to come home to,' I said, turning to look at him.

He nodded. 'Yeah, and I think Dad saw me as a burden after she'd gone. It's not easy coming home to the feeling you're not really wanted.'

And yet still he returned, every year he'd come back on some pretence of working to earn money. But I wondered if all he really wanted was his father's approval and he made the pilgrimage to this little Devon town each summer to try to win it.

'Mmm Mum always made me feel wanted, it was just everyone else she tried to scare off,' I sighed. 'It was like she was worried I was going to be kidnapped or leave her – she spent most of my marriage telling me Dick wasn't good enough, that he wasn't right for me, filling me with doubts.'

'Well, turns out she was right about that,' he said, turning to look at me, his eyes shining in the darkness. I could hear the sea rolling onto the beach and the cool, fresh air danced across my cheeks as he leaned in to kiss me. 'I hope Roberta's giving me good PR?' he said.

'Yes, as a matter of fact she rather likes you, which is praise indeed, you must be something special.'

'Do *you* think I am?'

I was surprised at his sudden seriousness. This was the guy who virtually had 'no strings' tattooed across his forehead. But here, now, with my chips going cold and the tide coming in I wondered if I'd got him all wrong.

'Well, do you think I'm special?' He was looking at me, searching my face in the darkness. 'I suppose what I want to know is… is it worth me sticking around after September?'

I was amazed, I'd never expected this. He didn't care what people thought, he lived his life, danced to his own tune and if you didn't like it you could leave. But here he was offering to give up his chance to go to Hawaii, his dream… for me?

'Is this a genuine enquiry?' I asked.

'Genuine. I want to know.'

'Wow, I didn't expect… okay, yes I like you, you're kind and fun and we have a good time together…'

'You could say that about a brother, what about your real feelings?'

'I thought you didn't do "feelings"?' I said, playing for time, scared to give too much away.

'I didn't do feelings …until you.'

I felt a rush of warmth, my heart began beating faster, yet I was still unsure, still vulnerable, after all this was the guy who had never committed to a location, let alone a person. And what if he was the kind of person who fell in love and then got cold feet?

'But you've always said we're mates, you've never acknowledged me as your girlfriend.'

'You've never acknowledged me as your boyfriend – but we're grown-ups and we don't need to have labels for each other. We both know how we feel, Ella.'

I could feel my heart thudding in my chest. This was exactly what I'd dreamed about hearing him say but I'd trained myself not to fall for Ben, I'd kept my heart locked shut and hidden the key somewhere because I didn't want to get hurt again. I also didn't want another man coming into my life at a crucial time and having to compromise, to give up or change what I had, however much I cared for him.

'In an ideal world, I'd like you to stay here forever...' I started. 'But it's not an ideal world, and unfortunately this isn't just about me or you and what we want now,' I said, the very thought of him leaving breaking my heart.

'I just think this is different... you and me. I know it sounds stupid, immature even, but I don't think I've ever been in love – so I don't know how it feels,' he said, screwing up his chip wrapper and aiming it in a nearby bin before putting his arm around my shoulder.

I couldn't believe he'd even mentioned the 'L' word but I didn't want to get carried away, after all he said he wasn't really sure how it felt.

I smiled, and he sat back down and took me in his arms and kissed me for a long time. 'You'll know how love feels when it happens,' I said.

'Then it's happened...' he sighed, 'and September is too soon.'

At this I was lost, and for a while we sat in silence, my heart swept out to sea. Was I ready to give Ben the key to my heart or should I keep it shut and protect myself because Ben was a free spirit? Did that mean he might get bored one day? He may think he feels this now but in a few weeks, months, when the weather had turned and our relationship was tested, would Hawaii be calling?

Eventually he spoke; 'I never realised it until now...'

'What?'

'What you said before, that losing my mum has made me scared of falling in love; it makes sense, it's obvious really, but sometimes you can't see it in yourself, can you? But you're right, I've always been scared of being close to someone – in case I lose them too.'

'I understand how you feel,' I said, recognising my own fears of being hurt, 'I lost my dad when I was younger and then Dick, and in a way I lost Sophia and Gina – it was never explained to me, these two lovely women who adored me were suddenly removed from my life. And there's always been this nagging voice in the back of my head. Was it my fault all these people left, will it happen again if I let someone in? And I know I'll be devastated when you leave.'

'I don't have to go, Ella.'

'I think you do.' I didn't want him to give this up for me. I wasn't going to change for a relationship, I'd been there and seen how soul-destroying it could be, and I didn't want to do that to Ben. I couldn't take him away from his travels and his adventures, he'd just grow to resent me, so I had to let him go… didn't I?

'I don't feel the same about going away,' he said. 'It used to fill me with longing, but now it makes me feel empty. I dread leaving you.' He took my hand and looked into my eyes. 'You remember the other evening when I was cooking dinner and you were making amaretto ice cream and we were together in the kitchen?'

I nodded.

'We were together, kind of side by side, doing different things, but like a team, and this… this feeling came over me. I can't explain it, but I thought yeah, I could be happy here, with her… forever.'

I was touched by this and my eyes filled with tears. 'Stop it, Ben, you're the one who said let's just do now, you can't change the rules.'

'I know,' he said, and I saw him touch his eye, knowing he was overwhelmed with emotion. I'd never seen him like this before and it was making me love him even more.

'I feel like a kid,' he said, 'happy and sad and confused at the same time – like your birthday when you're so excited you just spin round and round until you're dizzy.'

'I know, I feel like a little kid too,' I smiled through the tears.

'If I'm honest, this whole summer has felt like my birthday, Ella. And though the constant, excited spinning is slightly disorientating – I finally feel like I don't need to run away any more.' He smiled and held my face in his hands. 'Babe, I think I might just have this.'

He'd never called me 'babe' before; come to think of it he'd never used a term of endearment towards me or about me.

'But what about your dream, Hawaii – the dive – the final exam?'

'I don't know… I just don't know any more,' he said, and we looked at each other in the thick, dark silence, broken only by the sea.

This changed things, Ben now didn't see his future on some far-away shore with a group of strangers. Perhaps there comes a time in all our lives when we're ready to come home and face the truth, wherever and whatever that might be? But was Ben ready yet – or was he just scared that if he didn't stay, I might go?

That night I went back to Ben's for the first time. It felt special, like he was revealing the rest of himself to me, finally trusting me with everything. It was his father's house, a huge, white-painted walled garden kind of place bought with tears from the divorces, divides and deaths of Appledore. It was quite beautiful, if a little shabby, but Ben said it had never been quite the same since his mother died. 'She had a rose garden, it's overgrown now, but she spent all her time out there.'

His own room was in an annexe at the side of the house, self-contained and private.

'I didn't realise it was so nice and secluded,' I said, taking in the whitewashed walls, the clean, new furniture, the compact kitchen. 'I can't believe we've been friends for so long and you've only just invited me here,' I said, surprised at my own use of the word 'friends'. Was I more scared than Ben of committing myself to this?

'I never invite anyone. You're the first. Dad uses it for guests if ever his sister comes down from London, but other than that it's just me here – it means I don't disturb him if I'm home late. And he doesn't disturb me when I sleep late,' he smiled.

As a man who could be closed off when it came to his own life, being here gave a revealing glimpse of who he was. There were pictures everywhere from his travels, and framed pictures of him as a baby and as a little boy with his mum. It made me appreciate again how much he felt her loss all these years later. He'd been so young when she died and I knew how sharp that pain remained from my own loss of my dad. Ben was now a well-travelled thirty-nine-year-old man, and yet she was still a big part of his life.

He moved books and magazines off the sofa for me to sit down while he made coffee in the kitchen. The sofa was big and white and though it had seen better days it felt comfy and when he returned with the coffee we snuggled up together under a blanket.

'Hearing about your mum makes me feel so lucky to still have mine. She drives me mad but I wouldn't be without her,' I said.

Ben smiled. 'She's something else your mum, isn't she? I've never known anyone with so much energy.'

'Mmm "energy" is a polite way of putting it. She's fuelled by bitterness, resentment and strong tea,' I laughed. 'And yet I have to say I think she's softened while she's been here. Being by the sea, becoming Delilah's "assistant", and a new career as warm-up woman for the van has definitely changed her. She's gone all soft and squidgy… well, less prickly at least, she still won't have it that my Bellini ice cream made with Prosecco and fresh peach purée is a triumph.'

'She doesn't mean to hurt you, I'm sure, but if you're bringing up a family, running a business *and* making brilliant ice cream, there's nothing left for her to do.'

I loved the way Ben could see through everything, and gave others the benefit of the doubt. He'd been so kind to Mum and even when I moaned about her he came up with a cause for what, at times, seemed like rather unreasonable behaviour. And he was right again, Mum was reacting to what was happening around her, and as me and the kids had all gone off in search of life, she just needed to know she was still important to us all. She'd always needed constant reassurance that she was a good mother, which I never really understood as a child.

I recall telling her once that my friend Diane's mum was 'fun', and she'd shifted uncomfortably in her chair. 'Am I a fun mum too?' she'd said – and though that would never be a description I'd apply to my fiery, bossy, uptight mother – the look on her face had made me want to cry.

'Yes, you're really fun, Mum,' I'd said.

'More than Diane's mum?'

'Yes,' I'd said gently. Even as a young child I'd felt her desperate need to be loved and wanted by me, her daughter. I recognised this more when I had my own kids, and realised that your children's love is like oxygen. But I didn't feel the need to seek constant re-assurance and comparisons with other mothers as my mum had done.

'It might be the sea and the new job,' Ben said, gazing out into the darkness, 'but she's come alive, I think she just loves being with you.'

How like Ben to pick up on this. Having Mum around me was something I'd always taken for granted – at times resented even – but as someone who'd lost his mother he had tuned into this. We weren't demonstrative, and we bickered, she nagged and I sulked then we'd change it around – but ultimately neither of us doubted the love between us.

I just wished with this new freedom, she'd cast off past grudges and move on, but for some reason that didn't seem possible for my mother. I wondered if there would ever be the family reunion I'd always dreamed of; perhaps things had gone too far for too long? But right now all I wanted to think about was being here with the man I loved… because who knew how long this would last?

Chapter Twenty-Three

Gina's Film-Star Secrets

'Gina – you lied to me, you told me you'd consider letting me work at the café, you said you wouldn't sell without talking to me first. And you promised you wouldn't just leave without any explanation.'

Gina had turned up the day after her phone call as agreed. I was sitting on a bar stool, at the same pub we'd first met a few weeks earlier. Gina was doing her usual, drinking vodka and trying to flatter me by saying how lovely my hair was. This time I wasn't falling for it, I didn't want to be rude and was determined not to fall out, but I was going to confront her about the selfish way she'd acted.

'I was so worried, Gina,' I said, my eyes filling with tears. 'At first I thought you'd gone back to LA, but someone said they'd seen you in Westward Ho!. I'd even begun to think you might have been murdered or kidnapped… and you never called or responded to my texts and messages.'

'I'm so sorry, Ella, I didn't realise how much it would upset you. Darling, you have to understand, I've lived alone for a long time, only ever had to consider myself. I didn't give anyone a second thought – I needed time to think so I just took off – like I always do.'

'You must have known it would upset me... and while you were off "finding yourself" or whatever it was you were doing I discovered something else. You're divorced... why didn't you tell me?'

'Oh I know and like I said, I'm sorry; I wanted to forget about my problems, the minute you say "I'm divorced" people want to know the ins and outs. We divorced years ago, I don't talk about it.'

'So I see. Look, I understand you don't want to go over stuff like that – but it hurts that you didn't even mention it.'

She seemed upset, and that hadn't been my intention. I'd assumed she'd fight back and we'd just move on, but what I'd said seemed to get to her.

'Look, I'm sorry. I was just angry because you'd proved my mother right and I felt like a fool – I'm sorry you're divorced, I hope it wasn't horrible?' I said, handing her a tissue, her eyes looked damp, I'd never seen Gina cry before.

'It wasn't pleasant,' she said, gently dabbing under her eye make-up. 'Chad wasn't a big Hollywood director, he was an insurance salesman, and not a very good one,' she looked at me and gave a little laugh, her eyes brimming with tears. I was shocked at this, it had never occurred to me to question anything she'd told me, I'd assumed it was fact.

'He was a nice guy until he drank too much and then he wasn't a nice guy. I only stayed married to him because I believed in my vows. Being Catholic isn't a choice,' she sniffed and blew her nose.

'Oh God, Gina, I really thought you were happily married. That's so sad, that you stayed in a marriage because of some words you once spoke in front of a priest,' I said, taking a sip of the vodka she'd automatically ordered for me. For once, I needed it.

'Did you love him?'

'No. I guess I was just scared and lonely… and sad.'

'But I thought you were a big success in LA. We thought that you and Chad were the perfect Holywood couple – the director and the beautiful actress – Tim Burton and Helena Bonham-Carter, minus all the craziness of course. '

'God, no. I met Chad when I moved to LA, we lived in a disgusting one-roomed apartment and while he did nothing all day I walked the streets of Hollywood looking for work. Eventually, I was booked for a commercial. I was on TV lying on top of a giant chocolate fudge cake… mud wrestling for confectioners,' she laughed.

'That was good though, wasn't it? TV work must have paid well.'

'Not really, my agent fleeced me and I signed away most of the money, which was a pittance, I made the mistake of saying yes to everything and not looking at the small print. I was broke again six months later.'

'That must have been tough. So what happened?'

'I told myself it was my first step on the ladder to success but no one took me seriously after that. And as time went on I got the odd booking as a "soccer mom", but then I became invisible, and it was too late. I was suddenly too old. I couldn't make a dime, even had to borrow money from Mum to come back to Appledore most summers.'

She took another sip of her vodka; I thought she might cry.

'Mum's death felt like a watershed. I guess being old makes you think more about the past, what you did, what you should have done, and I'm here to right some wrongs, Ella.'

I continued to sit in silence, unsure of what to say, but aware she wanted to talk but was finding it hard.

'I'm so sorry, Ella, I lied to you, everything's been built on lies, but lying to you hurts me the most. I never starred in any films and I never lived in a mansion in Bel Air.'

'But I saw you, in the photos… I found them in an old carrier bag. You're sitting there like a film star on a sun lounger by your pool, oh and your beautiful bedrooms…'

'I shouldn't have sent those photos. They were as much for me as anyone else – I had too much pride to admit I was a failure. When I couldn't get acting work I became a cleaner working for a company who cleaned all the big houses in Bel Air – I asked the other cleaners to take photos of me around the house. We all did it – but while they did it for fun, I'd send the photos to my parents and our family in Italy telling them I was doing great.'

I didn't want this to be true; 'But the parties, they were real… you've told me about the parties… you met celebrities? I saw the photos.'

'Yes, I was carrying the tray of drinks; I was a waitress, Ella. I've been at some of the biggest and best parties in Hollywood, had my photo taken like a mad fan girl… but I was never *invited*.'

'So all the stuff your agent said about Leonardo DiCaprio?'

She was playing with her diamond rings, twiddling them around her fingers, shaking her head. 'My agent you spoke to in LA? It was me… and these diamonds? They're paste.'

I felt like someone had punched me in the stomach and at first refused to believe what she was telling me. Everything I'd thought about Gina was a big, fat lie.

'I'm sorry, Ella, I didn't mean to deceive anyone, I just wanted you all to think I was okay, that I was doing well. But it was all lies.'

I took a large gulp of vodka while trying to take all this in. Gina had always had a bigger impact on me than I'd realised. I'd modelled myself on this woman, even some of my mannerisms had been learned from her as a young girl. These were things people had remarked on all my life – the way I put my finger to my mouth when thinking, the way I walked with a slight swing, and the way I sometimes pursed my lips when I wasn't happy. It was pure Gina. And it was all lies, the Gina I'd thought I wanted to be didn't exist. Gina's life was the ultimate Facebook lie that people like me believed, and judged our own small lives by, constantly telling ourselves we weren't good enough. And a part of me could see why she'd lied to save face but whatever she'd done, she was still my cousin and I wasn't going to give up on her.

'So, when it didn't work out, why didn't you just come home, to Appledore?'

'I wasn't wanted here. I'd let everyone down.'

'But it wasn't your fault that you didn't make it in Hollywood; bloody hell it's the oldest story in the book! You're not the first and you won't be the last young woman to have her heart broken there. Gina, you didn't let anyone down.' I still felt stung by all the lies she'd told, but I kept in my mind those simple childhood summers in Appledore. They were real, and somewhere here among the fake Holywood tinsel and red lipstick the real Gina was a good person who was a victim of a society – and perhaps a family – who expected too much.

This was my role model, the woman I'd aspired to, I felt I'd let her down by giving up on my dreams and getting married. But here she was, telling me she'd amounted to nothing, had lied about everything – and in a way she'd given up too.

'So, Ella, I didn't expect to have this conversation, and I haven't said what I came to say,' she said, shifting the conversation.

I swallowed hard. Not more revelations.

'Is it about Mum and Sophia…?'

'No. I want to talk about the sale of the café.'

For once, I wasn't sure if I did. Having waited to have this conversation, I wasn't sure I was ready while still reeling from her revelations. Could I take any more?

'Gina, I have to tell you, you've broken my heart by selling it, I was hoping to make a life here. Of course the café is yours to do with what you want, but I just feel so let down that you couldn't even talk to me… you promised you wouldn't do anything until we'd talked. I may have been able to rent it, even pay a mortgage on it once my house is sold. What if the buyers are just using the land? The Ice Cream Café could be rubble by the morning… along with my dreams.'

'Such a drama queen,' she laughed. 'I think you're more drama queen than I am.'

I didn't laugh, I just continued; 'But this means everything to me – it isn't just a summer job, a stroll down memory lane, this is my future.' I was having such a wonderful summer, feeling worthy, fulfilled, creative – I wanted to continue to spend my days mixing lavender with lemon, roses with elderflower and calling it Summer Garden. I had to develop the new cocktail ices, keep hosting the ever-growing slimming club ladies on a Monday evening. And who knew the things I was yet to do with Nutella and crushed Oreos? Then there was basil... sweet, pungent, aromatic basil blended with ice cream and strawberries... just thinking about all my plans and dreams, now dashed made me want to cry.

'Ella, I never doubted your passion... but...' she started, but I wasn't letting her have her say. I'd sat by while she'd sold our past and my future and hadn't even had the respect to let me know first.

'I can't believe you'd sell your childhood, mine too – our heritage, Gina. Our grandparents built their life, their business through sheer hard work, their sweat went into it and – forgive me for the drama – their dreams built that café.'

'I know... you don't need to tell me.'

She didn't seem moved by what I was saying, just vaguely irritated because I was talking so much, but I wasn't stopping.

'And quite frankly it makes me angry to think you can just flog it to the highest bidder... it's selfish... and...'

'Whoa, I'll have you know this isn't the highest bidder, I won't be making a fast buck out of *this* deal.'

That angered me even more – she was just taking the first bid, without even giving me the option to make an offer. 'So that's it? You're just going to take what little money you can and run away again. Well I hope it brings you some happiness, Gina.'

My pitch hadn't worked, my dreams of expanding the business and reliving the glory days of Caprioni's were now buried in the sand for good. It was all too late, I picked up my bag and my jacket and stood down from the bar stool to leave.

'Ella, don't go…'

'It's okay, it's your café – your money, I understand…' I snapped, pulling on my jacket.

'No you don't understand…' she was standing up now too, and holding both my shoulders, her face in front of mine.

'Have you signed over the café?'

'Yes… I have, but…'

'Then there's nothing else to say,' I tried to walk on, but she pulled me back.

'Ella, listen to me…'

'I listened to you for years, and I believed everything you said, but you let me down. I offered to buy the café from you but no, you might have to wait a little while – and that wasn't fast enough was it?'

'Ella, stop! Look, I have a plan, and it doesn't involve rubble, fast money, crushed dreams or any other goddamn purple prose you can come up with…' She opened up her large handbag, took out a brown paper envelope and put it down on the bar, giving it an affectionate stroke with her long, red talons before looking at me. 'Open it,' she said, looking directly at me, a serious look on her face.

I turned from her gaze to the envelope then picked it up, opened it and pulled out a sheaf of paper. It looked like legal documents and I couldn't really make out what it was until I saw the words Caprioni's Café and realised these were the documents of sale.

'Why are you showing me this?' I asked. 'It really isn't necessary.'

'It is, because it seems you've come to your own conclusions about me and the café. But the truth is, I haven't sold it to the highest bidder, I haven't "flogged" it off and I'm not here to ruin anyone's life. I didn't expect Mum to die so suddenly, and I didn't expect to inherit the café – I assumed it would be left to Roberta, or you. At first, I won't deny I considered the "highest bidder" option, who wouldn't? I'm alone, I don't have any money, I have no assets and nothing to keep me in the US any more, so why not take the money and start a new life somewhere else? But then, for once in my life, I didn't put myself first. I thought it was time to consider other people, so I didn't run away, I stayed and decided to do the right thing.'

'So what's this?' I said, lifting the sheets of paper.

'It's the café. I thought about what you asked for, and I've decided to take you up on your offer to buy it from me. I had Mr Shaw draw up the papers last week, but I wanted to make sure it was the right thing for you… and for me. It's my dream too to resurrect the café, to relive those heady days of my youth when I'd strut along the prom like the Queen of Appledore, you at my side, the little Princess.'

I was in shock, just clutching at random sheets of paper, unable to speak.

'I can see you're a little overwhelmed by it all just now, but take a look at the documents and get back to me. My suggestion is that we share ownership, and I'll be a sleeping partner – I need money to live off, I have no pension. Technically I'll be retired and just sweep in every now and then wearing something fabulous and bringing a little glamour to the place. Meanwhile, you buy your half off me and do all the hard work.'

I was still sitting down, dazed and thrilled all at once, but I didn't want her to leave. 'Gina, stay, let's talk about this… I'm delighted, and it's what I want. I really appreciate your offer – but I may not be able to afford it yet.'

'Just do as I ask, take a look at the figures and get back to me.'

I agreed, and put the envelope in my bag to study when I returned to the apartment, and then walked with her to her hotel. Along the way I was asking questions about how much and how long, but she just kept shaking her head and saying 'read it and get back to me'. She was determined not to discuss it there and then, so we arranged to meet the following day.

We said goodnight and I almost ran back to the apartment, still clutching the papers to my chest as I closed the front door and immediately searched through them for the magic figure that would either make or break my dream. It was all very well Gina agreeing to sell, but if she wanted a huge lump of money all at once, or was asking for high monthly payments then I couldn't accept her offer. I landed on the sofa, frantically riffling through the sheets of paper, each one more confusing than the last, filled with instructions, legal jargon, things I just didn't understand.

Then I saw it. Like a little star glowing in a jargon sea of mesmerising text was the figure £5. It said, 'Total payable – £5'. Had someone mistakenly left the noughts off, surely it was meant to be £5,000 or even £50,000?

Mum must have heard me come in and appeared at the top of the stairs.

'You okay, Mum?' I asked, unable to take my eyes from the documents, still looking for the answer.

She smiled. 'Yeah, shall we have a cuppa?'

'I think we need more than a cuppa, Mum, it's good news... it's great news, I think. Gina's going to let me buy half the café – she's going to keep the other half and we'll be joint owners, but I'm just trying to fathom this... it says the total payable is £5, but that can't be right can it?' I held up the papers as she walked down the stairs.

'So she's finally done something good in her life?'

'Mum, now is not the time for this... we all *have* to move on. I talked to her tonight and she never lived an amazing life in LA, she doesn't have a rich husband and a pool and she isn't working on a film with...'

'Leonardo DiCaprio?'

'No.'

'Damn, I was hoping I could get her to say he ate our ice cream, thought she might even bring him along to Appledore.'

I had to smile; having hated the idea of coming here Mum was now completely invested in the business and the life.

'You love it here, don't you?' I said.

She nodded as she sat down on the sofa next to me.

'So let's make this work – Gina is handing us the golden ticket, Mum, so let's just embrace it, embrace her and all be a family again?'

'It will never work, love, too much water under the bridge. But I do want to stay here – I'm needed on deck every morning, and Delilah needs me,' she smiled at a semi-drowsy Delilah lying on the sofa in her baby doll nightie, her little tail wagging sleepily at the mention of her name. Along with everything else, I was dreading Aarya coming back and wanting Delilah. We'd have quite the custody battle on our hands and a tug of love over a Pomeranian was the last thing I'd need after this summer. Mum was right at me, 'You couldn't do it without me, could you, Ella… the business?'

'No I couldn't,' I smiled, putting my arm around her, she felt small and frail like a little butterfly. She was right, I couldn't have done it without her. My ice cream was good, but Mum had made it better – she'd added ingredients, ideas and flavours. We really had become a team. Then there was the whole social media element which she managed so well, putting us in front of people, making the community and the tourists aware of our presence. And thanks to Mum and Delilah people travelled for miles to buy our ice cream and meet our little furry girl.

'Just think, Mum, we can make a go of the café – it'll be like old times.'

'I don't suppose you'll want to work with me if you've got Gina,' Mum suddenly said, sounding like a slighted teenager.

'Just because Gina's selling me half the café, it doesn't mean I'm going to be in her pocket. And as you say, I need you,' I added. 'Gina won't be doing much work, she's talking about retiring, being a sleeping partner.'

'Mmm she's been a sleeping partner to quite a few if you ask me.'

After all this time I still couldn't fathom my mother. Here was Gina offering me everything I'd asked for at what seemed to be only £5 and still she had to have a dig at her. Mind you I was still bemused by the £5 and desperately hoping it wasn't a typo. I decided not to respond to her comment and I think she realised it was perhaps time to begin to embrace what was happening, if not for her, for me.

'We did well today, very busy,' she said, and started telling me all about Delilah's antics and the way her 'Summer Surpise Sundae' had sold out and what a godsend Ben had been turning up when she was really busy. And listening to her I thought perhaps this summer stint was her La Scala audition. It wasn't about accolades, awards and money, it was about doing what made you happy, and singing and being sociable and the centre of attention was Mum's thing. I hoped I could persuade her to come on board with the café, maybe she just needed a bit more time and like she had with the van, she'd find her place.

Eventually she went to bed and I noticed Ben had called, so I returned the call.

I wrapped a throw around me and, wandering out onto the now chilly balcony, just hearing his voice warmed me.

He asked how things had gone with Gina and I gave him the edited highlights – it would take too long to tell him everything. In all honesty, I wasn't too proud of some of the things I'd said. Then again, perhaps Gina needed to realise I wasn't the same little girl she could walk over any more.

'That sounds like great news,' he said when I told him about the £5 offer on the café. 'So you're definitely staying here?'

'It looks like it. At the moment I can't believe it and keep wondering if I'll wake up tomorrow and it was all a dream.'

'Actually I have good news too. I rang earlier to tell you that Dad said if I stay around he'll start bringing me in on the big accounts.'

I didn't answer him, I didn't know what to say. I was happy that he cared about me enough to want to stay here – but this was overwhelmed by my feelings of guilt that he wasn't chasing his dream. And it would be my fault.

'Did you hear me? It means I could stay and build a career here, and we could…'

'I know… I know…'

'So is that not what you want?' He sounded confused, hurt even.

'It's not just about what I want. It's what you want that worries me. You're Ben, you don't *want* to be holed up in an office 24/7 working on big accounts – you want the open ocean.' He was doing this for me, but I still wasn't convinced this was the right thing for him at this time. Would he resent me for this further down the line?

'Ella, things change, and if it means I can stay on here and be with you, then it's worth the sacrifice.'

As much as I wanted him to stay, the very fact he'd used the word 'sacrifice' in the same sentence as 'be with you' made me feel like this wasn't right.

'Ben, I don't want you to sacrifice anything, and I don't want you to change. That's why we work, because you're you.'

'I'll still be me.'

'No you wouldn't. That's why I love you, Ben, because you do what you want, you don't conform, you're not like everyone else.'

'You said "love" then.'

'Yes I did. And I do love you, which is why you have to go to Hawaii, you have to see that ocean, take your last exam.'

'I can't leave you.'

'Yes you can.'

'But what if you meet someone else?' I recognised the fear and sadness in his voice, I felt it too.

'You might meet someone else too, but we can't worry about the future, we have to do what's right for now. You're not ready to stop in one place yet, Ben, and I don't want to be the one responsible for you being here instead of on a barrier reef in the Pacific, I couldn't bear the guilt.'

'Is that it then…?'

I felt tearful, but I had to be strong. 'It isn't just about what's right for you, I have to find my own barrier reef too and I'm not ready to be swallowed up into another life. I just want to be me for a while, see how I fit into the world.'

'I don't want to say goodbye,' he sighed.

'Let's not make this a final goodbye, let's make it "see you later",' I said. 'You do you for a while and I'll do me and then, who knows, at some point in the future we might bump into each other on a beach somewhere.'

His silence killed me, and I was almost tempted to say, 'Please, Ben, stay, don't go, let's buy a small cottage and live by the sea together forever.' But I had to remind myself that I didn't want Ben to settle down with me and then twelve months, two years or more down the line suddenly want to go again. If we met in the future, and if we felt the same, I would know this was it – there were no sacrifices, just love. But for now, I had to let him go, because that's what loving someone means.

He put down the phone and I felt sore and empty inside, my heart was broken and I knew Ben's was too – but it wasn't the right time. I loved him more than anyone I'd ever loved, and because of that I couldn't ask him to give up his dream. He'd helped me to achieve mine, so how could I? I knew there would be no one else for me, but he'd made my summer. He was perfect for that easy, laid-back time of sunshine, ice cream and kisses and who knew what our tomorrows might bring.

This whole summer adventure had felt unreal and it was hard to trust our feelings. It had been like a wonderful holiday romance where we'd been thrown together through timing and geography and as someone who'd only ever had one relationship before I had to ask if that was what love was? A chance meeting, a sliding doors moment of fate? My heart was filled with Ben, but my head wondered if our mismatched lives would be enough further down the line. For now we had to accept that we both had independent journeys that might or might not end up in at the same destination. Our lives might not fit, but when we were together our hearts knew how to dance.

Chapter Twenty-Four

A Brioche and Beyoncé Boost!

The following morning, Mum and I set off for the beach early and as we drove she talked about the business, well, about watermelon juice to be precise.

'Beyoncé's invested in a watermelon juice company, I think it will be huge, a million-dollar brand. Let's get ourselves some of the action before those fat cats suck it all up,' she was saying.

'You've been watching *The US Apprentice* again haven't you, Mum?'

She nodded.

'So, in Apprentice-speak, how would that *translate* for us – Beyoncé's investing in watermelons so we could make watermelon sorbet?' I said. I was trying to be enthusiastic, but couldn't think about Beyoncé or her bloody juice, all I could think was that Ben would be leaving soon.

'Yes… sort of. I was thinking, a tropical sundae, or a frozen watermelon smoothie – a Beyoncé Boost!'

I didn't point out that there may be copyright or some kind of ownership of the name Beyoncé – then again, how would she find out? I couldn't imagine Jay Z and Mrs Carter turning up in Appledore at my van any time soon.

'Have you heard from trailer trash this morning?' she suddenly said.

'Mum, if you mean Gina, that's unkind...'

She huffed and folded her arms in a defensive gesture, which wasn't easy with her bust and her seat belt. 'We haven't seen her for thirty years and suddenly here she is, giving away businesses like a bloody magnate.'

'She's sharing the family business, it's quite a different thing.' I said, determined now to go for it, this was a fantastic opportunity. Without Ben around I would throw myself into it – and hopefully take my mind off missing him.

'I'm your mother and you don't even care what I think about taking up her offer,' Mum was now saying. 'You've made up your mind and you won't listen to me. How do you think that makes me feel? Invisible.'

'I know, Mum, I know. You don't want me to do this – but I think it's the right thing to do. You wouldn't want me to miss a chance like this would you?'

The realisation that she might hold me back seemed to calm her down; 'Ella, I know it's your dream and of course I'd never stand in the way of that.' And just when I thought we were winning, she added, 'But don't expect me to speak to her. Ever!'

I'd had enough, I was about to lose Ben and I couldn't cope with playing Piggy in the Middle between Gina and Mum again over some ancient feud.

'*Why* won't you speak to her? Mum, why will nobody talk about these sodding teabags?' I asked.

She shot me a look, and despite being only 4 foot 10 and weighing about 7 stone I felt myself wither under her gaze. Mum wasn't to be trifled with. But this clearly was about more than teabags and if we were all going to be working together it was now necessary to find out just what had happened all those years ago.

'I'm not a child,' I said, 'though sometimes you still treat me like one. You can tell me, you know? I mean if for example someone in the family had an extramarital affair in 1970s I am old enough to deal with it.'

But she didn't answer and I just continued driving to the beach where we silently opened and set up our van for the day. We muddled along all morning, the weather was mixed and when it began to rain I became ridiculously excited imagining how all the people who weren't coming out onto the beach would soon be able to come to the café. For a moment I forgot we weren't really speaking.

'Mum, you will work with me, won't you, when the café's up and running?'

'I don't know, you'll have to check it all with she who sleeps with the fishes.'

'Thing is, as I mentioned, Gina wants to retire,' I said, ignoring her comment, 'so you won't have to see her often.'

'I don't intend to…'

'No, okay, but we will need to be civil, and I worry that if she's dead to you or sleeping with any fishes it might make for a bit of an… atmosphere if we're all in the café at the same time. I mean, Gina doesn't have a problem with you…'

'Oh she does. Ask her.'

'I have and she doesn't.'

'Nice to know I'm being talked about.'

I couldn't win, everything around Gina was toxic as far as Mum was concerned.

It was now August, and if I had my way the café would be open before September so we could make the most of any late holiday-makers, but we had to find a way of working together. If I could find out just what had gone on all those years ago I might be able to talk them into forgiving and forgetting whatever it was. I was imagining the opening of the café – and Mum and Gina fighting over who would cut the ribbon. The last thing we needed were photos all over the *North Devon Journal* of Mum threatening Gina with the ribbon scissors.

We closed a little earlier that day, the weather was turning and by 4 p.m. there weren't enough customers to justify standing in a van on a rain-swept beach with my grumpy mother. Her resentment truly blossomed when I told her I was meeting up with Gina after work to discuss the business.

As I walked into the Seagate pub to meet Gina, I felt rough, like I had the beginnings of flu, but it was probably because I was already missing Ben. I bought a coffee and took a window table looking out onto the promenade and tried not to think of him, I had to throw myself into this life now.

The pub was busy with tourists and day trippers eager to drink up the last of the summer before their minds were filled with new school shoes and office desks. The pub was one of those lovely seaside places where everyone was welcome, including dogs, so Delilah came along in a rather fetching sailor suit with jaunty hat. Life had been pretty hectic and emotional recently, so I'd been a bit lax on the Delilah front regarding photos and while waiting for Gina I took the opportunity for a quick doggie photo shoot.

Delilah was a natural and posed happily for photos as I snapped her looking out to sea from the pub window. It was a moody shot, the light was going and there was a glass of wine in front of her. I put it on Instagram with the caption, 'Delilah enjoying the last of the day and reflecting on the summer she's had in Appledore'. I was becoming quite poetic with my captions, I also sent the photo to Ben saying Delilah was missing him – I thought he'd understand what I was saying.

Gina arrived late – she was always late and always beautiful. Her blonde hair was caught in a messy updo, with dusty pink lips and perfectly manicured nails.

I had a new-found respect for Gina, despite the act, she'd been as insecure as the rest of us. And that vulnerability shone through when she'd finally told the truth about her life. I was proud of her for opening up instead of running away again. 'Your hair is lovely like that – you are so… LA,' I said, hugging her. 'I feel a bit dowdy without my make-up.'

'Honey, you always look gorgeous,' she smiled, holding my hand and stepping back to look at me. 'I could do your hair like this if you like,' she said, touching her head and taking her seat opposite me at the table.

'Thanks, but I'm going to get mine cut, very short – keep the blonde, but make it more my own, you know?'

She smiled a knowing smile and looked at me; 'Yeah, I know, I guess the butterfly got its wings.'

The waitress arrived with menus and before she could ask, Gina had ordered a bottle of Sauvignon Blanc and I was glad I wasn't driving the van that evening.

'Gina,' I said, once we'd ordered our food and the wine had arrived, 'I've considered your offer and I share your dream, but that's what I want – to share it. I don't want you to "give" me half the café or…' She tried to respond but I spoke over her, I'd thought about this long and hard and had to make my feelings clear on this without offending her. 'Gina, I really appreciate your offer, I feel like you're my fairy godmother – but I have to pay you for my half of the café. I don't actually have a lump of money, but my own house has just been sold and when I get the money I could give you something as a down payment, then pay you monthly for my half.'

'It all goes to you anyway when I'm gone, I've done a will and everything,' she said.

'That's very kind, too kind. What about your friends? And what if you meet someone and want to leave everything to him?'

She smiled. 'Oh I won't be leaving anything to some man. If I've learned one thing in my sixty years – it's that men are not worth giving anything up for. By the way, don't tell anyone how old I am,' she winked.

I smiled back. 'Thing is, Gina, I want to feel I played my part – to genuinely feel like it's mine, like I earned it.'

She looked at me. 'Stubborn madam aren't you?' she smiled. 'But I get you. You want to do this your own way, make your own mistakes with no safety net.'

I nodded. 'That's exactly it.'

'Ha, we're thrill seekers you and I – more alike than you'd think.'

I'd never considered myself a thrill seeker, but perhaps in some ways I was becoming one, I certainly wasn't frightened of life. And as for doing something every day that scared me – well, these days it was rare if I hadn't done something that petrified me.

'Okay, so to keep you happy, put some money in my account every month,' Gina was saying. 'I sure as hell could do with the money; we'll work out a figure between us.'

'Great, that feels right. Sophia wanted you to have the café, not me.'

'Yeah, but she left you a portion of the business with the van and you've proved yourself,' she smiled. 'That's all Mum wanted to see.'

'Do you think so?'

She nodded. 'Oh yes, I know so. Mum once told me that whoever took over the café must love it like she did, I guess she knew that probably wasn't me,' she looked at me and shrugged. 'I'm the black sheep,' she sighed, 'but you're the golden girl. I wouldn't have come back for a heap of rust, but you're more caring – you still have a soul, so Mum left the van to you and the café to me. She told Ronald Shaw her dearest wish was for a family reconciliation, but she thought I might sell the café and go back to LA. Apparently she said it didn't matter, she wouldn't be here and I couldn't break her heart any more.'

'Oh, I'm sorry, that must have been hard for you to hear.'

'It kinda broke my heart,' she said, her voice breaking slightly. 'That's why I couldn't go to her funeral, I couldn't face her even in death knowing how much I'd hurt her in life. But you changed all that, Ella – when I saw you working the van it made me think of the good old days and your genuine goodness seeped into these cynical mean old bones. I've been too long in the Wild West, competitive people fighting for crumbs, and ending up with nothing – just someone else's toilet to clean. I thought I was different, that I could leave everything behind and start a new red carpet life of glitz and glamour and recognition for my brilliance – but I've realised, you only get that kind of recognition at home. At the end of the day, it's only your family who truly applaud you.'

She looked like she was about to cry, and I too felt tearful, for all her talk and her sparkle, she'd lived quite an empty life.

'So, look at us now, drinking wine and talking about the café – it's exactly what Mum would have wanted,' she said, discreetly wiping her eyes and rallying Gina-style.

'It's what all of us want,' I said. 'And no one's happier than me that you're staying here for the applause.'

She smiled; 'I could have run away, like I ran away before – but you take all the guilt and the hurt with you, Ella – because in the end, you can't run away from yourself.' She gazed out through the window at the dusky sea and tears came back to her eyes; 'Doing this… with you, it feels like I'm doing something right – and for the first time in my life, I actually like myself.'

I felt so sad for her, yet happy that I could be part of this; 'I hope they're happy tears,' I smiled.

'Kind of, but there's always the guilt…'

'About what?'

'Oh my mum, your mum… you… Oh Ella, it's all such a mess. I get glimpses of calm, whispers of how it could be, how things might have been if I'd been a better daughter and then… how can I ever hope to clean my mess up?'

'Gina, it's okay. Your mum loved you, she was proud of you, when I used to come for my holidays here she'd talk about "my daughter back from the States", like you were the queen.'

'Did she? I never really saw it myself, looking into my mother's face reminded me of the mistakes I'd made, the regrets…'

'Our mothers had fallen out when I was a baby, right?' I started. 'So tell me, how on earth did Aunt Sophia get Mum to allow me to stay with you here on those summer holidays?'

Gina shuffled in her seat, took a large gulp of wine, then shook her head, but now she'd begun to open up I decided to press on.

'I mean, Mum never let me do anything,' I continued, taking a sip of wine while watching her face to see if she gave anything away, '… always scared something would happen to me – even Dad sometimes said, "Stop being so paranoid about our Ella, she'll be fine." And yet she still allowed me to stay here for two whole weeks.' I didn't know what I was chasing, but there was something tangled up in all this that was starting to come loose, if only I could unravel it.

Gina shrugged and looked relieved when our food arrived, something to distract me perhaps?

'So, where are you going to get your hair cut?' she asked now, trying to change the subject. My heart sank and I had to let go of the tangled mess, unable to work through it alone. Gina always felt safe talking about the superficial things in life, here she was safe and nobody could hurt her. The beauty makeovers, the hair colours, the celebrities and the lipstick shades of life were where she made her conversational home. She poured the wine and talked avidly about my hair, my bone structure and raved when I showed her the photo of a short, blonde, choppy cut I had lined up for myself on my phone.

'You will ROCK that,' she squealed, a little too loudly. 'I wanted to be a hairdresser,' she continued once she'd calmed down. 'I sometimes wonder if my life would have been better if I'd stayed here, become a hairdresser and married the love of my life.'

'I didn't realise,' I said. I'd no idea Gina had a serious boyfriend in Appledore. Even when I used to visit, there was a parade of boys, but she never seemed to go steady with anyone.

'Oh he was my first love. I adored him, but life and people came between us… you know how it is when you're young, you don't have any say.'

I nodded. 'Yeah especially with mothers like ours,' I laughed, wondering if this was part of the secret.

'Love can hurt, but I hope *you've* been happy, darling?' she suddenly said, a wave of sadness coming over her like a veil.

'Yes, I wasn't happy in my marriage but…'

'But you had a good family. Our mothers always meant well, you know, Ella…'

'Did they become involved?' I said, bringing the conversation back.

She looked at me slightly puzzled.

'I mean, your boyfriend, is he the reason you went to LA?'

She smiled and patted my hand; 'I went to LA for lots of reasons, and yes our mothers were very "involved",' she said, her face tightening.

'Did they stop you seeing him?' I was eager to know the details, perhaps this love story held the answer I was looking for.

'Oh apparently he wasn't good enough for me. My mum hated him, my dad said he was "a lout", Roberta threw him out of the café and his mother said I was a tramp. Probably as well we didn't marry, the wedding breakfast would have been an awkward affair,' she laughed. It was a hollow laugh, the one she used when she was trying to make light of something that upset her. It seemed she still carried the pain of this time just under the surface.

I was trying to piece everything together, but there was still something missing. I tried to push her, ask more about it, but she'd made it clear she was closed off to any questions. I watched her now, just knowing there was something my cousin wasn't telling me but decided to save my questions about her first love for another day, I could see in her eyes it was a painful recollection, and we directed our conversation onto happier things.

We ate our meal together continuing to talk through ideas for the café, her excitement was infectious, and we made so many plans. Mum had warned me that she would do this and then just as it seemed I could count on her she'd abandon the whole project. Before Gina came back I might have put this down to Mum being mean or jealous, but I now realised Mum knew Gina, and said these things to help me. Mum didn't want to see me hurt and disappointed, and forewarned was forearmed – so I chatted along enthusiastically, knowing that I could cope if she walked away. On a practical level I didn't need Gina, I knew I would be fine and so would the café if she ever decided to leave again.

'I want us to spend time together bringing our grandparents' dream back to life – I want it more than any part I've ever gone for. I know we can do this, Ella,' she was saying. And I loved hearing it. We wanted the same thing – even if it might be just for now.

But that night I didn't worry about the tomorrows, I drank wine and glowed in Gina's light, her eyes sparkling as she talked animatedly of the future, and of bringing our past back to life. I just hoped it was the past of shared fun and ice cream and not of family secrets and hate.

We were standing outside Gina's hotel saying our goodbyes after the meal when I saw Cocoa, the chocolate Labrador from the beach. I looked up from the dog, who'd recognised me and was wagging her tail, expecting to see her owner Peter, but a younger man was walking her that evening and I realised it was monosyllabic Marco from the café. As they came near I bent down to say hello and Cocoa went mad, throwing herself around like a puppy, delighted to see me, so I made a big fuss.

'Hi Marco, I know this dog… it's Cocoa,' I said, by which time I was almost straddling her as she pushed between my legs. 'I feel I need to point out that I don't usually accost strange dogs on the street,' I laughed, knowing that Marco would be pretty unimpressed – it seemed to be his default position.

'Whatever floats your boat,' he said, raising an eyebrow. 'She's my uncle Peter's dog.'

'Where's Peter tonight then? Is he down the pub?' I said, feeling like a local, knowing folk by their first name.

'No. He's dead.'

For a moment I thought Marco was just being Marco. Was he going to add 'tired' to the end of the sentence? But he didn't, he just stood there, his face like stone.

'Peter? Dead?' I said, repeating him and sounding like a surprised parrot. I've never been very good at handling death – who is? But now I was even clumsier than normal. 'But he was on the beach yesterday, what happened?'

'He died.'

He wasn't making this easy – but then Marco never did.

'Yes… you said, but… how.'

'Heart attack.'

'I'm so sorry… and he's your uncle?'

'Yeah.'

'And you're now looking after Cocoa?'

'Looks like it.'

'What's your name?' Gina suddenly said.

'Marco.'

'Your surname?'

'Lombardi. Do you want to know anything else?' he grumbled.

I sensed tension, but after a few glasses of wine I was feeling warm and kind, even towards Marco. After all he had just lost his uncle so it was understandable he'd be spikier than usual – if that was possible.

'I didn't realise you were Italian,' I said. 'We must arrange to meet up with you, about the café?'

'It's closing.'

'No it isn't,' I announced. 'We are reopening it.'

Marco half-smiled, which was clearly a big deal. I'd met Marco a couple of times but never seen the glimmer of a smile.

'Nice to see you smile,' I said, pointedly, 'we'll need lots of smiles if you're staying on at the café. We're going to redecorate, bring in a new menu, fresh ideas… ice cream cocktails, brioche…'

'I can make brioche. I'm a baker.'

'Oh I didn't realise.'

'Sophia took me on when I was eighteen, paid for my day release training at college….'

This was the most I'd ever heard him speak. And perhaps it explained why he appeared so down; he was disappointed with the way his life was turning out. He'd hoped for an exciting future using his skills, being part of something – and here he was alone in a café going nowhere. Until now.

'Well I'm so glad we had this chat, why don't I pop in tomorrow and we can have a proper chat?'

He nodded, and there was an almost smile again.

'Such a shame about your uncle,' I sighed.

By now Cocoa was straining at the leash, she had seen a greyhound across the road and was keen to make his acquaintance so I said goodbye to Marco and turned to say goodbye to Gina. Her happiness from only minutes before had suddenly transformed into a shivering mess.

'Gina, what's the matter?' Had I said too much to Marco? Perhaps she didn't want me discussing business outside a hotel in the dark, which I could understand.

'I'm fine, darling, I'm just cold, it's really chilly and I need to get to my bed. Night night,' she kissed me on the cheek and suddenly disappeared into the hotel. I reassured myself this was perfectly natural, but she seemed odd.

Walking back to the apartment, I tried not to dwell on Gina's weird goodbye. Instead I just wanted to imagine the café, in pink and white, Reginaldo in matching colours, bunting rippling in the breeze, standing proudly by.

I phoned Ben as I wandered through the winding roads and told him all my news.

'I'm happy for you,' he said, 'you deserve this.'

'And I'm happy for you, when do you go?' I asked, my heart crumpling like tissue paper.

'I'm flying out first thing.'

'So soon? I thought you might be here a few more days…' I felt the ground moving underneath me, my world was shaky without him.

'There's nothing to stay for – and I hate goodbyes.'

'Oh Ben, I'll miss you,' I said, knowing this was the right thing for both of us – for now. 'But if you ever come back you've got ice cream for life at the café.'

'I'll miss you too, babe. And don't worry I will saunter into that café and sweep you off your feet all over again – after a hazelnut crunch of course.'

'Of course,' I laughed, my voice cracking. 'I can't wait, but I'm still going to work some days in the van if the weather's good, so look for me on my beach.'

'I will, and if you find yourself driving aimlessly, make it a road trip to Hawaii,' he said. 'I'll be waiting on my beach with a bowl of water for Delilah and an ice cold mai tai for you.'

I turned off my phone and walked slowly home. I couldn't think of anywhere I'd rather be than on that beach with Ben in Hawaii but my future was here, waiting for me under a big Devon sky.

Chapter Twenty-Five

An Ovaltine Tin of Secrets and Lies

I walked slowly back to the apartment. I wanted my eyes to dry and to be composed when I arrived home, in case Mum was up; I didn't want her to see me upset. I hoped she'd be up because I wanted to ask her about Gina's first love and to tell her all about the plans for her to work in the café. Mum loved the van, but I think she found it a little cramped on chilly days and would welcome the comfort of the café, where she could help out behind the counter in the warm. I didn't want her working too hard, so would make sure we had enough staff so she could be the maître d', welcoming people to their seats, chatting and just being the friendly face of Caprioni's.

'Coffee, Mum?' I asked, but looking at her, I immediately sensed her mood. Dark.

She shook her head, and I went and turned the kettle on, taking just one mug from the cupboard. She wasn't going to ask me about the café so I thought the best thing would be to just tell her, get it out there and she could dissect, warn and post-mortem all she liked. But I wasn't giving up on this dream.

I poured water on my coffee and went through into the living room where she sat on the big white sofa alone. She looked so tiny and forlorn, I was taken aback, so sat down and hugged her.

'Mum, I want you on this journey with me,' I said gently. 'I am so excited about this – and so is Gina, but she isn't you, she won't take your place. You're right about her, she isn't a hard worker,' I said. 'We can't count on Gina for the hard graft… but I'm counting on you to be there for me.'

'Gina was never around for the hard graft or the hard yards.'

My heart sank, I didn't want another anti-Gina diatribe. 'I know what you're saying and I agree, she'll probably fly away, and I'm ready for that, Mum – emotionally and practically.'

'I hope so, love,' she shrugged, but thankfully didn't add any more vitriol. She hadn't said she wouldn't work in the café either so I clung to this tiny flake of hope and continued. 'We talked tonight about working the van in other areas, it's our opportunity to spread the word – and if I'm going to be working the van, we'll need you in the café.'

I thought this would make her happy, but she seemed a bit defeated that night, like nothing mattered.

'Let's see shall we, love? I'm tired, it's been a long day,' she said, before kissing me on the cheek and heading upstairs.

I knew Mum would come round eventually, but could she and Gina ever be reconciled? When I'd questioned Gina, she'd taken on the same mantra as Mum that the past should stay in the past. But there was something tickling the back of my mind. Like chocolate and chilli, the first mouthful smooth and delicious segueing into something unexpected, slightly dangerous.

I was pondering this as I sat on the sofa cuddling Delilah in her nightie. I knew I wouldn't sleep, I was missing Ben and still going over the conversation with Gina, so I headed for the kitchen. I thought I'd seen Ovaltine in one of the cupboards, God knows how old it was but if it wasn't too out of date I would make myself a comforting drink.

Aunt Sophia had always given me Ovaltine when I'd stayed with her and couldn't sleep. I'd shared a room with Gina in their home over the café and Sophia would make me a camp bed. I'd lie there waiting for Gina to come home from dancing or a date, being scared of the David Bowie poster on the wall, a man/woman with one weird eye, the face painted in a jagged line – I thought it was a creature from space. I was always relieved when Gina arrived home in her sparkly shoes and beautiful dresses. I remembered her leaning out of the window smoking into the dark night, and then she'd tuck me in and kiss my forehead. I'd close my eyes, but the wonderful scent of perfume and alcohol mixed with woody smoke told me she was close.

Sometimes though Gina didn't come home and I'd wake in the night and look at the alarm clock by her bed. Once I could read the time it would worry me if it was after midnight, and I'd pad into Aunt Sophia and Uncle Reggie's room and say I couldn't sleep. Sophia would carry me down into the kitchen at the back of the café and take down the huge, catering size tin of Ovaltine. She'd always sing the song from the TV ad, 'I Can't Get over Ovaltine'. This always made me laugh and I'd join in until the hypnotic effect of the slow, soporific stirring of warm milk kicked in and my eyelids drooped.

As much as I loved being there, I was very young and without Gina in the bedroom I soon became homesick for Mum and Dad, but the Ovaltine always helped.

I remembered this as I rummaged around in the cupboards and after a while I came upon a catering tin of the stuff just like Sophia used to have at the café. I had to laugh, it was bright orange, enormous and still bore the trademark picture of the farm girl holding a wheatsheaf on the front. This had to be about forty years old, so I wouldn't be drinking it, I couldn't imagine what the Ovaltine would be like inside. It might send me to sleep, but would I ever wake up again? I reached for the tin with both hands, expecting the weight of this huge can of powdered drink to be something to grapple with, but was surprised to feel no weight at all. I brought it down from the shelf, looking at the long-forgotten label that resurrected those bittersweet memories of being soothed by my aunt when I was little and homesick.

I assumed the can was empty, but this was a piece of history and it might make a nice container for something. The retro style was very popular and perhaps I could use it at the café – a memento of Sophia perhaps? So I tried to open it. After breaking a knife on the lid, I tried the handle of a spoon and eventually managed to prise off the lid. Peering inside, instead of emptiness, I saw layers of faded pink tissue paper, which I peeled away gently, like rose petals, until my fingers reached the centre. There sat a tiny pair of pink knitted bootees, which I touched gently then lifted out from the crisp paper, puzzled and enchanted by these exquisite little woolly shoes. Then inside the paper scrunches, I spotted a little square card edged in silver which read;

19 October 1973

To my little girl on her 1st birthday. You'll never know how much I loved you. I may be far away, but know that I'm thinking of you every day and you'll always be here in my heart.

Love Mummy

Xxxx

I held the bootees to my chest, my heart beating. They weren't from my mother to me because Mum had never been 'far away' but something had been buried very deep in this family – because 19 October 1973 had been my first birthday.

Chapter Twenty-Six

Bruised Knees and Broken Hearts

'But... but if I tell you, I'll lose you,' my mother was saying as I stood in her bedroom holding the bootees. I'd gone straight up to Mum's bedroom and thankfully she was still awake, because I couldn't wait until morning to ask her what the hell this was about.

'Mum... I won't judge you, whatever it is. You're my mum and I love you.'

'I always knew this would happen, that you'd find out in the end. I wanted to tell you but Sophia said it would be best to make a clean start, your dad and I should move. "Just go..." she said, but you can't escape it can you, however far you run?'

'Mum, you're scaring me, escape what?'

I held my breath as Mum sat up in bed and put on her dressing gown.

'Is this about you and Sophia?' I asked.

'No, love, it's about you and Gina.'

'What is it, Mum? I don't...'

'The bootees,' she whispered, as she touched them lightly, like they might break. 'They're from Gina.'

'Gina? To a baby… her baby…?' I suddenly felt the ground move under me. 'Oh God… am I Gina's baby?'

Mum nodded.

I felt the earth tilt, everything I knew or thought I knew was suddenly washed away. 'My dad?'

'Some lad she was seeing…'

Then I realised, it must have been the boy Gina had told me about earlier that evening. Her first love, the love of her life – they'd had me and that's why it all became such a mess.

'She can only have been… sixteen, seventeen?'

'She was sixteen when she had you. It was a long time ago, she wanted to keep you and Sophia thought it could all work out. But times were different – oh the shame, I felt so sorry for our Sophia, good Catholic family, well-known local business, but Sophia said if she wanted to keep the baby she could…'

'So why? What…?' I sat on the end of the bed, my whole world had changed in a matter of seconds, my whole life had been a lie. Was I still me? And who was 'me' anyway now?

'Gina struggled, she was so young she couldn't look after a baby, and she still had a life to live. Sophia didn't want the father involved, said it would make everything more complicated. But Gina fought her to see him, I think he left, his parents sent him away – and then once you were born, she didn't want to sit at home all day with a new baby. Gina was young, she wanted to be out with her friends, drinking, dancing. I always knew it would be difficult, and Sophia was busy with the café, so as me and your dad lived nearby I offered to help. I was recovering from losing my own baby and when Gina had hers I was ready… so ready, I remember holding you in my arms for the first time and knowing I loved you instantly, as if I'd given birth to you myself. I started looking after you, until Sophia stopped it, she said it was preventing Gina from "bonding with her baby",' she said this in Sophia's voice, she'd obviously been hurt by this comment. I just sat on the edge of the bed listening, unable to move or think, just trying to take it in.

'Then one evening I noticed Gina had forgotten to take a blanket with her when she'd picked you up from mine earlier – I still looked after you when Gina wanted a break, we just didn't tell Sophia. So I popped to the flat over the café to drop it off – I was worried you'd be cold. Sophia and Reggie were both busy working so I just went up the stairs, but when I got there Gina wasn't around. At first I worried she'd taken you out with her – she'd done that before. But no, not this time, she'd gone one worse and actually left you alone, just lying in your cot. You were screaming, really distressed and hungry and judging by your nappy she'd been gone a while. I had to tell Sophia, she was furious and when Gina came back that night Sophia was waiting for her. She gave her an ultimatum, she said Gina had made her choice and she had to take responsibility, and if she didn't then Sophia would kick her out.'

'And so what happened?' I heard myself ask, a cracked raw voice coming from somewhere deep inside, still seeking answers.

'Well Gina was only seventeen, she wanted to meet friends and go dancing… always loved the nightlife did our Gina,' Mum added, in an aside, unable to resist making the point that Gina's priorities were, in Mum's view, rather skewed. Even in all this I realised I'd never heard her refer to Gina as 'our Gina' before.

'So, what happened?' I said, again, the only sentence I could come up with, my head devoid of any words other than the ones needed. My mouth was dry, and I could feel my pulse beating in my head.

'Well Gina did what she does best – she kicked off didn't she? The minute you try to pin down someone like Gina she rebels, and Sophia and Gina were both fiery, and both pig-headed. I see it in you sometimes,' she said.

Oh God, so this meant Sophia wasn't my aunt any more, she was my grandma. I was desperate to listen to Mum but was finding it hard to concentrate as the implications became clear. I tried to recalibrate my life and the relationships in it, unable to comprehend the changed family dynamics this news had brought with it.

'Anyway, things limped on for a few weeks, but Sophia and I were worried about you and about Gina. I would spend most days with you when Sophia was working and she would be there in the evenings, but Gina was like a caged lion pacing up and down all the time. In the end she realised what keeping her baby meant – and though she loved you, she couldn't look after you and she just ran. I'll never forget Sophia calling me in tears, it was just before your first birthday, Gina had gone missing along with money from the till. I went straight round there to look after you so Reg and Sophia could search for her, they got the police involved and everything. But Gina had planned her escape, she'd met a photographer who said she looked like a film star and he took her to London. From there they got passports and the next thing we knew she's calling from America and reversing the charges.'

'And that was it?' I wished I could say I felt something, but I couldn't. I was numb, just waiting for all this information to hit me so I could begin to work through it. Everyone around me had changed, my mother was my aunt, my cousin was my mother. Did this mean I wasn't me any more?

I looked at Mum… at the woman I knew as Mum, and she continued. 'Are you okay, love?'

I nodded, 'Yes, just tell me what happened next.'

'Well, Sophia was inconsolable at losing Gina, and there was I with three miscarriages behind me… and then Gina called one night to ask how you were. And out of the blue she asked if I'd take you.'

Oh God, it was all becoming clear now.

'It made sense, love – it was like fate – me without a baby, Gina with one she couldn't look after. Sophia had the café and Reggie took ill around that time, probably from the stress of it all.'

'And so Gina gave me away?'

'Gina parted with you because she loved you and wanted you to be safe and happy. She knew I had the time and all the love, and asked only that I let her have some time with you whenever she came back to Appledore. But when your dad got the chance of work in Manchester we moved. Sophia wasn't happy, she felt I was taking you away from her and also making it difficult for Gina to see you if she came back to Appledore and you were miles away up North. Sophia agreed to us moving, but it caused bad blood between us and she resented me for taking you away. But your dad and me wanted a fresh start and in a new city we didn't have to tell everyone you weren't ours; people just accepted us as a little family. That was all we ever wanted. And we were happy, for a while – but when Sophia told Gina she was furious we'd taken you away from Appledore. She and Sophia then came up with this idea and insisted we bring you back each year. They said if we didn't they'd call Social Services and get you back. We didn't know how serious they were, but they'd talked to Ronald Shaw about getting you back through the courts, so we didn't dare risk you not seeing her.'

'So that's why you allowed me to visit alone each year?' And that was why Mum didn't like Ronald Shaw, Ben's dad and told me not to listen to gossip in Appledore.

'Yes, we had no choice, but we didn't want solicitors involved, she just had to trust us that we'd bring you every year. Part of the agreement was that I wasn't around, Gina wanted you all to herself.'

I realised then just how much it must have torn Mum apart to leave me here every summer. 'You must have been distraught, worrying each time that she might want me back… run away with me even?'

Mum nodded; 'It was agony, not only did we miss you, we worried Gina would suddenly take you back to America… that was my greatest fear. I think the stress of it all killed your dad in the end, he loved you so much and Gina was always a dark shadow hanging over us. Even on the happy days – your birthday, Christmas, a holiday – it was there in our minds, if this might be the last time. As Gina grew older I could see how you two bonded, she was always fun, young, sparkly. She didn't have to tell you to do your homework, she could just be the fun "cousin". And of course you were like a moth to a flame, which is why I worried that if you knew the truth, you would choose to be with Gina. So I went from worrying she'd take you when you were little, to worrying you'd want to leave us…'

'Oh Mum…'

'I know it wasn't fair on you, I never gave you a minute's peace or freedom to make your own mistakes – because for me the price was too high.'

I understood in a way, and as a mother myself I think I'd have behaved in the same way Mum had.

'But my birth certificate… it has yours and Dad's name on it?' I said, still questioning this, still unable to really believe.

'It was the seventies, love, there were no computers, so forms went missing, or were processed without too many questions. Your dad knew someone at the registry office who was happy to put our names on the birth certificate for a few quid. It was all fine, until the thing we'd feared most happened – Gina wanted you back and this time she meant it.'

Mum wiped her eyes with a now well-worn tissue and continued.

'As bad as Gina could be, there was no doubting her love for you, Ella. She just had this unrealistic idea about motherhood, she wanted the pretty dresses, the birthday parties with pink candles, holidays by the sea. But she had no idea about what being a real mum entailed. I think by the time you were twelve she thought you'd fit into her life. You were a pretty little thing and I just knew she saw you like an accessory, a nice new handbag to show off to her friends. I knew she'd soon get bored with the responsibility, she's always done exactly what she wanted to do without any recourse. I blame Sophia – she spoiled her, allowed her to run wild while she was building up the business.'

I could see now why Gina ran away, she followed the brightest star, enjoyed the new toys, but abandoned everyone and everything when she'd had enough.

'So is that why I stopped coming here when I was twelve, you thought she was going to try and take me back?'

'Yes, she went to see Ronald Shaw and he talked to her about taking your dad and me to court to get you back – and she'd have done it too. My own sister was prepared to have my child taken from me – just because her daughter wanted a new trinket to play with. Like I say, she'd never said no to Gina and even now with the café, when she knew Gina wouldn't be consistent, that she was likely to walk away, she still backed her.'

I shook my head, this was wrong on Sophia's part, and as much as I'd loved Gina, it would have destroyed me to suddenly be taken from my mum. I sighed. 'What a mess.'

'I felt such betrayal, when it suited them I'd looked after you. I'd brought you up, loved you, made you safe, I've been a good mother, haven't I, Ella?'

I nodded, the need for reassurance now clear. 'Oh Mum that must have been terrible, so what happened?'

Tears were now falling down her cheeks. 'Well, your dad stepped in… he knew what Gina was like and he wasn't as easily swayed as Sophia. I was in a terrible state and he arranged for me and Gina to meet and he sort of mediated. He told me to be honest with Gina and I was, I said as one mother to another she knew the pain of losing her child, so how could she do this to me? I loved you as much as she did, but more than that I had been prepared to change my life to accommodate a child. I said you were loved and happy and settled, you had friends and a life up North and no mother would tear you away from that. I pointed out that Gina had given you away as a baby out of love – but how would she explain that to you? Typical Gina, she hadn't thought it through – she hadn't considered your feelings in all this. In the end your dad had the final say, and before we left he just said, "Gina, if you love her, let her be," and that was the last time we saw her. Until now.'

'So that was it?' I knew the right thing had been done, even now in the early hours of knowing it was clear Gina wouldn't have been able to care for me like Mum had. But still it hurt to discover my story was that my mother had given me away without a fight.

'About six months after that she called me. I almost died, I thought she'd changed her mind again and I felt sick when I heard her voice. It was late at night in America, I think she'd had a drink, and all she said was "Please don't ever tell Ella about me, I couldn't bear it if she hated me." She said she didn't want you growing up thinking badly of her... "just let me be her cousin," she said.'

I sat holding the bootees, working out the Rubik's cube of the past, of my life. Only now did all the letters make sense – they weren't Sophia's letters to Gina, they were Gina's letters to me.

Mum went on to tell me how Gina had lived for my holiday visits, often going without, so she could afford the airfare home to wait in the Ice Cream Café for her daughter. The last fortnight in August – every year.

'But the year after all the trouble, I told her you didn't want to visit any more, that you had a life at home and were bored in

Appledore. I couldn't risk her changing her mind again and wanting you back and I know it broke her heart, but I had to choose between your heart and hers. You were my priority, because I was your mum… I *am* your mum. I couldn't trust Gina again, or Sophia, and it would have destroyed both you and me to be parted. Even if Gina stood by her word, you were now a teenager, and you might be seduced by Gina's lifestyle, her glamorous ways, I couldn't risk it. She would have broken your heart, love – and mine.'

'I can't believe I didn't know.'

'Know what? That I'm not your biological mother? Would it have made any difference? I learned the day I took you home, it isn't about giving birth it's about being there and keeping you safe and fed and loved and happy.'

And I knew just what she meant. It was those first days at school when you leave your child at the door in tears, the bruised knees, the mean girls in the playground, the nasty colds and broken hearts. She was there for all that – keeping me safe, a box of plasters and a glass of milk – always there making sure I lived a good life…

'I hope I was a good mum?' she said, her voice small, almost a whisper.

'You were… you are. The best, Mum, the best,' I said the familiar line smiling through my tears.

I'd been trying to find me while I was in Appledore, but I didn't expect to find another mother. Was this the reason I'd always felt so drawn to the place, drawn to Gina? I'd always known there was a secret, one that had crushed my family like a huge, cleaving wave. I thought it might be about infidelity, lost love, even murder – and yes, for a while back there in the nineties I thought it might have actually been about teabags. But never this. Never a secret about me.

'I feel so guilty,' she said, tears now filling every crack in her face. 'But I couldn't risk losing you. It was my worst fear... I just wanted to be your mum, Ella.'

Her vulnerability was raw, no more drama, no TV catchphrases, just my mum, tear-stained, her heart swollen with love. How could I ever deny her that?

I leaned in and hugged her and we held onto each other for some time.

'Mum, I need to think about all this and I'll have to talk to Gina. Things have changed – but not between you and me, our lives together have always been so big and full and happy. I can't erase that, nor would I ever want to. I don't know what would have happened if you hadn't chosen to be my mum, but I know I couldn't have picked a better one.' We sat together on the sofa talking until very late and Mum went back to bed, leaving me alone to think about everything that had been said.

After a while, I had an urge to call Gina, I had to find out what happened from her. I was crying and said I needed her to come over immediately, and she got out of bed and ordered a taxi in the middle of the night.

'I know everything,' I said as I opened the door. I didn't need to say any more, she nodded and walked through.

'In a way it's a relief,' Gina sighed.

She sat down and I asked her many questions and she told me the same story Mum had, but from her perspective. And when she'd finished I had one more question to ask.

'My dad... who was he?'

'A boy... the one I told you about, the love of my life. But we were too young and my parents too Catholic, his parents hated me, they sent him away,' she had tears in her eyes.

'Did he ever come back? Do you know what happened to him?'

She stared ahead for a few seconds, trying to summon up the strength to explain. 'You've met him... recently I think.'

I was shocked, my stomach lurched. I'd met my own father? Wouldn't I have known? Would I not have felt something? 'Who?'

'It was Peter... Peter Lombardi.'

'Peter...? Peter from the beach with the dog, Cocoa?' I said, trying to assimilate this information. But no sooner had I heard it than I had to discard it. 'Gina... he died... the day before yesterday.'

She nodded. 'It broke my heart to hear that,' she said, big tears falling down her face.

'Oh Gina I'm so sorry,' I said. So that's why she was unnerved when Peter's nephew Marco had told us the news outside the hotel.

'When I came back, I asked around about him, if he'd ever married. "Carried a torch for a girl who used to live here," the guy in the pub said, and I knew that girl was me. I saw him on the beach with his dog, but it was from afar, he hadn't seen me. I loved Peter, I don't think I've ever loved anyone since – he used to write me poetry, long reams of beautiful words,' she sighed. 'It breaks my heart to think of the life I could have had, safe here with him... and you. When I'd seen him walking along the beach, that's why I had to take off for a few days, I had to think about what I wanted to do. And I thought about it and decided to give it a go, to stay in Appledore, sort the café stuff out with you and find him again. I was going to wander down onto the beach one morning when the tide was out and say "Hi, remember me…?"' Her voice cracked, she started to cry and I gave her a tissue and put my arm around her.

'I had this stupid idea about us even getting back together, Peter and me… I knew he was single, I'd asked around. Silly isn't it? He probably hated me for going away… but I just had this feeling about fate, you know?'

I nodded, and let her continue speaking.

'I thought wouldn't it be amazing if the three of us were all here, a family back where we started, where we should be… together at last.'

'Gina, he didn't hate you… he told me he used to write poetry for his sweetheart. He talked fondly of her and said she wasn't here any more, and he missed her so much – I assumed she'd died. But he was talking about you.'

'Oh Ella you've no idea how happy that makes me – I thought he'd never forgiven me for leaving. I wrote to you both when I left… he never responded. I sent them care of my mother because I didn't know where he was. When he never wrote back I assumed he'd forgotten me or hated me for leaving – but I wonder if he ever received any of my letters,' she said.

'There were lots of letters unopened from you in a carrier bag I foundbehind the freezer on the van. I imagine there are all kinds of letters in there, possibly the ones you sent to Peter. I can understand why Sophia would keep your letters to me, but why would she keep his?'

'It was all tied up in the shame of me being an unmarried mother, she wanted better for me. I think she hoped I'd become a film star one day and we could forget all about what had happened. She wanted to be proud – I wish I could have done that for her. I was a rubbish mum and a rubbish daughter,' she sighed.

'Gina, I love my mum and she'll always be my mum… but I'm sure in the right life you would have been a wonderful mother,' I said, putting my arm around her.

'I'd been a bit stupid in the past, tried to get you back, fight Roberta for you, but I loved you. I was bereft and I resented Roberta for being a good mother when I couldn't, yet I knew you were safe and happy which is all that ever mattered. To hear you say I'd have been a good mother means more than you'll ever know,' she smiled. And she looked happier than I'd seen her since she'd arrived.

We talked for a long time, both working through what the night had brought with it. We talked of the past and the future, and over the next few hours we began to see each other differently, but the same. She wasn't my cousin any more, nor was she my mother – but we still loved and cared about each other and this was the beginning of a new chapter.

Eventually, as the sun rose, Gina turned to me. She placed her hand on my wet cheek and smiled; 'You have his eyes, darling,' she said.

And I cried; for the past, for my childless mother, Sophia's lost daughter and Gina's lost baby. And then I cried for a man I never knew who'd died – who I'd met by chance on the beach, and who happened to be my father.

Chapter Twenty-Seven

Rolling Back the Years

Mum came downstairs to find us both asleep on the sofa and instead of huffing and tutting and complaining about Gina's presence, she covered us up and when we woke she made us breakfast.

I didn't open the van that day, we had 'a family meeting' instead where Gina, Mum and I discussed how we would move forward. Gina was now back in our lives and we had to find a way to make it work and for them to not hurt each other any more.

Once we'd worked our way through the tears and the blame and some forgiveness, we tried to make the best of the mess we were in. I knew it would take time, they would both slip, but perhaps now the secret was out, nothing was festering, feelings could be aired and they could move forward. I also had to move forward, and try not to dwell too much on the fact that Ben was leaving for Hawaii today, but it was so difficult. Everything reminded me of him, the beautiful ice cream cone necklace he gave me, the coffee machine he'd fixed, the freezer, ice cream, the sea. For me he was blue skies, Appledore and strawberry ice cream, and I would miss him like hell.

Over the next few days, Mum and Gina and I worked through plans, discussing colour schemes, menus, ice cream flavours and staffing. Despite it being prickly in parts, I was glad of their company because mediating a potential cat fight took my mind off Ben. It was interesting to see how the dynamics shifted and changed as the three of us struggled with new roles, while falling into familiar ones from the past. At one point I suggested rude ice cream cocktails and Gina swore making Mum reprimand us both affectionately. For the first time I saw a glint of something other than hate for Gina in my mother's eye and wondered if maybe she hadn't lost a daughter – but found another one.

After our day of talking – both business and personal – Gina suggested we go for drinks. Mum declined, she was tired and said she'd head back, and for once seemed okay about us going out together without her. I suppose her worst fear had already happened; Gina had returned and I'd found out the truth. But Mum had also realised that the consequences weren't horrific, she hadn't lost me as she feared she might. So Gina and I went to the pub, had a couple of drinks and talked, and then we laughed a lot – it felt good.

'Don't you two stay out so late again like you did last night,' Mum said the following day over early breakfast on the patio. 'I was worried to death until I heard you both stagger in at midnight.' Gina and I giggled, we had no problem playing the roles of 'naughty girls', reliving our teenage years and having the security of Mum to come home to.

There was a lot of work ahead to get the café reopened by the middle of August, but I was determined and over the next couple of days threw myself into it head on. Meanwhile, Mum's marketing expertise was in overdrive, she'd called the local papers, arranged a 'glamour' shoot for Delilah in the café with *Designer Doggie* magazine. She was Instagramming, Facebooking, Tweeting and even talking to Akahito her Japanese director friend about doing a reality show set in the café. Mum and Gina also bonded over a shared love of *The Sopranos* and *Mob Wives* – which I believe helped them to express themselves. There would for a long time be a residue of hurt and blame in their relationship, and often their bickering was real, but expressed in their own Mafia-speak it was funny and seemed harmless – I think!

'I'm street, so look both ways before you cross me,' Mum would say to bat Gina down and Gina would rise with a sassy shot across her bows like: 'Don't come for me bitch!' Which was hilarious, and they'd found a way to dance around each other and rub along in those sometimes painful, early days.

During this time I kept in touch with Ben, telling him the story as it unfolded, he said it was like a soap opera and couldn't believe all that had happened.

'I worry about you, I can come back,' he offered, 'just say the word and I'll be there.' But I wouldn't let him, this wasn't our time, I had too many complex relationships to work out before I was ready to add a man to the mix. I missed him, but the café reopening kept me busy and distracted along with all the ongoing 'relationship management' of Mum and Gina aka 'Mob Wives'.

During this time, Mum manned the van while Gina and I breathed life into the café, painting the walls peppermint, buying new, candy pink tables and rolling back the years. I had my hair cut and wore rings on my fingers and toes, and I was happiest walking around barefoot these days. My bohemian self was finally emerging, and after everything that had happened it seemed like nothing scared me any more. When you find out your mother isn't your mother, nothing surprises you ever again.

Of course in the middle of all this was Peter's funeral, which was incredibly tough. Gina and I went together, we stayed apart from the family who had no idea of our connection and probably just assumed we were paying our respects as local residents. It bonded us even more to share our grief for him, and for a life that might have been, if things had been different all those years ago. I found it hard to believe the lovely, gentle man I used to talk to on the beach was actually my biological father, some of the mourners my blood relatives, but in a small way it helped me to say goodbye.

Once work started on the café I threw myself into it and barely had a chance to catch up with my feelings, I was so consumed with the reopening. I was also keen to make up for lost time with Gina, aware that she might not stick around – and I could handle that, because I knew my mum would be there for me. It was a fine balance – I felt like I was managing international negotiations and at times 'the talks' almost collapsed. But we were all on a learning curve and Gina was trying to see things from Mum's perspective and Mum was being more sensitive to Gina's difficult and shifting role. Meanwhile I just woke every morning in shock, unable to get used to the strangeness and trying to come to terms with who I was.

'You've dealt with this so well,' Mum said to me one afternoon as we worked together in the van. It was a Saturday and busy on the beach so as Gina took deliveries for the café opening I spent a couple of hours helping Mum.

'I had no choice,' I said. 'I had to deal with it – though it still doesn't feel real. At the moment I'm just enjoying the fact that Gina's come back into our lives and we're a family again, I try not to think about the other thing... because the idea you're not my biological mum doesn't work for me.'

'Nor me,' she sighed. 'I used to watch all those programmes on TV about long-lost children turning up in their mother's lives and I used to think about Gina turning up in ours. It scared me to death, but instead of facing it, telling you – I put all that fear onto Gina and blamed her and Sophia. But you were Gina's baby and Sophia's granddaughter... they loved you too, and in my fear I was the one who took you away.'

I should have been told – one of them should have realised the impact this would have on me. But I couldn't spend the rest of my life blaming other people, there had been too much of that and now we were a family again I didn't want to lose anyone.

'You did what you thought was right,' I said. 'And by the way, I still have the best mum,' I smiled putting my arm around her.

We suddenly had a little rush at the van and though Mum could be eccentric and erratic, she worked well under pressure. She was able to focus and get on with things and just be there, which was as well because later that day Lucie called. She was devastated, her boyfriend had not only dumped her, but had stolen what little money she had along with her return ticket. Apparently she'd been calling all afternoon, but I'd been so busy I'd turned my phone off.

'Mum,' she was sobbing, 'I want to come home.'

I immediately dropped everything. We closed the van, I called the airport and Mum called the British Embassy – I didn't ask why, I don't think she knew herself she just panicked. She was scream-ing down the phone about her granddaughter being destitute and sold as a Thai bride, finishing with, 'If someone in that goddam office doesn't move their ass right now, I'm gonna pop a cap in it!' Her American TV speak had been made worse by the presence of Gina, for whom everyone was an 'ass', a 'doll' or 'trailer trash'.

So as mother threatened the nice man at the British Embassy with all kinds of physical abuse involving fire arms and baseball bats, I calmly booked an immediate return for my baby.

When we'd both got off the phone, we opened up the van to see Gina storming across the beach.

'Girls, what the hell? Why have you closed? Do you realise the queue's all gone to the deli for trashy ice cream instead of ours?'

'Sorry, Gina,' I said, 'but Lucie called, she needed to come home from Thailand, her boyfriend's dumped her and stolen all her money…'

Gina looked relieved. 'Shit is that all? I thought one of you had died in there,' she said, turning around and wandering back up the beach to the café.

I can't deny I felt a tinge of disappointment, hurt even, that Gina hadn't asked whether Lucie was okay.

I glanced at Mum, who knew me better than I knew myself.

'Don't feel bad, Gina doesn't really know what it's like to be a mum… or a nana… she'll get there, love.'

She smiled and served the next customers and I thought about how my mum had always been there, not just for the first days at school, the Nativity plays, the wedding – but for the stuff life is made of. Between the red-letter days and watersheds, she'd been there dealing with the fabric of life, cooking meals, cleaning floors, potty-training and soothing teething babies – first me then my kids. She'd laughed and cried with us, been covered in vomit and tears, watched endless hours of kids' TV and ached as much as we did every time we hurt our knees or our hearts. It didn't matter how her motherhood had happened – she was my mum, the kids' nan, and she'd earned it.

Lucie was due to fly in the following day, and knowing neither of us would be able to sleep, I suggested Mum and I go through the rest of the Italian carrier bag that evening.

'God knows what we'll find in here,' I said, elbow-deep in notebooks, though I was hopeful we might find Sophia's ice cream recipes. But sadly, after several hours, I had to concede what Mum had been saying all along – that Sophia kept all her recipes in her head.

The following day, after just a few hours' sleep, I met Lucie at the airport. She burst into tears and so did I as she hurled herself across Arrivals and we wrapped our arms around each other oblivious to everyone else.

I smelled musky perfume and sun oil in her hair and felt like a cat whose kitten had been returned smelling different and couldn't rest until it was washed off. I wanted to wipe away the hurt, the miles and all the missing, and gently pulled away slightly so I could check her for bruises or cuts.

'You haven't been hurt have you – he didn't attack you or anything?'

'No Mum, I told you, I'm fine physically... wow Mum you've changed. Your hair's amazing and you look – different, like a slightly cool version of yourself.'

I laughed, with relief that she was okay and with deep joy that in my daughter's eyes I was finally '*slightly* cool'.

We walked together to the car, arm in arm, my baby was back. It made me think again about Mum and Gina and all the pain of losing your child, or never feeling you really had them.

'So what happened, Lucie?' I asked as we reached the car.

'This guy I was seeing, he just took my wallet while I was sleeping.'

'Was it that Pang guy you're always photographed with?'

'No, Pang's lovely – he's such a sweetie, he was there when I needed him.'

'Oh I'm glad you had someone with you, darling.'

'Yes he's growing breasts and working as a pole dancer now, he wants to come to the UK and work. I said we'd help him... can we, Mum?'

I was a little taken aback, so Mum's gaydar was almost right, but perhaps her transsexual one needed updating? And how like Lucie to think of others when she was going through her own trauma. 'I would love to help Pang,' I said, 'but let's just put him and his pole on a back-burner until I get you safely home and settled. I have a café to open. While I drive, call your nan, she won't rest until she knows you landed safely. Oh and there's someone I want you to meet – a lot happened while you were away.'

And so we drove to Appledore together, and despite the fact Lucie had never been here before, I felt like I was bringing her home.

Chapter Twenty-Eight

The Cherry on the Sundae

Once Lucie was settled back at the apartment I called Gina who came over and we explained everything. Mum suggested we tell Josh at the same time, and organised the technical aspects of Skype. Waking him at some ungodly hour in Nepal to break the news that his nan was his great-aunt and his biological nan was a stranger to him wasn't the easiest – but it *was* the right thing to do.

Both kids just sat open-mouthed thousands of miles apart and Lucie kept hugging my mum like this meant she'd never see her again. 'But you're my nan,' she kept saying, producing fresh tears on top of the Thai ones.

Gina said she understood the kids' shock and looked forward to getting to know them. 'I'll never replace your nan,' she said. 'And anyway – who wants to be a grandma? I'd much rather be a glamorous auntie – and by the way if anyone asks I'm fifty. And if ever any of you tell anyone my real age you're dead to me,' she laughed, sounding more like my cousin than my mother. And it reminded me how we were all family; Gina may not have been in our lives, but there was a place for her in all our hearts.

Later Lucie asked if she could stay a while in Appledore and work in the café. I loved the idea of my daughter working in the family business, or 'the firm', as Mum liked to refer to it in Mafia undertones.

Meanwhile Josh, as I would have expected, took everything in his stride. He and Aarya were due back to the UK soon and both asked if they could come and stay in Appledore too.

First Delilah, then Mum turned up, followed by another mother and Lucie and now Josh and Aarya would soon be on their way. This was supposed to be my ice cream summer of freedom, my chance to see if I could make it on my own, away from everyone else, but it wasn't meant to be. Once Josh and Aarya turned up we'd all be together again, and despite what I thought I wanted – I couldn't have been happier.

The day of the café opening dawned and the weather was magnificent. Bright blue, cloudless skies told us it was going to be a blistering hot day.

'Mum used to call that "an ice cream sky",' Gina said as she threw open the doors and gazed out onto the beach. We were all hands on deck today with a new Assistant Manager, Dani, who was lovely and possibly the sanest person on the staff, but with Gina, Mum, Marco, and Sue now threatening to come and work for us, it was a low bar.

As I chatted to Marco that first morning as he baked the fresh brioche (and yes, can he make bread!) I kept thinking, this is my cousin, which was so weird. Of course I didn't tell Marco of our connection; Gina and I decided to keep my heritage private out of respect to Peter.

But the icing on the cake – or the cherry on the sundae – emerged during Marco's first kitchen shift. I asked him if he knew where Sophia's recipes might be.

'Sophia never wrote them down because she made them up as she went along,' he said. 'She always said each ice cream was a work in progress and could always be improved or altered. "Everyone brings something else to the ice cream," she used to say. "A different perspective, a different flavour, a different experience."'

And suddenly I got it. This was a creative, living, moving process, and it couldn't be pinned down to a list of ingredients. Good ice cream was like any good baking or cooking, it was about the love, the passion and the spirit of the person creating this wonderful stuff.

Sophia was right, everyone brought something different and she wanted me back at the café bringing more ideas, introducing more flavours to new customers. She'd never wanted the rift, she wanted us all to be reunited – and she'd done this by leaving me the van, knowing one way or another Reginaldo would come through. In my view there is such a thing as fate and when people we love die they don't leave us, they stick around and leave clues every day to guide us.

'It was just another of Mum's tests – for you to find your own way, make your own recipes,' Gina said. 'You've put a bit of yourself into all this and now it's about Ella's ice cream – not Sophia's. It isn't about the past,' she said, 'it's about the future, and you're the future, honey. I know it's what she'd have wanted, for her granddaughter to carry on the business and make it fly – so you go girl.'

And I did.

The opening of the Ice Cream Café was a huge success and for what was left of the summer long queues stretched down the front, tables were booked days in advance and the forecast for the future was good. Thanks to Mum, our ice creams were featured in magazines, radio, online and on TV. Delilah was the original ice cream diva, photographed with children, local celebrities – and always, always with ice cream. She now featured on all our posters and had outfits to match every flavour, and trust me, her plum ginger designer coat with frosting hat was to die for.

Now I finally had a Facebook page worth looking at; sumptuous ice creams, heady cocktails and Devon sunsets – I had the lot! But the irony was, after all those years looking at other people's bloody Agas and Dick's sunburn in Marbella – I didn't look at other people's Facebook photos any more. I didn't have the time or the inclination, because I was living my real life on a beach with the biggest sky – and you couldn't capture the joy of that on a screen.

Josh and Aarya returned from Nepal at the end of August and we rented a big house overlooking the bay and filled it with family. Sue arrived in a flurry of sequins and dress jewellery and moved into the apartment. She's renting it off Gina for the next six months, and loves it – who wouldn't? As she says 'It's got all the modern contrivances.' Meanwhile our new assistant manager Dani is about to move into the flat above the café, she lives for ice cream and like Gina she's come back to Appledore having run away as a teenager. She's funny and friendly and very sweet, but there's a sadness behind her laughter – I wonder what her story is?

How ironic that this was to be my summer of escape – running away from home to start a new life – yet here we all are, they ran away with me! The kids are going to work in the café, Gina's planning to stay on a little longer and Mum's in her element. Best of all, I have my van; Reginaldo was my knight in shining armour and rescued me from another life, bringing me to a better one. Mum, Gina and I are contemplating a road trip with Reginaldo – it might be fun to travel to Italy, where it all began. We can catch up with family, sample real gelato and be inspired by Sorrento – where the lemons are as big as your head.

In the end it had been Sophia who had inadvertently revealed the family secret. I sometimes wonder if it was just a coincidence that Sophia hid the bag of secrets in the van she then bequeathed to me. Was this my aunt's way of finally unburdening the secret and helping me to find out the truth about myself? I like to think so.

I've realised since I came here that family, heritage, and the happiness of my childhood and love for my children gave me strength and confidence to chase my dream. I'd stayed in the same place physically and emotionally for too long and until this summer I'd been scared to make the break. Appledore has taken me to its heart – without me realising, some special people were waiting here for me and made sense of my life. My anchor is here in Appledore, I'm not tied to it, I can go anytime – because I know this is my forever and I'll always come back.

Epilogue

Today I sit with Delilah in my van on the beach, it's early autumn, the weather is closing in and I don't have many customers. Delilah's asleep and everyone is at the café serving hot chocolate, decadent sundaes and warm breakfast brioches made fresh by Marco, sandwiched with cool, creamy ice cream in one of the many flavours we offer.

I love my new life and it isn't closed off like the other one because I can always head off into the sunset in my van in search of adventure. Sometimes, when we've been really busy, or Mum and Gina are bickering and the kids are making too much noise, me and Delilah drive along the open beach, a big sky above us and a never-ending sea in the distance. We park up among the sand dunes where Ben and I once kissed, and sometimes I'll phone him and ask how it is in that great big blue Pacific and he talks to me about the sea.

I sometimes fantasise about him turning up on my beach, or better still, I could turn up on his. And who knows, one day Delilah and I might just keep driving until we get to Hawaii, two girls in search of an adventure, our futures spread before us, though we'd need to make sure Delilah had enough outfits packed first.

My ice cream summer has given me so many gifts – I've discovered a talent for ice cream and business and international relations (Mum and Gina!). I rediscovered my Mum, Roberta, who is bright and funny and clever, and of course the best mother in the world. I also found another mother, a wonderful woman who has always been there, watching from afar – and who will continue to enrich my life and that of my children.

Marco is also a kind of gift – albeit a monosyllabic and sometimes quite rude gift – but he passed on Sophia's advice, to make ice cream from the heart, not from a recipe. He also happens to make the best Brioche in Britain – and what's more, in a weird way I kind of like him. I lost a cousin in Gina and found a cousin in Marco and knowing this gives me faith in the world, that there is a kind of equilibrium and it will all come right in the end.

I remind myself of this on the days when all I can think of is Ben, and what might have been. And I remember what he told me: 'Hold your breath, dive in and let the water take the weight, give yourself up to the universe and know she has your back.' And from my little van I look out onto a vast sea, a huge sky and then down at Delilah in her prettiest dress – and I just know we have some great adventures ahead of us. All we have to do is hold our breath, and dive in.

Ella's Ice Cream Recipe

This is so simple and you don't need an ice cream maker just a plastic freezer-proof box. I often whip up a batch of this vanilla while I'm in the van, with the blue sky above, and the endless sea ahead.

For flavoured or 'adult only' ice cream, I add up to 3floz/85ml of fruit puree and/or alcohol to the egg yolk mixture. If I'm adding any delicious extras like choc chips, chopped nuts, praline or any little sweeties, I just fold them in before freezing. So gather the ingredients, put on some Italian music and imagine you're in Sorrento – where the lemons are as big as your head!

Ingredients

- 2 eggs, separated
- 2oz/60g caster sugar
- 10floz/300ml double cream
- 1-2 tsp vanilla extract

Start by beating the egg whites until stiff, then beat in the sugar a spoonful at a time until the mixture is stiff and glossy.

In a separate bowl, beat the double cream until pillowy but not stiff.

Mix the egg yolks and vanilla extract.

Now, gently fold the whipped cream into the meringue with a spatula. When it is almost incorporated, slowly fold in the egg yolks one spoonful at a time.

Pour the ice cream into a plastic freezer-proof container and pop in the freezer for a minimum of 6 hours, until the ice cream is solid.

Take the container out of the freezer 10 minutes before serving, and scoop into cones or dishes then add toppings.

Enjoy!

Ella x

A Letter from Sue

Thanks so much for reading *Ella's Ice Cream Summer*, I hope you enjoyed the delicious ice creams and didn't mind waiting in the long queue at the van! If you've enjoyed this story, please feel free to pop in to the Ice Cream Café in my next book (out in June) to meet a new heroine, with a new story, and catch up with Ella's adventures too.

Delilah the Pomeranian is the star of this book. Little Delilah was a rescue dog who'd had a difficult life until she was adopted as 'an older lady' by my friends Michael and Vic in San Francisco where she lived with her brother Chuggaboom, a miniature Pinscher. Sadly, Delilah and Chuggaboom both died in 2016, but they will always have a place in the hearts of those who knew and loved them. Delilah still has a Facebook page where her daddies keep us up to date on the adventures and crazy antics of her siblings, Popcorn, Little Eve and Millie Milkshake. You can find them all here on https://www.facebook.com/DelilahPom

If you'd like to meet up again with Ella and Delilah in my next book you can sign up to my mailing list and I'll let you know when it's released. I promise I won't share your email address with anyone, and I'll only send you an email when I have a new book out.

If you want to taste a little of *Ella's Ice Cream Summer*, do try Ella's easy ice cream recipe and let me know what you think!

www.suewatsonbooks.com/email

www.suewatsonbooks.com/

www.facebook.com/suewatsonbooks/

Twitter @suewatsonwriter

Acknowledgments

My thanks and the biggest chocolate sundaes EVER to Oliver Rhodes, Claire Bord, Jessie Botterill, Kim Nash, Emily Ruston, Jade Craddock and the rest of the delicious Bookouture team, who turned this ice cream story into a Knickerbocker Glory!

A very big thank you and lashings of hot fudge sauce to my lovely American friends Michael Angelo Torres and Vic Spinoza. Their very special little girl, Delilah the Pomeranian, turned up in this story in a doggie bikini, twirling and barking and stealing my heart, and they kindly allowed her to stay. Sadly, the real Delilah isn't with us any more, but wherever she is there's an extensive designer doggie wardrobe with tasteful accessories – and I know she'll always make her daddies very proud.

I have so many blogger friends who take the time to read and review my books and I love all of them. Unfortunately there isn't enough room on the page to thank everyone individually, so for now I'd just like to say a waffle-cone, heartfelt thank you to those who are always, always there for me, many from the beginning, who welcome each book and cheer me along my journey. Kathryn Everett, Sarah Hardy, Dawn Crooks, Suze Lavender, Rachel Gilbey, Kaisha Holloway, Ana Tomova, Sara Steven, Bethany

Clark and Anne John-Ligali – thank you for being such lovely friends and wonderful champions of my writing, I would be lost without you.

Knickerbocker Glories to all my fabulous new friends at the Book Club at Mim's; plus lashings of whipped cream and a special cherry on top for Marie 'Mim' Deakin, proprietor of Mim's Café. With her bubbly warmth, amazing talent for making everyone feel at home, and creating wonderful sweet stuff, Mim was my inspiration for Ella's story.

To my girls, Lesley McLoughlin (and the late and lovely Cocoa, who also appears in the book), Alison Birch, Louise Bagley, Jan Newbold, Sarah Robinson, Jackie Swift and Sheila Webb; thank you for providing regular scoops of ice cream for the soul, and for reminding me there's a big and wonderful world outside my writing shed.

To Liz Cox, an enormous, calorie-free sundae for 'the funeral scene', for always making me laugh, and for inspiring me for so long, in so many ways.

Last, but never least, swirly vanilla cones with chocolate flakes and raspberry sauce to my Mum, Nick and Eve. Thank you as always for your love, patience and humour – and for allowing me to 'research' ice cream every day, without ever mentioning the word 'diet'!

Made in the USA
Columbia, SC
06 September 2017